PUGILIST FROM SHANDONG II

~Rebellious Dragon~

Thomas J Haase

反抗龍樣板

[Type here]

Thomas J Haase

1702 W. Cass St. Tampa, FL 33606

Printed in the United States of America

First Edition 2021

ISBN: 978-1-7332759-3-4

For ordering information contact:

Thomas J Haase.com/orders

Website: Thomas J Haase.com

Cover art: Map: Between 1855 and 1870 loc.gov/item /gm7100507

Cover image: Thomas J Haase

Contents

Epigraph

Moment by moment, the journey continues.

Each containing a fathomless expanse.

Behind drifts away, and is consumed by the dark.

Ahead, effortlessly appears,

out of the light.

Preface

Writing this second part of the series, naturally evolved out of the initial publication, which painted a story in words, describing various aspects and events in the life of Li Yutang.

Rebellious Dragon takes the reader through the life experiences and encounters of Yutang's teacher, Cheng Yangban.

1. SHAOLIN BURNING

"Grandfather, do you remember when they burned the Shaolin Temple?" young Yangban asked his elder while sitting on the ground near the front door.

"Shaolin, yes, I remember the story my father told me when I was young about that dreadful event." his grandfather said as he leaned back against the wall while sitting on the small stool.

"When I was just a little older than you, my father told me the story of how the emperor sent his General to deal with the monks at Shaolin." Old Cheng said, leaning forward and putting his hand on the boy's shoulder.

"He said there was this General in the Imperial Army named Yao and the Emperor sent him a message to come to the Forbidden City."

"I have come to see the emperor." The General dismounted his horse and walked up to the sentry standing guard at the large front gates of the Forbidden City, as the gentle breeze silently lifted a wisp of fine dust from the ground and carried it past the motionless guard.

"And what is your business with His Majesty?" the guard solemnly asked.

"The emperor has requested my presence to discuss the Shaolin Temple." He slowly removed his gloves and sword before handing them to his assistant standing near his horse.

"Wait here while I inform the court." The guard turned and walked over to knock on the secured gate.

"Boom, boom, boom," echoed through the interior compound, signaling the presence of an official visitor waiting to be granted an audience with the Ruler of the Middle Kingdom under Heaven.

"Someone will be out to see you."

"Slam!" the general, assistant and guard heard about an hour later as the bolt securing the Forbidden City from the outside world was

slid back. Slowly and ever so quietly the gate began to nudge its way open barely enough for a person to slip through.

"I'm the Imperial eunuch in charge of interviewing all potential visitors. Who dares to disturb the Ruler of all under Heaven?" the eunuch looked away while asking.

"I'm General Yao from the Emperor's Imperial Army.

"His Majesty under Heaven summoned me to discuss the Shaolin Temple." He proudly replied while stepping closer to the eunuch.

"Do you carry the official scroll requesting this audience with the Great Ruler under Heaven?" he coldly asked while turning his head and looking down the street.

"Yes, I do." He held out his hand and waited.

The General's assistant quickly stepped forward and placed the scroll in his hand, Yao then stepped even closer, shoved the scroll in the eunuch's face and said, "Here!".

"Well!" the eunuch scowled while turning to look at the General.

Slowly he untied the silk ribbon and carefully unrolled the delicate fabric.

"Hmm! And where did – You - get this!" he condescendingly demanded while reading the contents.

"From that other one of -you- that came to my camp!" General Yao leaned in closer while staring in his eyes.

"Well!" the eunuch quickly looked away and rolled up the scroll.

"Wait here!" he turned and quickly slipped back inside the gate.

"Slam!" General Yao heard the moment the gate finally closed.

"Ha!" echoed through the tunnel as the eunuch yelled.

General Yao slowly turned to look at the guard standing by the wall. "Hmm." He said as they both smiled.

"Screech, boom!" the three heard an hour later as the large bolt was slid back to allow the gate to be opened once again.

General Yao stood up and walked towards the gate which again was opened very slowly and barely enough to slip through.

"Okay, you may enter." The eunuch coldly mumbled as he stuck his head around the gate while looking at the sky.

"Good!" General Yao yelled as he leaned to within inches of the eunuch's face.

"Well!" he pulled his head back.

"Follow me." The eunuch opened the gate slightly further to allow the outsider entrance without touching the Imperial property.

"Screech, boom!" echoed through the entranceway; signaling that the outside world was once again barricaded out.

"This way." The eunuch directed the moment he finished closing out the world.

Quickly he turned and began scurrying through the tall meticulously sculpted archway. For several seconds General Yao stood captivated by the large wooden gates adorned with evenly spaced horizontal rows of large round brass cones. Additionally, he realized, he was for the first time inside the hallowed Forbidden City, and sensing what the eunuchs felt when the world was locked out.

"Hey, follow me!" he turned and yelled.

"Sorry."

As the General stepped out of the archway and into the vast open courtyard, he again stopped to absorb the magnitude and beauty of this initial reception area. The entire area was stone paved leading to several stone bridges spanning a deep trench and leading to the first stairway. Each bridge consisted of ornately carved stone railings separating each new level rising upward. On each side of the stairway were giant granite lions guarding the steps to the next reception hall.

"Hey!"

General Yao rushed to catch up to the eunuch who was half way across the first bridge. He looked to the side, saw several eunuchs under the overhang rushing in the opposite direction, while pointing at him before giggling.

"Don't be stopping again!" the eunuch said as they reached the second bridge.

As they crossed the second bridge, General Yao turned to look back at the entrance gates and momentarily paused, then quickly turned and kept his pace with his guide. Later as they reached the steps leading to the initial breezeway, General Yao was amazed at the height of the jade-colored lions Each lion stood approximately twelve feet in height and was carved with an intricate maze pattern that seemed to continue on all four sides.

Reaching the top of the steps, they walked into a large meticulously painted breezeway with dragons chasing a golden sun painted on each supporting header. The large columns were painted bright red while the ceiling was covered in gold dragons and multi-colored lotus flowers. As they reached the opposite side and stepped out into the sunlight, General Yao was startled by the grandeur and immense size of the courtyard in relation to the previous one.

"Keep walking. We're on a busy schedule." the eunuch said as he began walking down an even larger stone stairway.

Ten minutes later the two finally crossed the last open area, climbed another stone stairway and found shelter from the sun's heat inside another elaborate hall. Unlike the previous buildings, this structure was closed in between the columns with meticulously carved wooden screens consisting of interconnected hexagons and at the bottom of each panel were raised gold dragons set on a solid raised wood panel.

"Stay here!" he snapped while pointing at the large carved wooden bench against the long wall and then scurried off around the corner.

General Yao looked around at the elaborately decorated overhang and quietly walked over and eased his way down on the bench, making sure not to disrupt anything by moving too fast. Looking up he observed the craftsmanship of each painted dragon and lotus flower; all were identical to the next without the slightest deviation in pattern or shape.

An hour passed before the eunuch suddenly appeared from around the corner and ran up to the General. "Quickly, the Emperor will see you now!" he said while struggling to catch his breath.

Instantly General Yao stood up and followed directly behind his guide as he hurried around the corner, down another long hallway and finally reached the entrance to the emperor's reception hall. As the eunuch reached up and slowly began to open the elaborate doors, General Yao once again stopped to glance at the grandeur and intricacy of the entrance.

"Hey! Remove your headdress, and when you enter these doors make sure you move slowly and don't look up at the emperor!" he sternly whispered while looking back and continuing to open the large wooden doors.

"Sorry."

"Hmph."

The eunuch pulled the doors open further, and General Yao noticed that the immense columns supporting the roof were painted with brightly colored dragons coiling from top to bottom and a gold-colored sun just beyond the dragon's reach. Strangely, there was no sound from the movement of the doors, not even the slightest squeak, while inside all sound and voices momentarily ceased as the outside world was temporarily granted access. Numerous eunuchs continually scurried silently along the long marble walkways surrounding the main platform as the emperor sat patiently waiting.

"Heavenly Emperor, your humble servant has arrived." A eunuch positioned half way down the corridor yelled to the Ruler sitting in a large intricately carved throne on the opposite end of the room as the general stepped inside the room, while the emperor's many court eunuchs sat behind him at a distance and whispered among themselves.

Without saying a word, the emperor signaled for his visitor to step forward. Instantly General Yao humbly made his way up the long walkway, with his headdress tucked securely under his arm and the other arm pulled tightly in to his stomach. Upon reaching the designated area, he knelt down on one knee, placed his fist on the floor, and continued looking downward while saying, "Your humble servant has arrived, oh great Yong Zheng, ruler under Heaven."

"So, you have news about the subjects at the Shaolin Temple?"

"Yes, oh great Emperor, I do."

"So, what news do you bring me?" he looked away.

"I have evidence that the monks have been assisting in an attempt to overthrow you oh great ruler." He said while lowering his head even further.

"What? They're working to overthrow me?" he screamed while standing up. Then he stepped forward to the edge of his platform and stared at the general.

"Are you serious?"

"Yes, oh great ruler under Heaven."

"I have always been kind but cautious towards those monks." He yelled while pounding his fist into his other palm.

"When I began my reign in 1722, I told them they would be allowed to continue their training as long as they remained loyal to me." He paced back and forth across the wide platform.

"Obviously I have been way too tolerant of this group over the past three years!" he walked back to his throne, sat down and remained silent for several minutes.

"I want them crushed within six days of the new year." He eventually said while stomping his foot on the floor and twisting it as if there were a bug underneath.

"I don't want to start another year with them conspiring behind my back.

"How many men do you have here with you?" he leaned back in his chair and signaled for a eunuch to approach with his writing scroll.

"I can have three hundred men ready to go when I return to my encampment."

"Good. Take them and go to Shaolin." He began to write on a delicate scroll.

"This scroll will be your orders. Take it and keep it safe.

"Once you arrive, I want you to kill all the rebels and burn the temple to the ground." He said as he finished writing and handed the scroll to a eunuch.

The eunuch slowly bowed, backed away and then quickly walked over to General Yao. As he approached, the General reached up without looking and allowed the eunuch to place the scroll in his hand.

"Go now and do not fail." The emperor stood up and walked away.

"I will not fail, oh great ruler under Heaven."

Cautiously General Yao stood up, slowly backed towards the door while continuing to look at the floor and when he reached the doors, the first eunuch ushered him outside.

"Go… now!" he commanded as he pushed the General outside just before closing the doors and forcing the General to find his own way to the front gates.

Minutes later General Yao pushed open the large wooden gates, walked over to his assistant, and grabbing his gloves and sword, quickly mounted his horse. While turning towards the north he heard, "Hey what about the gate?"

"Close it yourself, you have nothing else to do!" he said while strapping his sword to his side.

"Well!.. Boom!" he heard as the gates were once again secured from the outside world.

After several hours, he arrived back at his encampment, and summoned his subordinates while dismounting from his sweaty horse.

"I am leaving at first light for Shaolin.

"I want three hundred men armed and ready to march at sunrise." He walked inside and began removing his armor.

"This will be several months and I want enough supplies to last the trip." He sat down to wipe off his sweat.

The following morning as the late autumn sun began slowly rising above the horizon, General Yao walked out of his tent and said, "Is everything ready for today's march?"

"Yes, General Yao, we have all the men in formation with all their gear. Behind them we positioned the carts with all the supplies" the lieutenant replied as he pointed towards the back of the long line of men and carts.

"Good, then let's get on our way. I want to be in Dengfeng city just after the winter solstice." He mounted his horse and rode to the front, turned around to inspect the group standing in formation, signaled the flag bearer to begin the march and turned to lead the soldiers towards the edge of the city and begin the long trip south.

As the last troops exited the city walls, the first snowflakes effortlessly floated in the air before touching the ground. The fields in the distance that months earlier were bright green and bursting with life had now resigned to a long deep sleep. All the workers they had seen over the years feverously harvesting their bounty before the cold Siberian air moved in and froze the ground were gone except for the lone man and his cart slowly spreading the manure from the animal pens sparingly across the brown hard soil.

The air was still with a thick layer of dust and humidity clinging tightly to everything, while each step the soldiers marched created a dense cloud for the trailing men to navigate. As each step of the troops stirred up even more dust, the entire battalion almost disappeared except for the continual clatter of weapons, armor, and supplies in the carts. Continually the sound of the horses and the clatter from the weapons rushed across the empty fields and echoed back from the walls of the ancient village, while the chatter of hungry birds dancing and weaving around the men in hopes of a scrap of food added to the echoes. Day after day as the formation marched forward, their dust cloud and noise pierced the stillness and tranquility blanketing the family villages they passed, momentarily ceasing all their activities and curiously joining together in order to decipher the dust and commotion of the passing formation. For the villagers, the only clue about the interruption was the flag bearer at the lead silently announcing the emperor's army on assignment.

Week after week the group continued their pace and soon the snow silently began to accumulate, making the march harder and slower. Eventually, the detail finally arrived on the outskirts of Dengfeng city, *"We will stop and make camp here for several days while the men rest."* General Yao said as he dismounted his horse.

"Inventory our supplies and send out scouts to the local farmers so they can replenish what is needed." He removed his headdress and scanned the horizon.

"It is two weeks until the new year, so I want to make preparations for the day we arrive at Shaolin.

"Inform all my Lieutenants that tomorrow we will have a meeting about our strategy." He stood his long halberd against a nearby tree.

The following morning as the sun finished the final moments of its ascent, General Yao walked out of his quarters and said to his officers, "In several days we will march to Shaolin. We will stop within two miles of the temple, make camp and then send out our scouts to assess the situation."

"Make sure no one leaves the detail without my permission. I don't want anyone informing the monks of our arrival or intentions." He stared at each officer.

Days later the group began the last section of the march and the next afternoon were setting up their camp near the temple. Quietly a group of scouts were dispatched to begin observations of the temple. After three days the scouts all returned to give their reports.

"General, we watched the temple from a short distance and noticed that all the monks were still there and remained inside the temple walls preparing for the upcoming New-Year celebration tomorrow." The scout said as he knelt before his superior.

"Good, tomorrow we will march to the temple and finish this assignment. All the fireworks and celebrating will be a great diversion for our arrival.

"I want everyone ready to go at sunrise and make sure they have their weapons ready for battle." He slapped the small table with his hand and then saluted each officer.

"Send in one trusted runner." He pointed at his lieutenant.

"I'm writing a progress report for the Emperor and I want you to begin the trip back to give him my assessment." General Yao said as he began writing on the scroll.

"Don't stop and don't fail me." He handed the scroll to the runner and patted him on the shoulders.

When the first light from the sun began to illuminate the cold night sky, General Yao walked out of his tent, turned and looked down the path where the remaining tents had been erected. "We leave in one hour." He said to his assistant. "Make sure everyone is ready and tell them to be careful of these monks because they are very skilled at fighting." He turned to begin tying on his armor.

The moment General Yao settled into the saddle on his trusted steed, he turned towards the soldiers and said, "Let's begin." and then pointed in the direction of the temple.

Hours later the shadows began to creep away from the base of each tree and stretch across the dirt path, signaling the eventual end of another day would be arriving soon. The detail arrived at the entrance to the Shaolin Temple and spread out to surround the walls.

Confidently General Yao walked his horse up to the front steps of the temple and yelled, "Shaolin Temple, this is the army of the great ruler under Heaven, Emperor Yong Zheng.

"We are here to arrest the traitors!" he shook his sword in the air.

For several minutes only the chirping birds broke the silence. Suddenly, the large wooden doors to the temple began to slowly open and an aged monk stepped out on the landing.

"I'm a humble monk from this peaceful temple." The monk said as he bowed while positioning one open palm in the center of his chest. "My master would like to know who it is you seek?"

"I'm here on behalf of the great ruler under Heaven. And he wants everyone!" he said as his horse reared up on its hind legs while whinnying.

"Send your master out here now!" he commanded as his troops raised their weapons and took one step forward.

"Please, please I will tell him." He turned and slipped back inside the doorway.

After several minutes the monk returned with an elderly monk in a gold robe.

"Sir I'm the abbot of this humble temple. Who is it you seek?" he slowly bowed.

"We have information that you are assisting in a rebellion against the Emperor." He pointed at the monks.

"What? I assure you no one here has done anything to assist in such an unworthy cause."

"Liar!" Yao pointed at the abbot.

"Please, please sir I'm telling you the truth."

"Enough! Everyone will come out here now or we will kill everyone and burn this place to the ground!"

"But sir, we have done nothing wrong."

"Arrest them all!" he said as he forced his horse to climb the steps.

"Boom, boom, boom" the drums sounded and signaled to the army to approach the walls and arrest everyone or kill those who resisted. Instantly the troops marched closer and closer to the temple walls. As they approached, they could hear the screams and desperate cries by the monks for reinforcements.

The first troops breached the temple wall, instantly setting off a frenzied attack by the monks to secure the location. Unfortunately, more and more troops stormed over the walls at various locations and soon the monks were driven out into the courtyards where they were forced to fight to survive.

"*Protect the meditation hall!*" *a monk pointed at the distant building.*

"*Make a wall and drive them back!*" *he turned and struck the soldier with his long sword.*

"*Don't let them in!*" *he spun to avoid the soldier's spear.* "*Keep fighting and don't give up. We must protect the sacred scrolls!*"

"*Behind you! The soldiers are coming behind you!*" *a monk yelled as he pointed to the rear of the temple grounds.*

"*Monks, stay together. Don't let them separate you!*" *an elderly monk said as he grabbed the robes of the young acolytes and pulled them closer.*

"*Master, there's too many for us to fight!*"

"*Fight anyway, don't let them win.*"

"*Give up and you will be spared!*" *General Yao yelled as he rode through the courtyard. Unfortunately, the cries of the monks to fight and the chants of the soldiers to attack and kill drowned out his command.*

As the battle raged on, minutes seemed like hours and slowly the monks became outnumbered. One by one they perished at the hands of the emperor's troops. First the younger inexperienced members succumbed to the invasion and were killed with minimal effort by the troops. Next the elders who were too feeble to compete with the younger invaders were eliminated in the adjoining halls. Finally, the experienced and formidable senior monks continued fighting until the last one stood alone against the remaining troops. Eventually, his valiant efforts were extinguished and the General finally stood victorious in the open courtyard.

"Burn this place to the ground!" he yelled to his bloodied and weary troops.

"Ahh!" they yelled in unison before lighting numerous torches and running from building to building to start it on fire.

Eventually, as the sun sank behind the large trees surrounding the temple grounds, the intense heat and flames from the ancient timbers lit up the sky and overshadowed any indication that the night would be upon them soon.

"Gather everyone together so that we can take an accurate count of who has survived and how many from the temple were exterminated." General Yao stood outside the temple near an old tree.

"General, we have taken an accurate count of all the monks and it appears that three are missing." The officer bowed while handing his superior the report.

"What do you mean, three are missing?"

"Yes sir, our count is accurate and three are missing."

"We have not been able to locate three of the senior monks. We found their quarters and the remnants of their belongings, but we cannot find their bodies." He bowed and stepped back.

"We also found a secret tunnel in the back that had been recently opened."

"Search the area and find those three!" Yao said as he stepped forward and slapped the officer with his gloves.

The Lieutenant turned and grabbed two of his assistants and said, "Divide the troops up into groups of five and begin searching the area where you found the tunnel!

"They can't be very far away."

For the next two hours the teams searched the surrounding area, and finally when all light from the sun had disappeared and the large new moon appeared over the trees General Yao walked towards the large stone steps, stared at the smoldering remains and said, "cancel the search", turned and grabbed the reins of his horse while shaking his head. "Gather the troops and head back to the camp," he said as he mounted the stallion, turned and slowly walked away.

The following morning while the last embers from the fires continued to smolder and release faint trails of smoke in the distance, General Yao ordered the surviving troops to begin the long 600-mile march back to the Forbidden City. Many were injured but could still walk, while others were placed on makeshift stretchers and carried.

As the tired and road-weary troops finally approached the outskirts of Beijing, the early April warm weather had melted all remnants of snow and now the new growth in the fields was beginning to show.

Hours later they arrived back at their encampment and began unloading the wounded along with the remaining supplies.

"Make sure everyone is well fed and given time to rest. I'm going to see the emperor.

"I hope he doesn't want anyone disciplined for losing those three monks." He looked at his Lieutenant and shook his head.

As General Yao rode up the main gates of the Forbidden City, he dismounted his horse and walked up to the guard standing near the opening and said, "I'm General Yao from the Imperial Army and I'm here to see the emperor." He handed the reins of his horse to his assistant.

"I'll inform the court." The guard turned and pounded on the large wooden gates.

"Boom, boom, boom" echoed through the interior courtyard.

After about an hour, the general and his assistant heard, "Screech, slam" as the inside bolt was pushed back.

"Squeak!" the gate slowly moved.

"Who dares interrupt the Great Ruler under Heaven?" the eunuch looked up at the sky.

"I am!

"And don't give me that – who are you crap!" Yao stepped directly in front of the eunuch.

"Well!" the eunuch turned away with one hand on his hip.

"I'll see if the emperor has time for an infidel." He quickly turned and slipped back inside the gate.

"Screech, boom!"

"Ha!" his voice echoed through the archway.

The general turned and looked at the guard and his assistant, shook his head and walked over to sit in the shade of a tree.

"Screech, boom" pierced the quiet about an hour later. As the gate slowly began to move, the eunuch slipped through the narrow opening, looked at the small clouds and said, "You can see him now." and then quickly slipped back inside.

Immediately General Yao stood up, walked over to the opening and pushed open the gates far enough to easily walk through without effort.

"Hey, pull that gate shut so no one else gets in. One outsider is enough!" the eunuch snapped as he watched Yao enter the city.

"If you want it shut, do it yourself." He headed towards the first courtyard.

"Well!"

"Screech, boom"

Two hours later as General Yao was sitting on the carved bench outside the reception hall, a eunuch walked hurriedly around the corner, stopped in front of the main doors and said, "He will see you now." Slowly he opened the two large doors and bowed as he stepped inside.

"Oh, great ruler of all under Heaven, your humble servant General Yao has returned." A eunuch further down the hall announced.

"General, you have returned.

"Step forward so we can talk." He motioned for Yao to approach his platform.

"Tell me, what is your report about the Shaolin Temple." He slid forward in his chair and rested his arms on the armrests.

"Oh, great ruler under Heaven, I engaged the enemy at their doorstep.

"I then demanded that all traitors be brought out and handed over. Unfortunately, they refused to comply, so I burned the temple to the ground."

"And what about the traitors inside?" he stood up and stepped forward.

"I killed all but three, oh great ruler."

"What?

"You let three live?"

"No, oh great ruler, they escaped through a secret tunnel at the back of the temple."

"So, I sent soldiers to track them down."

"Good, I want a full report about their capture or death." He turned and sat down while motioning for the general to leave.

General Yao bowed, slowly stood up and backed away from the platform. When he reached the doors he bowed, turned and stepped outside, then quickly walked back to the main entrance. "Screech, boom," he slid the lock back and pushed the gates completely open.

"Are you going to close the gates?" the eunuch snapped as he caught up to the officer and looked at the wall.

"Close them yourself, you've got nothing else to do!" he said as he mounted his horse and rode away.

2. WAKING THE DRAGON

Just as the sun began to slip behind the distant mountains, a woman let out a sharp cry that echoed throughout the village, signaling the birth of another child. Suddenly a man ran outside to announce to everyone the news. "It's a boy, it's a boy! After years of trying, we finally have a boy!" he yelled while running down the street with his arms waving in the air.

"Congratulations, congratulations, Cheng Zhangfu" the neighbors replied as he excitedly ran past and continued further down the street.

The year of 1785 in Pingdu was a time of continual turmoil and strife. The reign of the Manchus had been a thorn in the side to everyone and especially those in the working class, beginning with the edict requiring all males to wear their hair in the traditional

Nanais style, which attempted to undermine and eradicate their Han culture. Unfortunately, all it accomplished was to draw the Han closer together and fuel their hatred towards the Manchu rulers.

"What are you going to name him?" his neighbor asked as soon as he returned from the excited trip through the neighborhood to let everyone know the news.

"Well, we were thinking that if it was a boy, we would call him Cheng Yangban."

"Wow, that's very auspicious!" his neighbor replied.

"Yes, we are hoping that it will serve him well and bring him good luck." He stepped through the front door of his house.

Three years passed quickly and Yangban was growing fast.

"Yangban, come with me outside. I want to begin your training." His father walked to the door

"Yes, Father," the boy answered as he ran to catch up.

"Today I want to teach you the basic stances we use in our family's long-fist style." He demonstrated the first position.

"Now you follow along." He gestured for the boy to imitate his movements. "Good, good. Now here is the next position."

"Like this Father?"

"Yes, yes that's good."

Yangban followed his father and one by one he quickly learned the basic stances that would be the foundation for his future training. "Let's go over by the tree and sit in the shade." He took his son by the hand.

"Father, does everybody learn these?" He sat and leaned against the aged pillar standing motionless while casting shade on the ground.

"No, these are only in our family style. Other styles of Kung Fu have their own unique versions and the movements they do are specific to their style, so they need stances that fit with the movements."

"Really?" the boy scratched his head.

"Yes, but I will explain it again when you are a little bit older. For today we will practice the movements without all the details."

"Can we do them again?" the boy jumped up.

"Just a couple more times and then we will begin learning the punches."

"Great!"

"I think we have practiced the stances enough for today." He handed the boy some water.

"Thank you, Father."

"Now I want to teach you our hand positions and how to root your feet as you use them."

"Father what is rooting?" Yangban looked at the clouds.

"Well, remember last week when you were playing in that puddle and got stuck and your mother had to come and pull you out. Then when she pulled you out, your shoes stayed in the mud?"

"Yes, I remember. It was so much fun."

"That moment of being stuck is like rooting."

"Huh?"

"When you root your feet to the ground it's like they are stuck there and glued to the earth. And no matter how hard someone tries to move you, they can't.

"Like when I pull on the small trees and they don't come up?" he grabbed a tall weed and tried to pull it out.

"Yes."

"Hmm"

"It's okay if you don't understand, it took me years to figure it out and we will talk about it again." He patted his son's shoulder.

Over the next five years Yangban trained daily and his progress quickly increased. The various stance positions strengthened his legs and joints while teaching him how to remain stable to the ground as he moved through the numerous basic routines. The jumping techniques taught him to relax as he floated through the air like a bird, and when he landed, his body should become heavy like a large boulder partially buried in the ground. Daily he practiced his leg sweeping technique to imitate a large broom sweeping the leaves away from the door, in order to become extremely fast and proficient.

"Today Yangban I want to teach you some of the basics for the broadsword." His father began circling the weapon around his body.

"Most kung fu styles try to imitate the movements of Yan Qing from the Water Margin stories. He was very short and an exceptional master of the sword so everybody was afraid of him."

"Is this one of his sword forms?"

"No, what we have are movements from our style executed with the attitude, spirit and tenacity of Yan Qing." His father jumped, kicked and spun in a circle.

"Wow! And that's what I'm going to learn?"

"Yes, but first we are going to talk about the parts of a sword and how it is used. How many parts are there?"

"I see only two, the handle and the sharp blade."

"Really? let's look closer. Here is the blade edge, the back, the guard, the handle and the butt end. Each one of them has a purpose."

"Wow, five instead of just two."

"Yes, with the blade you can hack, slash, chop and slice." He showed an application for each.

"Now the back is good for blocking, barring and deflecting another weapon. The guard keeps your opponent's weapon from hitting your hand, while the butt end is good for striking your opponent when you're closer. Also, always remember: if your opponent has only one sword, you need to watch his empty hand and if he has two swords, watch his footwork."

"Really?" the boy looked at the sword.

"Yes, the empty hand is good for grabbing and punching, while the steps you use when you have two swords, will either set you up for an effective counter attack or make you vulnerable for an attack." His father performed a series of intricate steps.

"Now follow me."

For the next two hours Yangban learned and practiced all the fundamental techniques and finally the prearranged series of movements in the form.

"I want you to practice for another hour by yourself, so you can remember the movements. Tomorrow we will go over everything again." He turned to walk away.

"Yangban, come quickly so we can bow to our ancestors." His mother said as she walked past her son's room.

"You slept late today." His father began lighting the incense.

"I stayed outside until after dark practicing my sword form," he bowed.

"That's good. It'll help speed up your progress." He placed the burning fragrant sticks into the aged urn.

Following their morning meal, Yangban and his father reviewed the sword form and characteristics until he heard his mother yell, "You two have been out there for several hours. Are you hungry yet?"

"We'll be right in." his father said as he turned towards the archway.

"Father, why is the roof curved at the ends?" the boy pointed at the arched ridge with the evenly spaced dragons facing towards the end.

"That's designed so the evil spirits won't sit on the rooftop and try to come inside through the cracks. And all the figures on the curve help to chase them away. Our ancestors always believed that the evil spirits would sit on the roof and scare everybody. So, they started building the roofs curved at the corners to keep them away. All the deities on the edge help to make sure they stay off the roof." He pointed at the two ends of the roof to show all the figures.

"What are they? they all look different."

"The first one at the end is a phoenix with King Min of Qi from the Warring States period sitting on its back. My father told me that King Min was caught between the devil and the deep blue sea

31

after he was defeated by Yue Yi, a general of Yan. Suddenly, a phoenix flew by and carried him across the river and away from the devil. Afterwards, everyone believed that the immortal riding a phoenix placed at the end of a ridge symbolizes - being unexpectedly saved from a desperate situation. Also, like the immortal riding a phoenix, at the tail of the ridge beasts there is another beast with two horns which is called chuishou (hip beast)."
He pointed at the end of the ridge.

"The next one is a dragon and they control the rain and water and symbolize imperial power. So, it could protect the palaces and temples built of wood from fire, but it also shows the supremacy and dignity of imperial buildings.

"Behind the dragon sits a phoenix. They're regarded as the king of birds throughout our country. For centuries the Phoenix has been believed to be an auspicious omen that the country is in peace and its people will live a happy life.

"The lion following the phoenix is a symbol of the power of the Buddha's teaching. It embodies valiancy and majesty and when a lion roars, other animals are frightened and dare not give out their cries. Our ancestors also believed that lions could drive away demons and ward off evil spirits.

"A marine horse and a heavenly horse come after the lion and both are symbols of auspiciousness, bravery and loyalty. What's more, the marine horse can roam in the deep seas while the heavenly horse will soar in the open skies freely. Because of this, they embody the omnipresence of royal dignity and virtue which can reach as deep

as the sea and as high as the heaven. They look quite similar to each other but if you look closely, you'll see the heavenly horse has wings.

"Behind the heavenly horse sits Xiayu, a marine beast that rules over the fish. It has a shield on the body and a fish tail. People believed that Xiayu could also produce rain and could protect buildings from fire.

"Next is Suanni who looks like the lion but is even fiercer and can eat tigers. It has a long mane and represents stateliness, goodness and good luck.

"After Suanni is Xiezhi, who has one horn on its head like a unicorn. Legend has it that Xiezhi owns the mysterious power to tell rights from wrongs and butt the one in the wrong with his horn when seeing people in conflict. So it is a symbol of justice.

"Behind Xiezhi is Douniu who has an ox's head and a dragon's body. People say that it often comes out on rainy days and it can prevent misfortunes, disasters and protect buildings.

"The beast at the back is called Hangshi, (ranking the tenth) and it looks like a man but has a monkey's face and a pair of wings. He's always holding a vajra in his hands and it's believed he can vanquish demons. Also, he has an image quite similar to the thunder god, so Hangshi is said to protect a building from lightning.

"Are there any evil spirits up there now?" he carefully scanned the roofs.

"No usually they only come out at night. That way most people can't see them."

"Oh good," Yangban began running towards the kitchen door.

"Yangban slow down! Why are you in such a hurry?" his mother asked as she looked out the kitchen window.

"I want to make sure I get inside before the evil spirits try to sit on the roof and scare me!"

"Ah you're lucky, one of the early ones was right behind you." She turned away and smiled.

"Really?" he cautiously looked around while sitting at the table and beginning the simple meal.

"Before you go back outside, I want to see your writing." She continued stirring the pot of steaming vegetables.

"Do you know why I ask you to practice your writing so often?"

"Not really."

"Because it helps your Kung Fu and your Kung Fu helps your writing."

"Huh?"

"Practicing each character helps you develop very exact muscle skills, and those same muscles help you with the precision needed for your weapons. it also helps you to visualize what you are doing and *where your opponent is located." She placed more of the steaming vegetables in front of him.*

"Do you understand?"

"Kind of" he struggled to pick up the noodles with his chopsticks.

"Think of the idea like this: if you are writing the character "Hua" which means flower, you need to visualize a flower and then you will see the flower in the character. And the same thing happens when you're practicing your sword." She imitated wielding a sword.

"But I have to jump around and roll when I do my sword form."

"That's true, but each movement with the sword should be as exact as the characters on your writing paper."

For the next hour Yangban practiced his writing and focused on trying to visualize the imagery connected to each character and one by one he slowly began to understand the connection between the two.

"No Yangban write those again!" she slapped the back of his head.

"You're starting to get in a hurry and the characters are very sloppy!" she pointed at the paper.

Another hour passed as he repeated all the writing until his mother was satisfied. Now his fingers were beginning to get tired while his legs became restless and longed to run and jump.

Okay you can go outside and practice with your father." She pointed at the door.

"Great!" the young boy jumped up from the ornately carved stool and rushed out the door.

"Yipee!" he jumped up and down while running across the open courtyard towards the arched entrance.

As he passed the large fish-pond, he stopped to wave at his friends gently swimming under the growth of lotus leaves covering the far side of the stone structure. One by one the fish appeared at the edge and waited for the boy to give them their daily treat.

"Sorry, maybe later." He turned and ran towards the opening.

"Father, can we practice the sword again?"

"For a little while and then I want to show you a form that teaches a lot of elbow strikes." He executed the first part of the series.

Yangban quickly picked up his sword and began performing the series that he learned several hours earlier. Cut, kick, block, roll, cut in a circle and circle the sword tightly around the body.

"No, Yangban, that isn't how the sword should be used. When you're cutting or chopping you need to watch the sword so you have the correct angle of the blade. Otherwise, it will never cut correctly." He tilted his hand to show the proper angle.

"As you cut, the sword is most effective when the blade is at a specific angle to the part of the body you want to cut. When you cut across the stomach, the sword must be at the same angle as the ground. If you are cutting down across the body from the shoulder to the opposite side of the hips, the sword should angle like when

you cut through bamboo. Remember last week when you tried to cut down that small bamboo sprout behind the kitchen and when your knife hit the trunk it bounced and made you drop the knife on your foot?"

"Yes, I remember, it made my hand hurt all day." He rubbed his wrist.

"That happened because you didn't have the correct angle between the knife and the bamboo. Now try again." He stepped back.

"Be aware of your empty hand. It's not there to just flap in the breeze and scare the flies. Always remember the words of the ancestors — When encountering a single sword; watch the empty hand and when encountering double swords; watch the feet." He quickly stepped through an intricate footwork pattern.

"What did they mean by that?"

"If you have only one sword, your empty hand should be just as useful and as busy as the sword. It needs to attack and defend just like your weapon. But if you have two swords, then it will be your steps that help to make the swords deadly or not, because they will be setting you up to attack or defend. Do you understand?"

"Um…"

"Think of it this way. If you attack me with your stick I can block over my head and stop you from hitting me, and at the same time I can grab the stick and keep you from hitting again. So, it's my empty hand that also stops you. Now if you strike and I have two swords, I won't be able to grab the stick, but if I step correctly, I can avoid the stick and strike back with my swords." He slowly walked through the movements to demonstrate.

"Oh, so if I had two swords, I would step to the side and then I could kick instead of grabbing the stick!"

"Yes, but make sure when you have two swords that you use them correctly. Just because you step to avoid the attacker's weapon doesn't mean you'll automatically be out of the way."

"Huh?"

"When you step you need to use the swords to help keep the other weapon away while you attack with your swords." He positioned his swords to demonstrate.

"Now when you only have one sword, like I said, you can grab with the empty hand. But again, you need to be aware of where your sword is and what it's doing. Blocking must be done with the edge of the sword and not the flat sides."

"But when I do that, it always hurts, because the blade is so skinny."

"So, get used to it, because if you don't learn to block correctly, you increase your chances of getting injured or killed."

"Ai-yaa!' he turned and looked around.

"Bring your sword over here." He pointed at the tree nearby.

"I want you to chop at the tree like you're hitting someone."

"Thwack, clang!" he hit the tree and instantly dropped the weapon to grab his elbow.

"Ouch!" Yangban began to rub the joint vigorously.

"What happened?"

"I don't know, I hit the tree like you said and then my arm hurt."

"Do you know why?"

"No."

"It was because when you swung the sword you didn't focus on how the sword was positioned when it hit the tree. Consequently, all the power from your strike came back at you and hurt your elbow." He said while gesturing the process.

"When you strike, your weapon needs to be at a certain angle in relation to your target. Otherwise, it won't cut through your opponent. It'll only bounce off. Also, as you attack you need to focus on what is called "follow through" or projecting past your opponent. That means whenever you strike, you need to see your weapon go through your target and beyond so that all the energy follows through and doesn't come back at you. Do you understand?" he put his hand on his son's shoulder.

"Kind of..." Yangban looked at his elbow and then at the clouds slowly drifting overhead.

"Let's go back and practice some more without hitting the tree."

For the next two hours they reviewed every routine the young boy knew and then discussed the basic theory for application. Soon the sun began to shine directly downward between the trees, so Zhangfu turned towards Yangban and said, "Okay son, I think it's time we went inside to see what your mother has made for us to eat."

"Yes!" the boy excitedly replied.

"When we come back out, I want to tell you about how to use your stick." He rested his arm on the boy's head.

An hour later as the shadows began to creep back out from under the trees and search for a distant home for the evening, Yangban pushed the door open and enthusiastically jumped through the opening before running across the courtyard. Several seconds later his father walked out, turned towards the main opening and casually walked across the open compound.

"Yangban, did you bring your stick?" he pointed to the weapon still standing by the kitchen door.

"Oops, I forgot." The boy turned and ran back to get the weapon.

As they walked out to the open grass, Zhangfu said, "Yangban, the first thing I want to teach you is about how to correctly use your stick. Many times, as I watch you practice, it's obvious how little you understand about your weapon." He held his stick out for the boy to observe.

"Your stick has many uses, it's not only for striking. You can block, poke, trap, and lock all while defending yourself. Does that make sense?"

"Umm..."

"Let me explain those points one at a time," he said.

"When you first pick up the stick, your mind thinks it's for hitting in one way only, but actually a stick can hit in nine directions, straight in, up, down, sideways left and right, and angle down left and right, and up left and right."

"Wow."

"And it can block in just as many directions, in addition to trapping and locking, which are done by slipping behind the other weapon and pinning it to the ground." He pushed his son's weapon to the ground with his stick and held it down.

"I want you to practice for a little while and see if you can figure out some of those ideas while I train over there." He pointed to the shade near the big tree.

Over the next two hours, the young boy continued training and researching the ideas his father previously explained. Eventually, as the shadows crept further across the open grass area and began to crawl up the distant trees, his young body began to tire and slow down its movements.

"Yangban, let's go back inside for today before I have to carry you, because at ten years old you're getting too big for me carry".

"Okay," he slowly replied and began walking towards the compound.

Two years later, as Yangban walked across the family compound, he turned and watched, as two young squirrels chased each other around the base of a large tree, before quickly climbing the trunk of the aged warrior and resting on the first outstretched limb. Continuing forward he slowly opened the weary door and stepped into his father's office before sitting in the old chair. "Father, I was wondering when I could learn the spear. I have always liked watching you when you practiced your forms and special techniques and would like to learn them."" He sat straight up in the chair.

"Yes, I've noticed for a long time how you always seemed to find a way to be positioned to see what I was doing whenever I would practice with the spear."

"You knew I was watching?" he asked embarrassingly.

"Oh yes. So how about if we start tomorrow? I'll find your grandfather's spear and you can use it."

"That would be great!" he jumped up and rushed towards the door.

The following morning Yangban walked across the open compound and saw the old rooster heading towards the fence to jump up and crow. Quietly he stopped, watching as the old feathered sentry effortlessly jumped and landed softly on the shaky weathered boards. "Erh, erh, erh!" he announced while looking in all directions. "Erh, erh, erh!" he repeated to make sure everyone knew he was up and on duty.

Two hours later, his father turned the corner by the compound entryway and strolled up to the big tree. "Good morning, I see by the way you're sweating that you came out to train early today."

"Good morning, yes I did. I wanted to make sure I was warmed up and ready when you arrived." He leaned his worn sword against the tree trunk and drank from his small container of water.

"Let me loosen my legs a bit before we start." His father swung his leg up on the trunk of the tree and leaned forward to grab the foot.

"Have you been practicing any of the techniques that you saw me perform?"

"No, I've been focusing on the sword movements you showed several weeks ago."

"Do you have any questions about what I taught you?" he switched legs and continued stretching.

"No, I'm just trying to improve the timing as I jump up and cut, before landing in the low twisted position."

"Ah, keep practicing, you'll figure it out just like I did years ago."

After thirty minutes Zhangfu stepped away from the tree, picked up his spear, walked out into the grass area and said," Okay, I think it's time to start your lesson."

"Yes!" he clinched his fists as he turned and ran to retrieve the aged weapon.

"First, I want to show you several basic movements that are crucial to perfect whenever you're wielding the king of weapons." he held his spear out in front of his chest and shook it.

"The first is called "coiling dragon spits its tongue" and it looks like this." He demonstrated the technique at full speed.

"You start this movement from your basic horse stance as though you're sitting on your horse and striking in front of your knees. Next, as you step forward, your spear blocks in front to clear a path for your next step. Follow this movement with sitting on your horse again while twisting the spear to trap your opponent and instantly follow up with an explosive thrust to their chest with the sharp tip.

"Wow, that's so incredible and it's only the first movement!" Yangban stood with his hand pressed against his forehead.

"Now you try so that I can watch and make adjustments."

Yangban immediately jumped out in front of his father and tried to imitate what he saw.

"No, you need to always keep one hand at the very end of the spear, because it gives you more reach with the tip and it keeps your hands from being hit with a weapon."

His son tried again and struggled to maneuver the long weapon with his hand completely at the end. Eventually, after his father made several more corrections, he understood the concept and began to move the spear in a more comfortable manner.

"Good, good you're getting the idea and the spear doesn't appear to be such a foreign object in your hands. Now the next technique is called "Lihua removes her helmet." He showed his son the technique.

"The key to this movement is in how well you can feel the tip as you throw it up in the air. Your wrist and fingertips must be relaxed and sensitive and don't pull the weapon towards your body as you lift the tip. The spear must go straight up in order to catch it behind your back and you must catch it at the very end of the weapon. Also, make sure to keep your body upright so you don't fall over and your knee is pulled up as high as you can. Now you try."

Yangban grabbed his spear by the sharp tip, pointed it straight out to the side and attempted to throw it up behind his back. "Thwack, ouch!" the spear hit his thumb and then his head before dropping in the dirt.

'See, it takes a sensitive touch while lifting, but don't worry. You'll hit yourself many more times before you figure it out!" he laughed and shook his head.

Over the next three hours, Yangban focused on perfecting the two fundamental movements. The "coiling dragon" technique required focusing on numerous body parts simultaneously and developing an acute sense of precise timing between the body and the spear's sharp tip. Additionally, his stances were required to be exactly timed to the motions in order to maximize the generation of power from the ground. Finally, he turned his attention towards the second technique and spent two of the three hours trying to correctly throw and then catch the seasoned weapon. "Thwack, ouch, thwack, ouch!" echoed through the trees as the hard wooden shaft continually hit his head, fingertips and ribs. Finally, determination and dedication persevered and he repeatedly caught the spear without hitting himself or dropping the ancient warrior in the dirt.

"Yangban, come inside and eat." His mother yelled from the edge of the compound.

"Did you get those movements figured out yet?" his father asked as he stepped into the kitchen and sat at the table.

"Yes, finally. It took a while to quit hitting my fingers, but I got it," he said.

"After we eat, you can show me how they're coming along and then I'll show you several more movements." Zhangfu said as he stirred the bowl of rice and vegetables.

Thirty minutes later the two walked outside into the bright light from the glowing yellow ball high overhead and headed towards the training area.

"Show me the techniques from this morning." He stood his weapon against the tree.

Yangban quickly performed the first series of steps to imitate the dragon technique and turned towards his father.

"That was good. It appears you're getting the concept of how the body and spear must become one in order to effectively execute the technique. Now show me the second movement."

Again, Yangban quickly positioned himself and demonstrated the technique.

"Hmm, that's not too bad. If you keep practicing, you'll have it down in no time." He raised his thumb.

"Now the next technique is called "circling whirlwind releases the poisonous snake." Zhangfu spun around and thrust the spear outward.

Yangban tried the technique and suddenly fell backwards, "Thud" he hit the ground and dropped the spear.

"Hmm, it looks like your iron broom sweeps are in need of some serious help." He tilted his head back and smiled.

"I'll let you practice that technique while I go in and check on the horses." He slowly walked away.

After an hour his father returned and asked, "So, how are those sweeps coming along?"

"Sometimes they're good and sometimes they're not." He stood up and brushed off the dust from having recently fallen on the ground.

"Keep at it, you'll get it. Now the next movement is called "twisting body, coiling snake." He grabbed his spear and demonstrated.

"I like that twisting type of movement and then falling into a low stance. Now I just have to figure out how to do it correctly and powerfully." He began stepping through the movement slowly and methodically while trying to orient himself to the directions of the motion. Two hours later he sat under the large tree and drank some cool water as he watched the large white clouds silently drift across the blue sky and disappear behind the distant hills.

They don't seem to have a care in the world and their movement is so smooth and continual. he thought as he leaned back against the trunk.

Maybe I'll try to move like they do and see what happens. he decided while slowly standing up.

Casually he walked through the series of movements while trying to imitate the soft clouds. Wow, when I act like the clouds it seems so easy to perform the techniques and I don't struggle with balance or falling. He scratched his head.

Throughout the next several years, Yangban trained daily and soon his years of training began to become apparent. His body had changed dramatically since his youth. His strength, balance, awareness and control were now honed to a fine edge. Each technique was becoming powerful, pinpointed and deadly while the control of his mind continued to tighten and his experience with a variety of weapons expanded daily, until he was proficient in all eighteen classical weapons. He was on the verge of becoming a true warrior.

3. FLOWER OF DEATH

In the late 1600's, England began establishing relations with China in hopes of establishing a trade agreement. Initially, all their efforts were defeated by the Portuguese who had already established trade relations with China years earlier. Gradually, over the next one hundred years, England earned the right to trade on a small scale. Unfortunately, this arrangement didn't last too long after the realization of profits from opium became apparent.

"Lower the sails," the captain pointed at the shore.

"Lower the sails!" his first officer yelled to the deckhands.

"Creak, creak," the wooden pulleys slowly turned and released the large canvas catching the early morning breeze. Minutes later as

the English 1100-ton Northampton finally stopped, the captain gave the order, "lower the anchor."

"Lower the anchor." The first officer pointed at the chain lock. "Rattle, rattle, splash!" the 3000-pound iron weight pierced the calm water's surface.

"Gather the landing party." The captain wrote in his log book.

"Gather the landing party and lower the boat. We will be leaving shortly." The first officer climbed down the steps.

"Creak, creak, splash," the boat settled onto the still water.

One by one the ten-man party climbed down the rope ladder and carefully maneuvered towards an oar. Finally, the first officer climbed down and stood at the helm.

"Push off," he pointed at the starboard side oarsmen.

Immediately after the boat was far enough from the Northampton, the men began rowing towards the shore. After thirty minutes the bow skidded into the sand and the first officer quickly jumped out into the shallow water.

Reaching dry sand he turned and said, "I want you four to come with me and the rest need to stay here and guard the boat." He turned and began walking away.

The first four men jumped out and rushed to catch up to their superior, while the remaining crew pulled the boat further up the shore and secured it to an old log.

"Ah... land at last," an oarsman said while sitting on the soft sand.

It was now 1805, and for many years England had been smuggling opium into China through a small barrier island off the coast of Guangzhou called "Lintin Island." Its position and physical characteristics supplied the incoming ships with excellent cover from the authorities in Guangzhou. It was tall enough to shield the height of the ship's mast and wide enough to obscure the size of any docking ship. The English ships would regularly arrive in the early morning to utilize the position of the rising sun and dock close to the large rock formation. The local traffickers would then quickly sail their well-armed junk boats out to the ship and offload their newest bounty of opium pods before hurriedly sailing back to shore to avoid detection. From there the bounty would be quickly transported to a secure location before being sold to local traffickers and shipped throughout China. Because of the immense trade deficit that England had accrued over the years, they required payment in silver only.

"Goumin, how are you?" the lieutenant waved from the landing party boat.

"Good, good sir."

"Are you ready for my men and their boats?" he politely bowed.

"Yes, the captain is waiting."

"Good, good. Signal him to start bringing it to the deck."

"Do you have the silver?"

"Yes, yes."

"We have 150 crates, how much silver do you have?"

"Enough for 200."

"Good, I'll signal the captain." He turned, pulled a long white flag from his pocket and waved it several times towards the ship.

"tell your men to start sailing and quickly. We need to be finished and sailing out to sea before the noon hour." He began walking towards his boat at the edge of the water.

"I see the signal, so start bringing up the crates," the captain yelled to the deckhands.

Suddenly, the deck of the foreign ship came alive with activity, "Open the cargo well, swing over the pulley and hook, untie the crates and get ready to hoist them up!" one by one the crates of opium were raised to the deck, stacked, counted and by the time the junk boats arrived, the entire deck was filled with crates stacked as high as possible.

"Goumin, welcome and come aboard so we can settle up." the captain held the rope ladder while his guest climbed up to the deck.

"Hello, Captain, nice to see you again." He slowly bowed.

"Goumin, come inside so we can finish our business." As they began climbing the steps the captain turned, *"I want you two to go down and count the silver while we conclude our business."* He pointed at two of his senior officers.

"Do you want us to bring it on board?"

"No."

"Goumin, please have a seat while we talk." He pulled back the chair.

"Thank you, captain."

"Your lieutenant said you have 150 crates."

"Yes, that is correct, but unfortunately the cost of production has gone up."

"Oh, how much?"

"Ten silver bars per crate."

"What? Ai-yaa!"

"Would you like me to sell it to someone else?"

"No, no I'll take it."

"Good, then we have a deal?"

"Y-yes, okay"

"I knew I could count on you to buy the pods. Let's go out and tell them to start the exchange." The captain put his hand on Goumin's shoulder.

"Lieutenant, start bringing the silver on deck and offload the crates on the other side." He leaned over the railing.

"Creak, creak," the pulleys lowered the large iron hook.

Immediately the deck came alive with activity, as the opium crates were lowered to the junk boats while the silver was raised from the other side. Two hours later the last opium crate rested on the junk, the hook was released and Goumin bid the captain farewell, "Good-bye, Captain, I'll see you when you return with another shipment." He bowed.

"Yes, yes, I'll see you then." The captain bowed.

Goumin climbed back down the ladder and instantly began yelling in Chinese at the men on the junks. The men at the oars immediately lowered the oars and began pulling on the oars as fast as they could.

"Raise the anchor!" the captain yelled to the first officer.

"Raise the anchor!" the officer yelled down to the deckhands.

"Raise the sails!" he pointed at the large mast.

Once again, the wooden deck sprang to life as everyone rushed to fulfill the orders. The old worn pulleys once again creaked and complained about moving from their quiet position as the heavy iron chain was pulled from the seabed and rattled continuously as it fell down into the depths of the hull.

"Hurry, hurry, we need to get to our hiding place before anyone sees us!" Goumin yelled at his oarsmen.

An hour later the junks moored safely in the secluded cove and began unloading the precious cargo.

"Hurry, hurry and get those crates off the boats and into the wagons!" Goumin darted nervously back and forth.

"Zoufei, make sure all the crates arrive at the warehouse."

"Yes, boss." He secured the ropes on the overloaded wagon.

"Hurry, hurry, get those crates off the boats!"

An hour later the last crate was finally unloaded and quickly disappeared up the narrow dirt path. Minutes later the secluded beach was again empty and quiet.

"Zoufei, send one of your men to tell your friend that our cargo has arrived and he needs to come tomorrow." Goumin continued counting the crates.

"I want all the cargo to be gone in several days."

For years this scenario continued and slowly the demand increased as the addiction spread further and further across the Middle

Kingdom. Eventually, every major city had an opium den and its pressure was no longer perceived as an unknown establishment. Now everyone knew where they were located and who their primary patrons were, by their frequent visits.

The Qing government repeatedly tried appealing to the English leaders, in hopes that they would realize the devastating effect the drug was having on the people, and how its smuggling into the Kingdom was destroying the economy. Unfortunately, the English white devils were making an incredible profit from the opium, so they had no interest in the health or lives of the lowly Chinese. And to consider abandoning all the potential profits for the sake of the Qing economy was totally out of the question.

"Goumin, Goumin! My friend is here to buy some opium and wants some extra," Zoufei placed his hand on the shoulder of his friend.

"How much does he want?" Goumin asked without looking up.

"Five extra crates."

"He can buy them but the white devils raised the price."

"That's okay, he's opening a new market in Shandong."

"Really? Good, good. Here is the price and if your market up there works out, I'll give you a better deal next time." Goumin stood up and bowed.

"Zoufei, what happened to your cousin from Henan Province?"

"Ai-yaa! He was running his mouth about the success of his business and almost got arrested. So now he's lying low." He squatted next to a crate.

"Is he still buying?"

"Yes, and hopefully he'll arrive next week."

"Hey, Chouma, it's about time you showed up, I was getting worried." Goumin turned and shook his papers.

"Sorry, sorry, I had to get some of the houses to pay up and all they wanted was to buy on credit." He shook his head.

"Do you want your usual amount?"

"Yes, and maybe two extra crates if you have them."

"I do, but the white devils have raised the price, so do you still want them?"

"Ai-yaa! How much extra this time?" Chouma looked down and shook his head.

"Ten bars per crate."

"What, that's robbery!" he slapped his forehead.

"I know, I know, but you'll make it back from the houses because their clients will never quit smoking." Gaumin put his hand on Chouma's shoulder as he leaned in close to whisper.

"Okay, okay I'll buy it. When will your next shipment arrive?" He waved for his helper to bring the money.

"About five weeks." Goumin pulled on a crate.

"Good, hopefully by then I'll have another house open in Fukien Province."

"Great, I'll keep your name on the top of my list." Goumin bowed.

"Excuse me, are you Goumin?" the visitor bowed.

"Yes I am."

"Great, I'm Shao Bendan from Panyu."

"Who sent you to me?"

"My cousin knows Zoufei and said you could supply me with some opium."

"How much do you need?"

"Maybe one crate until my business expands."

"Okay that'll be fifty bars."

"What, my cousin said they were thirty!" he slapped his forehead.

"They were, but the white devils just raised the price."

For several minutes Shao Bendan stood and appeared to be figuring in his head, then turned and said, "Okay, I'll take it."

"In five weeks, I'll have more so if you come back and buy more than one, I'll give you a better deal." Goumin bowed.

Day after day, a steady stream of customers arrived to purchase the illegal drug and transport it to their local distributors before it was delivered to the growing number of smoke houses. Finally, after five weeks of daily transactions, the warehouse was empty and Goumin could rest and prepare for the next ship to arrive with another shipment, only for the process to begin again.

Year after year, the demand for the flower of death steadily grew and the Qing government soon tired of the foreigners' continual smuggling and its effects on their economy.

"What news do you have for me today?" the emperor leaned back in his ornately carved wooden throne.

Oh, great ruler under heaven, I bring you news about the foreign devils." The eunuch knelt and bowed.

"And what news do you bring?"

"The foreigners are still smuggling in the opium and the demand is continuously growing."

"What do you mean, the demand is growing?"

"We have reports of the drug being sold here in the north."

"All the way up here from Guangzhou?" the emperor stood up and stepped forward.

"Y...yes, oh great ruler under heaven."

"Where?"

"It's here in Beijing."

"Are you serious?" he turned and began pacing back and forth in front of his throne.

"Send in my scribe," he said while returning to his chair.

"You can go." Immediately the eunuch bowed, slowly stood up, bowed again and quietly backed away. Minutes later another eunuch scurried to the hall while carrying several tightly wrapped scrolls. Silently he walked over to the reception walkway, bowed and quietly moved forward with each foot barely stepping past the last until he reached the end prior to the steps of the emperor's platform. Kneeling on one knee, the eunuch bowed and said, "I am your official scribe and have come to write your great words of wisdom."

"Prepare your scrolls."

The eunuch carefully unrolled the first scroll, removed the writing brush and ink well from inside his sleeve and patiently waited.

"Send this to the leaders of the land of England. I am the Duoguang Emperor and ruler of all under heaven in the Middle Kingdom." He leaned forward and looked around the room.

"For years we have allowed you to enter our great land and purchase our tea, silk and porcelain. Recently my representatives reported that your ships are continually smuggling the deadly opium into our southern port of Guangzhou and now it has spread throughout our great land." He sat back while waiting for the scribe to finish.

"This "flower of death" is rapidly undermining the moral fabric of our people and tearing apart our economy. We hope you will consider these important facts and refrain from any further smuggling of this deadly drug in our great land." The emperor leaned forward in his throne, gestured for the scribe to leave and turned to look away. As soon as the scribe finished writing, he carefully rolled up the scroll, slid the brush and ink well back into his sleeve, bowed and then stood up and slowly backed away.

Months later when the English ship arrived in London, the captain delivered the official scroll to the King. "Your Highness, I bring you an official letter from the ruler of China, and I took the liberty to bring in a translator." The captain bowed as he handed the scroll to an assistant.

Turning towards the King, the assistant walked closer, unrolled the delicate fabric and held it for the translator to interpret.

"To the rulers of the land of England." He began as the king stood up.

"I'm the Duoguang Emperor…" he continued as the king casually walked around his large throne chair.

"We hope you will refrain from smuggling...."

"What?" the king stopped and looked at the translator, slowly walked closer with a puzzled expression.

"Did you say they want us to refrain from smuggling?" he leaned in close to the shaking underling and looked him in the eyes.

"Y...yes your highness. That's what they ask."

"Hmm, interesting request." He stood up and walked back to his throne.

"They only wanted to trade on their terms and sell more than they bought." He sat down and leaned back in the chair.

"And now that we owe them for all their goods and have figured out how to balance our debt, they complain about the affect our cargo has on their people and economy." The translator bowed and slowly backed away while the assistant silently rolled up the delicate scroll.

"Interesting." The king slowly stroked his beard while looking at the ceiling and appeared to be contemplating the words he just heard.

After several minutes of silence he spoke, "Fetch my senior official." He stood up and straightened his thick robe. Twenty minutes later a man dressed in an expensive suit hurried into the room.

"I'm here, Your Highness," he said while walking up to the throne.

"I want you to send a message to my officials in India that we will begin shipping more opium to China." The king continued walking around the large chair.

"If we stop now, we will soon owe them our entire country, and I will not be bullied by the backward yellow dogs!" he sat back down and pounded on the thick arms of his throne.

"Send the letter now!"

4. THREE MOVES

"Creak!" the old door yelled as young Yangban forced it to move from its comfortable closed position.

"Father now that I am twenty years old, I would like to start working as an escort." He walked over and sat in the worn chair of his father's office.

"Are you sure?" his father removed his glasses and looked at his son.

"Yes, I have thought about it and I would like to travel some."

"You realize there are some dangerous people out there and they are very good at their kung fu skills?"

"I know that."

"And many of them have no problem with killing you or any other person."

"I know that also. I remember you telling me about them many times over the years."

"I just want to make sure you know what you are getting yourself into." His father leaned back into his chair.

"You have taught me our family Kung Fu very well, and I think I will be able to survive because of that." Yangban sat straight up.

His father turned and gazed out the window. After a few minutes he turned back towards his son, "Very well, where were you thinking of working?"

"I thought about asking your friend Old Li."

"I'm going to visit him tomorrow and I know he is always looking for escorts he can trust, so I'll ask him." He picked up his writing brush.

"Thank you, Father."

"He told me recently that someone had been caught stealing."

"While they were working?" Yangban scratched his head.

"Actually, he caught them before they left for Weifeng." His father shook his head. "And I don't know if he found anyone to replace them. I suggest you go and focus on your training until after I have a chance to speak with my friend." His father began writing.

"Okay, I can think of several techniques that need improving." He stood up.

Yangban walked into the center of the compound, looked left at the small sapling and began charging towards it with a series of powerful kicks and punches. When he neared the silent opponent, he began punching directly at the trunk while touching the tree but not shaking the leaves. Kick, kick, jump, kick, punch, punch, and lean, the techniques continued.

"Yangban, come inside and eat. You have been out there for almost three hours!" His mother walked inside.

"Yes, Mother." He wiped the sweat off his forehead.

"So, your father told me you want to work as an escort?" Yangban stepped into the kitchen. "Yes Mother, that is correct. I have been thinking about it for a long time. I would like to see some of the other places in Shandong and be able to help father's business at the same time." He sat down.

"Do you understand the risks? There are many thieves out there. And they have been training a lot longer than you." She placed the hot vegetables in his bowl.

"Yes mother, I realize they have been training longer, but I know how strong out family style is. And I have been focusing on the aspects that are the weakest. I think now would be a good time to test my abilities." He straightened his back.

"I don't know. But if fighting bandits is what you want to do...." She placed her bowl on the table and looked out the window.

"Thank you for your concern," he placed his hand on hers.

The next morning, Yangban rose early, gathered his weapons, and trained in the courtyard the entire day. Just as the sun began to slip behind the trees, his father walked through the arched entrance.

"Yangban, I had quite the talk with my friend Old Li." He approached his son.

"Really?"

"Yes, we talked about his business and then about your future." He sat on the ground under a tree. "He is willing to allow you to try being an escort. But he is worried that you may not understand what it involves. And he doesn't want you to get killed."

"Will I be the only guard?"

"No, he wants to send someone with more experience along to help you on the first few deliveries."

"Okay, then I'll be fine." he sat down next to his father.

"He did say that recently someone tried to steal the cargo and the guard had to kill the bandit."

"I have thought about that." He leaned back against the tree. "And I have tried to visualize what I will do when I am forced to kill someone."

"How do you think you will feel afterwards?"

"I'm not sure." He looked up at the clouds. "Killing an animal for food, I understand. But, killing a person?"

"Ahh…. good, you thought about it and the lack of a solid answer means you've learned from the years of practice. Otherwise, you might enjoy the act or be too scared to follow through and end up being killed." His father said.

"Truthfully, I am scared about the idea, but I also know I will survive."

"Good, he wants you to start tomorrow." His father stood up

"Okay" Yangban sighed deeply while standing up.

"Try and get some sleep tonight," he walked away.

Yangban stood up and looked at the sky, the trees and the ground for several hours as his mind jumped from one scenario to another. Soon the sky had turned black and the moon crept its way over the horizon.

I guess I'll try and get some sleep. He picked up his weapons.

Lying in his bed, his mind raced all night.

"Er, Er, Er," he heard the rooster crow just as he finally fell off to sleep.

I guess it's time. He sat up and looked around the room.

"Are you ready?" His mother asked as he walked outside.

"Whew, I guess so." He shrugged his shoulder.

"Be careful, and watch the road, and keep your spear ready, and...."

"Okay, Mother" he put his hand on her shoulder. "I'll see you when we return."

"Promise?"

"Promise." He looked her in the eye.

Yangban turned and walk across town to the Li family compound.

"Yangban, it's good to see you." Old Li said.

"Good morning, Old Li. It's good to see you." He placed his spear on the ground and formally bowed.

"Come inside so we can talk." Old Li opened the ancient door.

"How is your son Xiaoshu doing with his Tan Tui training?" Yangban asked as he stepped through the door.

"Some days he trains really hard for seven years old, but then other days, well...." He sat in his chair.

"It sounds like you're worried about his future."

"Yes, I am." He lit the long pipe. "Someday he will be in charge and I worry about his children."

"Would you like for me to talk to him? Or could I spend some time and train with him. Then he will understand where he will be in ten years and possibly grasp the importance of his training."

"Thank you. That would be great. I think it would help him understand all of the things I have been teaching him. Because then he would hear it from outside the family."

"Okay, I'll stop by tomorrow."

"Now Yangban, let's talk about your ideas about your future." Old Li placed his hands on the young man's knee.

"I would like to work for you as an escort." He sat up straight. "I know I am young and lack experience, but I believe my training and honesty could be a valuable asset to your company."

"I see." He leaned back in his chair and puffs on the pipe. For several minutes, Old Li sat and smoked on his pipe while the young guest sat nervously and waited.

Eventually Old Li sat up in his chair and said, "Here's what I think we should do. I will let you ride as an escort with one of my senior guards. If there is a problem, you will have someone more experienced to help out. Also, they can let me know how you handle any bandits on the trip. So, if you are interested, I have a shipment that needs to go to Qingdao in a couple of days."

"Great, I will be here!" Yangban stood up.

"Come back on Monday morning. They will be expecting you and be ready to leave by the noon hour." Old Li turned and picked up a stack of papers.

I think I will put in some extra hours of practice for the next couple of days. He imitated several hand positions while walking.

"Father, Old Li said I could accompany his group on their trip to Qingdao." He stepped inside the office door.

"Good, when are they leaving?"

"On Monday morning, so I'm going to train all day for the next couple of days."

"Wise decision," he turned back to his papers.

For the next several days, Yangban trained all day with an added sense of enthusiasm, since he knew the areas of his training that required the most improvement. The days raced by and Sunday evening arrived too soon.

"Are you ready for tomorrow?" his mother asked as she placed the hot soup on the table.

"I think so, I wanted to practice more on my weapons, but I didn't have enough time." He slowly fanned the hot bowl.

"Well, be careful. And don't try to fight everybody by yourself. There are others going along who are much more experienced." She put her hand on his shoulder.

"Okay."

Yangban rose early the next morning, gathered his belongings, trusty weapons, and headed out of the compound before anyone else was awake. An hour later just as the sun was beginning to peak over the trees and announce the arrival of a new day, he walked up to the archway of the Li compound. He stopped and read the calligraphy etched in stone. "Tsai yun man hsien" (colored clouds are rising in the South; the family is being blessed by good heavenly signs).

Hmm…I like that saying, I know it will help me on this trip, he thought as he walked under the archway.

"Hello Old Li", he said as he placed his weapons on the ground and bowed.

"Good morning, you're here early. That's good," he stopped and bowed. "Come inside and you can help with the packing. Go through that door to where my son Shoushan is organizing the cargo. You can ask him what he wants you to do." He pointed at the door leading to the back storage area.

Yangban walked out of the office and through the storage area to a small enclosed compound where the cart was waiting to be loaded.

"Hey Shoushan, I haven't seen you for a while," he waved at his friend.

"Yangban, Father says you are going with us to Qingdao," he turned and bowed.

"Yes, that is correct, we plan to leave before the noon hour. I need you to carry all these crates outside so they can be loaded on the cart." He pointed at the cargo."

Several hours later the last crate was loaded and secured to the cart. Everyone in the group was ready and began walking out of the compound.

"Yangban, do you want to guard the front or the back?" Shoushan asked.

"I'll go up front," he ran past the cart.

The autumn sun was now directly overhead and the shadows were tucked tightly underneath the trees. Thirty minutes later the group passed the remaining building on the edge of town and turned down a small dirt road towards Nancun. All the birds had found a branch in the cool shade earlier and were patiently waiting for the heat to follow the sun behind the distant horizon. Fortunately, the breeze kept the intensity of the mid-day sun at bay and allowed the group a steady pace throughout the afternoon. As the sun began to touch the horizon, Shoushan yelled from behind the cart," Hey Yangban, run up ahead and find a spot where we can stop for the night!"

"Okay," he waved and began running ahead. After twenty minutes he returned. "I found a spot not too far from here." He pointed in the direction.

Later, after the sky had turned black, the stars silently announced their position, and all was quiet.

As the first rays of light arrived from the distant star, the next morning, the group slowly rose and prepared for another section of their journey.

"Yangban, I'll lead the cart today." Shoushan said.

"Okay."

"Make sure nothing falls off the back of the cart. I don't want to lose any time because we have to stop and pick up the busted crates."

"Okay." Yangban checked the ropes securing the cargo.

The hours slowly drifted by, as the group continued on the dirt road. Suddenly a man jumped out of the tall grass and stood in the road.

"Yangban, watch the cargo!" Shoushan yelled as he turned his head towards the cart.

"Okay, and I'll look for any other bandits behind us." He turned around to check the road.

Shoushan drew his sword from its sheath and approached the stranger. "You need to move off to the side so we can pass."

I'll move when you give me your cargo. And if you don't, I'll kill everyone."

"Ha! You aren't getting anything and we will see who gets killed today."

"Ai-yaa!" the stranger raced forward swinging his stick wildly. As he neared Shoushan, he raised the stick over his head and instantly Shoushan jumped forward, rolled past the stranger and cut his leg as he stood up. "That's one move, two more and you will be dead." He turned and watched the stranger wrap his wound.

"It's only a scratch. Now you will feel the power of my Hua style."

"Is that what the first attack was, I thought maybe you learned it from some little kids playing in the street."

"What, little kids?" He charged forward swinging the stick from side to side.

Shoushan stood motionless until the bandit neared and then quickly stepped back; avoiding the stick.

"Yaa!" the bandit jumped high in the air, landed in a low crouched position with his stick flat on the ground and imitating a technique that everyone knew from the Shaolin style called "Squash the snake."

Shoushan instantly stepped to the side and kicked the stranger in the face; sending him rolling backwards and dropping his stick. As the bandit struggled to his feet, the blood streamed from his nose and stained his tattered shirt while he staggered and shook his head, Shoushan yelled, "Here, you might need this!" and kicked the stick at his face.

"Thwap!" the weapon hit his reddened chin; causing him to stumble back even further.

"You got lucky, ptooey." He said while spitting, as the blood began to run into his mouth.

"No, you got lucky that I didn't kill you just now!"

"We'll see who gets killed." Instantly the bandit rushed forward.

Shoushan automatically charged forward while dragging his sword in the dirt behind him. The moment the bandit swung his stick to attack, Shoushan flicked his sword forward; sending dirt towards his opponent's eyes. Instinctively the fighter raised his hand to shield his face, and as he did Shoushan spun to the side while chopping the exposed arm. "Thud!" the sword hit into the bone near the elbow.

"Ahh!!" the bandit dropped his stick and grabbed the deep wound.

"I planned to cut your head but decided to attack the arm instead." He stepped back and wiped the blood from his sword.

"So, consider this your lucky day." Slowly Shoushan turned towards his friends and said, "Bring the cart," then looked one last time at the stranger frantically trying to stop the bleeding before heading down the road towards Qingdao.

"Yangban, you walk up front until nightfall."

"Are you sure?"

"Go!"

Just before the sun sank below the trees, Yangban turned and yelled, "Shoushan I can see Nancun." He pointed at the city.

"Good. We'll walk until we get there and then stop for the night."

"Yangban you looked a little nervous earlier when I wanted you to walk in front of the cart." He sat down next to a tree as they neared the city walls.

"How come? All you had to do was watch me keep that idiot from stealing our cargo."

"True, but after all my years of training at home, I never experienced that kind of situation.

"My father and other relatives always told me about the thieves on the road, but I guess it never really sunk in until today." Yangban sat down next to his friend.

"How did it make you feel, besides nervous, to watch the fight?"

"Scared, cautious, and a little bit humbled."

"You didn't get excited from watching?"

"No." he began to scratch the ground with a small stick.

"Good, because that means you will be less likely to want to hurt or kill someone with very little reason or just for fun." He put his hand on Yangban's shoulder.

"Did that happen to you when you first started?"

"Yes, and it took several trips before I got used to the situation. Don't worry, you'll get past it. But I know you'll have plenty to think about for the next couple of days."

As the other members of the group sat next to their small fire and talked about the events of the day, several solitary clouds drifted across the sky and momentarily dimmed the light from the moon.

"It's the tenth hour and all is well," the town crier reported from off in the distance.

Early the next morning before the other members were awake, Yangban and Shoushan walked out into a large open area and began their daily training; several minutes of standing meditation, then stretching, and finally practicing and researching their family forms. Yangban then used a nearby tree to pinpoint his aim with the spear-tip, working to hit a smaller and smaller spot while just touching the bark, followed by driving the razor-sharp spear past the edges of the tree and continuously slicing the same groove in the bark.

Shoushan meanwhile focused on techniques with his sword; stabbing forward and touching the same piece of jagged bark. Afterwards, he attacked the sides of the bark-covered opponent by chopping at its sides at the height of a thief's ribcage. Each chop needed to be at a precise angle in relation to the point of impact to achieve maximum affect. Any miscalculation in angle caused the sword to roll upon impact and only slap the opponent.

Two hours later they walked back to the campsite and saw that everything had been packed in the cart and the other members were waiting to begin another day's journey.

"We should be in Qingdao by tonight if we leave soon and don't encounter any more thieves." Shoushan said as he adjusted his sword and looked at the sun that had slowly crept over the distant trees.

"Yangban, you take the lead." He pointed down the dirt path in front of the horse.

One by one the group followed the horse silently pulling the loaded cart towards the distant port village. The late autumn cool air pleased the aging steed, offering him the opportunity to pull the cart without profusely sweating and continually searching for a cool drink of water or a shade tree.

Soon numerous farmers began entering the dirt path on their way to the day's harvesting efforts. All the tools needed for the removal of golden ripe corn cobs from their dying stalks before cutting down the brown and decaying stems were precariously dangling over the sides of the wheeled platform. Once the workers arrived at the field and neatly stacked the corn in the cart, they would begin tying the long stalks into bundles and stacking them by the edge of the small drainage ditch separating the dirt path from the fertile soil. Field by field the routine continued for several weeks until all crops were harvested and the fields left bare for the winter's eventual arrival.

As the group continued their steady pace, they could feel the air begin to moisten from the nearby sea. Occasionally a lone seagull could be seen soaring high overhead in search of a small morsel of food, followed by several more chasing after the first in hopes of stealing the bounty. Suddenly all the fields of corn that had covered so much of the landscape were now replaced with low lying wheat and millet. The golden-brown grains perched at the top of each delicate stem eagerly awaited the upcoming harvest to end their summer's long efforts.

Yangban casually walked over the top of a small hill and stopped as he observed the images of a coastal village for the first time. "Hey Shoushan, Qingdao!" He turned and pointed at the village below. Soon, the group entered the outskirts of the village and steered the horse towards the shop near the dock.

"Ahh…. Shoushan, you made it," the store owner said as he walked outside and saw the group stopping in front of his store.

"Just like my father promised."

"Yangban, after we unload the crates, we'll go down to the pier and have some fresh fish."

"Great, I've never had any seafood fresh off the boat," he said as he untied the ropes and threw them over the cart.

One by one the crates were carefully unloaded and carried inside so the owner could open each one and inspect its contents. Eventually, after the shipment was completely unloaded and inspected, the group all sat on the floor to rest as the shadows began to stretch completely across the street. After thirty minutes the two fighters strolled outside and headed towards the pier.

"I've never seen a sailing ship before and they're much bigger than I imagined!" He excitedly pointed at the vessels moored at the dock.

Walking along the worn wooden planks in front of each ship, Yangban continually stopped at each vessel to observe its construction. The length, width, and height of each ship in addition to the height of the center mast struck him with complete awe. He could hardly fathom how so much cargo could be stored inside each vessel and still allowed to float along with all the crew and their supplies.

"Are all those crates going into that one ship?" He pointed at the cargo, looked at the ship and then scratched his head.

"Yes, and there will be more tomorrow." Shoushan said as he stepped inside a shop cooking seafood.

"That flag over there says they are here from Guangzhou. That's a long distance."

"Yangban, they have some fish from the water down by Guangzhou, do you want some?"

"Definitely!" he quickly turned and headed towards the doorway.

"It's now the eighth hour and all is well!" the village crier's voice echoed through the streets, signaling to the two men that the morning light would soon be appearing on the horizon. Casually they walked back to the small shop, found a suitable place on the store's floor to sleep and quickly lost the sounds from the streets as their minds drifted off.

"Clang, clang, clang!" the men on the ships began pounding on the metal clasps supporting the crates as soon as the first rays from the sun crept over the horizon.

"Are these all the crates we are taking on our cart?" Shoushan asked as he stepped out the back of the store.

"Yes, and this one is very delicate, so be careful."

"Does everyone have all their belongings?" Yangban asked while tying the last rope.

As Yangban finished, the driver shook the reins and the horse slowly began walking down the dusty street. An hour later the group was once again at the top of the small hill on the edge of the village. "Interesting place." Yangban turned to look back at the streets below one last time, pulled his coat closed and buttoned it shut before walking down the hill towards his home.

After several days, the outskirts of Pingdu could be seen on the horizon and instinctively the horse began to increase its pace.

"Hey Old Li we're back!" Yangban bowed.

"Any trouble on the road?"

"Nothing we couldn't handle." Shoushan rested his sword against the wall next to the small desk.

"So how did it go with our new recruit?"

"Ha! It was a vivid flashback of the first time you took me along."

"Oh really?"

"He was that scared?" Old Li leaned against the wall and shook his head.

"So, you're saying Shoushan was more nervous than me?" Yangban leaned on his spear and smiled.

"I'll bet he left out that last half."

"Wow, I'm feeling better already." Yangban stood up and placed his hand on Shoushan's shoulder.

"I knew you would enjoy hearing that from my father."

"Yangban, I think you need to go home and see your mother." Old Li said.

"Really?"

"Yes, she was here every day while you were gone. I haven't seen her that much in years." Old Li shook his head.

"Okay."

"Come back tomorrow and I'll pay you.

"We can talk about Shoushan's little brother."

"That sounds good, I'll see you then." He turned and walked away while waving his hand.

Early the next morning as Yangban stepped up to the archway, he reached over and brushed the leaves off the auspicious poem on each side. Looking up at the sky he noticed nine solitary clouds brightly illuminated by the morning sun. "Hmm, that's interesting nine clouds and nine characters on the arch."

5. METAMORPHOSIS

"Creak!" the worn door groaned as it slowly swung open.

"Hey Old Li good morning." Yangban bowed after closing the door.

"Yangban, how are you?" the aged man replied as he turned from his desk full of papers to see who had entered his small office.

"Good, and my mother says thank you." He sat on the wooden stool.

"Thank you, for what. I didn't do anything. I stayed here. You were the one out on the road dealing with all the bandits." He gestured to show where he had been just before standing.

"Come with me, I need to check some inventory and we can talk while I'm counting." He slowly walked towards the back door.

"Oh, I almost forgot, here is your pay for that trip."

"Thank you, thank you." Yangban bowed.

As soon as they stepped through the door Old Li grabbed the board hanging on the wall with the inventory papers clipped to the front and headed towards the first row of shelves.

"I need to count all these, so if you count this side, it will really help."

Each crate contained numerous items, so Yangban had to open each crate, verify the number of items inside in relation to the total on the outside and then reseal the crate. Fortunately, the crates filled with the larger items were easy to verify, but the crates filled with numerous small items required each box be unpacked, counted, repacked and then sealed shut.

"Do you want to talk to Xiaoshu today?" Old Li asked.

"Yes, as soon as we're finished, I'll go find him."

Several hours later, after the inventory was finished, Old Li walked back into his office while Yangban headed out into the courtyard to find the young boy.

"Shoushan, have you seen Xiaoshu?"

"Yes, he just walked out the front gate."

Yangban hurried through the open courtyard towards the arched opening in hopes of finding the boy before he could disappear. Fortunately, he found Xiaoshu sitting under a large shade tree.

"Xiaoshu, come out here so we can practice" he pointed at the open area between the large old trees.

"Let's use this tree to stretch against before we start." He said while placing his foot up on the trunk and leaning forward.

"Yangban, did you have fun on the trip?"

"It went really well."

"How has your training been going lately?"

"Okay I guess," he dropped his leg and leaned against the trunk of the large tree.

"You don't sound very excited about it."

"My dad keeps telling me I should practice more, but I just want to play with my friends." He looks at the clouds.

"Do your friends practice at their home?"

"Yeah, but I'm not as interested in it."

"I remember when I was your age and my father made me practice every day and many days, I didn't want to practice at all. But I practiced anyway because my father said it was good for me and one day I would understand."

"Really, my dad says the same thing."

See, it's not just you who hears things like that. Now that I'm twenty years old, I realize the words my father said were completely true. Just like one day you'll feel the same way."

"I guess." He pushed away from the tree.

"How about if I practice with you today?"

"Sure, that would be great."

Yangban placed his hand on Xiaoshu's shoulder as they walked out into the open area.

"Show me the routine you recently learned." He watched the boy nonchalantly execute the series.

"Hmm, can I make a suggestion?"

"Okay."

"As I watched you perform the routine, it appeared as though each movement was completely empty of spirit and focus. Do you understand why you're doing each movement?"

"Um....."

"Let's go through each movement and I'll explain the application. Now show me just the first three movements."

Xiaoshu executed the movements as strongly as he could.

"When you're doing the first movement, you're punching an enemy in the chest. Your arm and wrist should be straight so they don't get broken." He knelt down and placed the boy's fist against his chest.

"Now squeeze your fist really tight. See how strong your arm and fist feel?"

"Oh, okay." he scratched his arm.

"The second move you showed me was a heel kick to the stomach. Remember when you kick you need to pull your toes back all the way so that it keeps them out of the way from being broken." He lifted Xiaoshu's foot and placed it against his stomach.

"See, if your toes stick out when you kick, they'll break really quick or get bent backwards." Slowly Yangban bent the toes backwards to show the position.

"The next movement was a block to the side. Here, I'll hold my arm out so that you can do the block against my forearm."

"See how your fist bends over when you hit my arm. That means your fist isn't very tight, so try again and tighten it as much as you can."

"Like this?"

"Yes, that's much better and now that block will actually be effective against a punch."

For hours they reviewed each movement and discussed their applications. Soon, the warm sunlight began to fade as the distant star began to slip behind the treetops, and Yangban knew it was time to stop.

"Okay Xiaoshu, I want you to practice all the techniques we talked about over the next two days and then I'll come back and we can continue with all the remainder of your training."

"I'll see you then." Yangban turned and began walking towards his family compound. As he reached the main archway he heard "It's now the ninth hour," from the distant town crier. Slowly he continued into the kitchen and boiled some water for a cup of tea. Afterwards, he carried the steaming cup outside and sat on the nearby step looking up at the distant stars while sipping the hot beverage.

Days later, as he entered the Li compound, he yelled to Old Li standing by his office, "Old Li, how has Xiaoshu's training been going?"

"Better, much better. He really liked how you explained the applications of each movement."

"I'm sure the words I used are exactly the same as the ones you have always told him. But hearing it from someone else seems to make it sound different."

"Yes, that's true. Oh, next week I have an order that needs to be delivered in Jinan. Are you interested in the job?"

"Sure, what day will we be leaving?"

"Probably early Wednesday morning."

"I'll be here at sunrise." Yangban said while looking around the compound.

"Old Li, do you know where Xiaoshu is?"

"No, but if you ask his mother, she'll know what he's doing." He pointed towards the kitchen.

"Mrs. Li, have you seen Xiaoshu?" Yangban asked as he looked in the front door.

"Yes, he's sitting here practicing his writing." She pointed at the table in the adjacent room. "Good, I can talk to him about the connection between writing and Kung Fu practice." He walked in and sat down on a stool next to the boy.

"Xiaoshu did you know writing the characters is just like learning a new Kung Fu form?"

"Really?" he looked up.

"Yes, because both of them require that you become mentally and physically part of what you are doing."

"Huh?"

"When you write the characters, you need to memorize what it looks like and then train your muscles to write it correctly, just like when your father teaches you a new form. As you learn the new sequence, you must memorize the movements and then train your body to perform exactly like you saw your father perform." He gestured several techniques.

"Okay, now I get it!"

"Soon it gets easier and easier to execute and then it starts to become as natural as tying your belt. When it gets to this point, the techniques will just flow from one to another and your fighting skills will really improve."

Xiaoshu picked up his sword and excitedly rushed outside to practice. Unfortunately, after only several minutes he was ready to stop and sit under the shade tree. "Clang," the sword hit the tree root as the boy dropped it and quickly sat down.

"You need to practice longer than that if you want to succeed." Yangban shook his head as he watched the boy relax against the tree trunk.

"Maybe tomorrow." He looked off at the distant horizon where the large band of clouds marched silently towards the sinking sun.

"Xiaoshu, did you brush and feed the horse?" Old Li pointed at the stall while walking towards his son.

"Do I have to, can't one of your workers do it?"

"No, I told you to take care of the horse, so get going or I'll get my bamboo switch!" he reached down and grabbed the boy by the ear.

"Ouch, okay, okay, I'll go."

"Make sure you do everything I told you to do because I'm going to check after you say you're finished." He looked at Yangban and sighed while shaking his head.

Slowly the boy sauntered off towards the stall and stopped several times to pick up a rock to throw over the compound wall. As he reached the enclave and climbed over the worn wooden fence boards, he grabbed the small wooden bucket and filled it with fresh feed. Turning around to return the bucket to the corner inside the pen, he was greeted with several "Nays" and the shaking of his head by the solitary horse as if to say "It's about time and thanks."

Instantly, the horse stuck his head into the bucket and began lapping up the sweet grain with his tongue, and as he did, Xiaoshu stepped to the side and began brushing the dirty matted hair hanging from the aged animal's neck. Soon the tangled mess was smooth and straight so he moved on to another area and began the routine again until every part of the horse was groomed.

"Good, I can go back inside now." He quickly placed the brush on the shelf.

"Did you finish everything I told you to do?"

"Yes, Father." He slumped onto the small stool in the kitchen.

"Good. Tomorrow I want you to help me clean the pen and spread the manure in the field."

"Yes Father." Xiaoshu leaned forward and looked at the floor.

"It'll be several more days before they leave for Jinan, so I want you to take care of the horse every day, and I don't want to have to come looking for you, because if I do, I'll have the bamboo switch in my hand!" he grabbed the boy by the ear and made him sit up straight.

Immediately, after his father left the room Xiaoshu stood up and quietly slid the stool back under the table and rushed outside. The sun was beginning to slip behind the distant line of trees covering the hill, and he knew it wouldn't be long before his mother was calling him back inside. He dashed out towards the main archway in hopes of finding one of his friends. Standing in the open street, he looked to the left and saw no one, turned and looked right.... still no one, "Hmm I'll go over to the Cheng family compound and see if my friend Wuwei is busy." He ran down the street, turned the corner and headed for the main archway.

"Wuwei, Wuwei are you here?" he yelled as he stopped and looked in all directions.

Slowly he began walking further into the compound and finally saw one of the elders.

"Grandma Cheng, have you seen Wuwei?"

"Yes, he's out back helping his father fix the roof." She said while pointing towards the back buildings.

"Thank you." He instantly began running in that direction while waving his hand over his head.

"Wuwei what are you doing?" Xiaoshu asked as he looked up at the repair site.

"We're patching this hole to keep the rain out."

"Can I help?" he stepped on the first rung of the ladder.

"Sure, bring up some of those roof tiles." Wuwei pointed at the stack of tile sitting by the tree.

"They're heavy!"

"Be careful not to break any of them because we only have enough for this small patch." Wuwei's father yelled as he continued securing the underlayment.

Slowly Xiaoshu began carrying the tiles over to the ladder, then carefully climbed up with a delicate clay tile tucked tightly under his arm until he reached the top and handed the piece to his friend. One by one he continued until he finished carrying the entire stack of thirty tiles up on to the roof.

"That was fun!" he said as he stood on the top of the ladder and watched the repair project.

"Can I help on the roof? I like doing stuff like that."

"No, we better not get any more weight on this section of the roof until I'm finished." Wuwei's father said as he secured one of the tiles to the roof.

"But you can stay there on the ladder and watch how it's done."

"How come the tile doesn't slide off when you let it go?" He shifted his position on the ladder while pointing at the tile.

"See that little piece on the back?" He turned it over. "That catches the edge of the tile board and keeps them in place."

"Wow!"

"Wuwei did you know all that?"

"Yes, my father taught me about them last year."

"Are you going to fix anything else when you're done with this?"

"No, not today, Wuwei and I need to go and practice before it gets dark."

"Oh… okay. Will you be doing anything tomorrow?" he climbed down the ladder.

"Yes, I have some repairs to do on the stable."

"Can I help?" he kicked a rock across the courtyard.

"Sure," he grabbed another tile to install.

"Great! I'll come over after my writing practice." He turned towards the entrance archway.

"Bye, Wuwei!" he waved as he ran across the open courtyard.

"Xiaoshu, where have you been?" his mother stood in the doorway with her hands on her hips.

"I was over helping Wuwei and his father fix their roof." He said while walking through the main archway of their family compound.

"Your father was looking for you while he was practicing. Did you brush the horse like he told you yesterday?" she shook her finger at him.

"No, I forgot." He stopped and looked at the ground.

"Well, go and do it now before your father finds you, and no complaining!" she turned and walked back inside.

"Yes, mother." Slowly he turned and headed towards the stable while kicking stones along the ground.

An hour later Xiaoshu was finishing his chores, as the sun left the last remnants of light in the courtyard.

"Xiaoshu, you missed our practice today, so tomorrow make sure you are there so we can make up for today."

"Yes, Father." He slumped down on the small wooden stool.

The following day, as Xiaoshu was finishing his writing practice, he heard "Rumble, rumble crack, splat, splat!" as the rain began to turn the grey dusty courtyard black and muddy.

"Great, it's raining so maybe I won't have to practice today." He thought while looking out the open window.

"Xiaoshu, come quickly so we can practice in the barn." His father closed the office door.

"O....kay." He slowly lowered his head, stepped back from the opening, walked out the door towards the office in the falling rain with his shoulders slumped forward, opened the door and stepped

inside. Looking around he saw his father standing in a basic stance imitating riding a horse while vigorously turning his waist with his arms extended to the sides. With each turn he forcefully exhaled at a precise moment in the turn and his feet never moved as if they were glued to the floor.

"Come here, Xiaoshu, I want to teach you about generating torque when you punch, kick and throw." He stood up and motioned for the boy to come closer.

"Torque?" he scratched his head in confusion while walking.

"Yes, that's how you can make strength more effective." He demonstrated the concept.

"Huh, more effective?"

"Come here, and grab my arm." He extended his arm.

"Grab tight, I want you to try and hold me here." He said while gently pulling back and forth.

"Now if I try to escape by using my arm and shoulders, it feels like this." He slowly pulled back by using his arm only.

"If I use the ground and my body, it feels like this." Xiaoshu struggled to hold the arm.

"What happened?" Xiaoshu released the arm.

"That was the effect of using torque instead of strength. Strength is in the muscles and they only have so much, but even if I add several muscles, they still only have so much. Now if I root to the ground

and use all the muscles in their natural direction, which is a spiral, I can make them enormously strong with less effort."

"I see!"

"See, how when I tried the first time you could feel all the effort coming from my arm and shoulder? And then when I used the ground, it was very hard to distinguish where it was coming from or how to deal with it?" his father pointed at the ground, then his shoulder and finally his arm.

"If you practice diligently, you will be able to do this, but you need to practice every day and not go running off to the Cheng family compound."

"But I like to help with the construction!" he looked at his father with a saddened expression.

"Ai-yaa! I'm trying to teach you the family Kung fu style so you can work for the escort business. How are you going to defend yourself while escorting our cargo, if you don't practice?"

"But I don't want to fight!"

"Ai-yaa! Practice your forms until I tell you to stop, and don't say a word!" Old Li sat on the bench in the corner.

For two hours Xiaoshu continually practiced each routine and each time he made a mistake, his father stopped him, corrected the technique and made him repeat the movement twenty times before continuing.

Outside, the rain finally stopped as the dark menacing storm clouds finally relented, allowing several rays of bright sunlight an opening to merge with the moist soil.

"Taishan, Xiaoshu are you going to eat?" Mrs. Li yelled through the rain from across the compound.

"Yes, we'll be in soon. I'm trying to get Xiaoshu to practice." He yelled from inside the office.

"Don't be too long or all your food will be cold!"

"Okay."

"Xiaoshu, do your forms again and make sure they are correct and then we'll go in and eat. Otherwise, we'll stay for another hour or two." His father said as he turned to sip his tea.

"What, longer?"

"Yes."

Twenty minutes later, Xiaoshu finished and stood sweating profusely while leaning over and looking at the floor.

"Good, now we'll go in and eat." Taishan stood up and headed towards the door. Slowly Xiaoshu raised his head, watched his father open the door and step outside and gradually began to follow behind.

Xiaoshu dejectedly followed behind from a distance, sauntered inside and ate his evening meal before quietly escaping to his room.

The following morning, long after the sun rose above the horizon to announce the fresh new day, Xiaoshu slept.

"Have you seen our son?" he asked as he stepped inside the kitchen door.

"No, I thought he was out training or helping you." She said as she washed the wooden bowls.

"No, I haven't seen him all morning."

"Xiaoshu, are you still sleeping?" she yelled as her husband stood near the door.

"Huh?" he stirred in the bed.

"Get out here, now! Your father is looking for you!"

"Okay."

"When he's finished eating make sure to send him outside immediately!" he turned and walked out the door.

Minutes later Xiaoshu begrudgingly walked into the kitchen and sat down at the small table, propped his elbows on the table and placed his chin in his palms.

"Your father has been waiting for you outside for some time now. Hurry up and eat so you can go out and help him." She placed the bowl on the table and turned back to her fire.

"Yes, Mother." He looked down at the steaming bowl of rice and vegetables.

"Father I'm here." He said as he walked into the office.

"It's about time. The horses have been waiting for you to feed them for some time, so hurry and get their feed."

Xiaoshu walked out the front door of the office to get the wooden bucket and as he turned, he heard Yangban say, "Hey, Xiaoshu, how are you doing today?"

"Good morning, Uncle, I'm fine."

"Do you want to help me with my training?"

"It will have to be in a little while, I got up late and have to finish my chores."

"I'll be outside the compound by that big tree training, so when you're done, ask your father if you can join me."

"Okay."

"Father, I just talked to Uncle Yangban and he asked if I wanted to go out and train with him by the big tree."

"After you finish all your chores, you can go, but I'm going to ask him about what you did while you were out there." He pointed his finger at his son with a scowl on his face,

Thirty minutes later the boy rushed into his father's office and said, "Father, I finished my chores."

"Very well, you can go, but remember what I said." He continued writing on the delicate fabric.

"Bye." Xiaoshu rushed out the door without closing it. As he ran across the compound, reached down, picked up a rock and threw it up on the roof and kept running.

"Hey Uncle, I made it!"

"Good, you must have worked really fast to get everything done already." He stopped and turned to look at the boy.

"Can I sit and watch you for a while?"

"No! you're here to train, so that's what we're going to do."

"Really?"

"Yes, and if you think I'm going to let you sit and watch and then go running off to play, think again."

"Yes, but...."

"I don't care what you thought you were going to do, you're here to train, so get busy!"

"Okay." He looked at the ground while slowly walking out to the open area.

"I want you to go through all your basics."

"Yes sir." He kicked a small twig.

"I finished." He said, as he walked up to Yangban.

"Good, now show me what you were working on with your father." He put his hand on the boy's shoulder.

Slowly Xiaoshu began demonstrating the movements with the sword that his father taught him recently.

"It looks like you're still having trouble with the flower movement and the wrapping the sword around your body."

"It hurts when I hit myself." He stopped and scratched the ground with the tip of the weapon.

"Remember when we talked about this before, and I told you not to be so afraid of getting hit?"

"Yes, but it still hurts."

"Keep practicing, in time you'll figure it out."

"How long will we be out here?" he asked after several more attempts at the technique.

"Several hours, so don't be thinking about asking to leave."

The sun was now rising high up into the clear sky and chasing all the shadows into the small indentations under the tree roots near the trunk of the old sentry. Xiaoshu was sweating profusely and the fine dirt had become caked to the back of his shirt following the attempts at rolling with the sword. Meanwhile, Yangban remained focused on the techniques with his spear and occasionally glanced out of the corner of his eye to see what the boy was practicing.

"Xiaoshu, bring your sword over here so I can help you with the techniques." He leaned his sharp weapon against the tree.

"I noticed when you were blocking with the sword that your sword was not properly positioned."

"Huh?"

"When you're blocking you need to pay attention to the sword and how it's positioned. Otherwise, it'll never be able to protect you. Whenever you're blocking, you must keep the blade positioned so it will remain strong and not bend, which means the blade must point at your opponent's weapon."

"But when I do that and somebody hits my sword it hurts."

"Which would you prefer, a little pain from blocking correctly or a lot of pain or death from blocking poorly?" He leaned over to look the boy in the eyes.

"Training in kung fu doesn't seem to be very important to you does it?"

"Ah, I guess I like it."

"Really, then how come you have so much trouble focusing and always want to go play?"

"I don't know."

"Since I saw you last it doesn't appear as though you've made much progress. Which tells me that you haven't been training very seriously. It's more like you only practice because your father makes you."

"Um…"

"I'm leaving tomorrow for another job and today I came by because I wanted to help you with your training, but it's obvious you're still at the point where you were last time. So how can I help you if you don't practice or take it seriously?"

"Um…"

"Tell me, what kind of things do you like to do?"

"Well, I like to help Wuwei's father fix things on the house, and I like to build things with piles of stones."

"See how excited you got when I asked you what you liked to do, and you explained those things to me?"

"Yes."

"That's how excited you should be about your kung fu training. Or it'll never be good enough to save your life while you are out guarding the cargo."

"Have you told your father that you like to help the neighbors build stuff?"

"No, I know he would only yell at me for not wanting to train."

"Someday you're going to have to tell him and if you don't, he will always expect you to take over guarding the cargo."

"What? really?"

"Yes."

"So that's something for you to think about. Now let's go back to the office and see what your father is doing."

"Do I have to tell him today?" Xiaoshu asked in desperation.

"No, I'll let you decide when to tell him. But you must tell him. Otherwise, it's not fair to him or you."

"I will, I promise."

"Good. it's a shame you don't want to train and improve your kung fu, but it's good that you know what you want to do." He patted the boy's head before placing his arm on his back while they walked.

6. AGITATED CRANE

Creak! The old door slowly opened while complaining about being forced to move.

"Good morning Shoushan." Yangban bowed.

"Good morning."

"How is your wife feeling? "

"Oh, she says it'll be any day now, because she can feel the baby drop more and more."

"Well then you will be a father again when we get back from Jinan."

"Yes, that's true."

"Yangban, could you check the cart and make sure everything is secured?

"I'm going to get the paperwork from my father and then we'll be leaving"

"Okay." He walked out towards the back of the building and saw the other workers busily securing the ropes to the sides of the two wheeled cart.

"Is everything on the cart? Shoushan is getting the papers and then we need to leave."

"Yes sir, we checked it three times."

"Well let's check the ropes one more time." Yangban grabbed a rope.

"Good, now we're ready."

"Shoushan, are you ready to leave?"

"Yes,

"Did you check the cargo?" He picked up his sword and tied it to his back.

"Yes, they verified everything three times.

"And I rechecked all the ropes," Yangban picked up his spear and began walking towards the compound main entrance.

"Okay, let's get going so we can get close to Weixian by tonight."

Slowly the driver turned the horse with the reins and guided it towards the main archway. As they walked through the opening, Shoushan turned to see his father who was standing in his office door.

"See you when we get back." *He waved and turned back towards the cart.*

The early autumn air still had a slight chill and the morning dew was clinging to the tips of the leaves, while the sun finally rose over the treetops. As they walked further from the small village, they saw a lone farmer tending the crops in the field. His oxen stood patiently while the worker methodically removed the encroaching weeds from the hearty corn stalks. Within weeks the summer-long toil of tending to the crops would be coming to a close, once the ripened corn cobs were harvested and the stalks cut, chopped and returned to the field for fertilizer.

"Yangban!" *he motioned him to come to the front.*

"So, tell me, how do you feel about this trip?"

"Well, I guess I'm a little anxious and cautious."

"Because of the last trip?"

"Yes." *He shifted his spear on his back.*

"Like I said, it will take several trips to get comfortable with the concept.

"But you'll get there." *He placed his hand on Yangban's shoulder*

As they walked, more of the local farmers arrived on the road with their carts filled with tools on their way to the waiting fields. "Rattle, rattle, clang, clang!" echoed from the carts as the wooden wheels dropped and returned from the numerous holes and trenches in the path, shaking everything within the wooden side boards.

The aged horse pulling the worn cart continued its steady pace, one step after another on the same daily route as the previous months. Numerous farmers didn't have the luxury of a work horse to pull the cart; they struggled along pulling the cart themselves or with help from a family member.

Soon the sun was directly overhead and all signs of the morning dew were gone. Now, the warmth from the distant star dried the loose soil and caused a subtle cloud of dust to linger behind the slow-moving cart. Seconds later the dust slowly settled back to the ground and returned to its stillness.

"Let's stop over there and cook some rice." Shoushan pointed at the trees ahead.

"I'll run up and find some wood to burn." Yangban ran ahead.

An hour later, everyone finished their meal and the group began another section of their journey. The air remained calm while only a few clouds dotted the sky as a distant eagle quietly soared across the sky and scanned the ground for an unsuspecting victim. Off in the distance a single stream of smoke from a small fire in an open field stretched straight up into the open sky. Field after field and turn after turn in the narrow road passed as the cart and its travelers ventured onward.

"Yangban, can you see that hill over there in the distance just below that single cloud?" He pointed at the cloud.

"Yes."

"We should be able to make it there today. Just on the other side is the village of Kuocun and that is half way to Weixian, so we'll stop there tonight."

As the group rounded the base of the solitary hill and neared the outskirts of the village, Yangban said "Ah, at last!"

"Yes, we have stopped here several times.

"It isn't very big, but it's a welcome landmark and the people are very friendly.

"While you get everything organized for the night, I'm going into the village and talk to a friend that lives here."

Casually, everyone helped setup an encampment, build a fire, begin cooking a long-awaited meal and slowly settle in for a good night's sleep.

"Here you go. My wife made us some dumplings." Shoushan handed everyone a portion of the gift.

The sun had slipped behind the horizon and was replaced by a sliver of the moon. Overhead the entire sky was engulfed in twinkling from distant stars, while the only sounds were an occasional dog barking.

"Ehr, ehr, ehr!" A lone rooster from the village announced the new day.

"Yangban let's check the ropes while they make some rice." He pulled on a rope.

"Tonight, we'll be in Weixian and it is larger than Qingdao, so it'll be a nice change."

"Great!" Yangban retied a rope.

As the horse stepped out onto the dirt road leading west, the sun began to rise over the horizon and send its first long shadows racing up the walls. Yangban and Shoushan led the group and for several hours casually talked and pointed out unique formations in the landscape.

"There is a swampy area up ahead so we need to be careful as we get close and especially while we're crossing over it.

"It's always a good spot for bandits to ambush a cart." He pointed ahead at the area.

"Whew." Yangban adjusted his grip on the spear.

As the group neared the thick grass, the two fighters began to carefully scan the sides of the path adjoining the thick growth. The grass was now tall and turning brown, so anyone with darker clothes would hide easily. Suddenly the horse stirred and began to snort wildly, Yangban turned and saw a lone bandit scrambling out of the grass and run towards the back of the cart.

"Shoushan!" He yelled and began running.

"Go! I'll watch the front"

As the bandit neared the cart, Yangban cut him off and stood motionless with his spear pointing directly at his opponent.

"Hey, get out of my way!" The thief pointed at his opponent.

"You're not getting anything from this cart, so leave now!

"I said leave!" Yangban took one step forward while shaking the spear just enough to make it rattle.

Time suddenly froze and all sounds ceased. The two stood only feet apart, but neither moved. Yangban had his spear pointed directly at the bandit's face, while his opponent continually switched his gaze from Yangban to the spear.

"Leave now or die!"

"Ahhh!" the bandit turned and quickly ran back into the grass.

Yangban remained motionless while scanning the grass for signs of his opponent.

"Are you okay?" Shoushan yelled.

"Yes."

"Good job." He motioned for the driver to continue.

Yangban began to retreat and continued to scan the grass as the cart slowly moved forward.

Eventually, the cart began to move away faster than he was able to walk backwards, so when he concluded the area was safe, he turned and ran back up to the front.

"Were you scared?" Shoushan put his hand on Yangban's shoulder.

"Ohh…yes."

"Relax. It's okay now."

"Whew! that was intense." He shook his head.

"Let's stop over there by those trees and eat some rice." Shoushan pointed ahead.

Later, everyone was sitting in the shade and talking about the encounter while waiting for the rice water to heat up, the driver just sat and shook his head.

"I've seen so many bandits like that on these trips and it still amazes me." He looked at the ground.

"Shoushan, remember last year when we were going to Taian and those three kids tried to stop us?

"The moment you told them they were going to die, two of them dropped their weapons, one wet his pants while the other stood and cried, and then they all stumbled to pick up their sticks before running off?" He looked up and chuckled.

"Ha! Yes, I remember.

"My dad laughed for days about that."

"I remember one day I walked into his office and he was almost in tears.

"When I asked him what the problem was, he said he couldn't stop thinking about that incident. The more he thought about it the more he laughed." He shook his head and smiled.

The sun was beginning its slow descent towards the trees and the shadows were stretching longer. As the group headed down the road once again. Minutes later Yangban noticed a distant structure, "What's that Shoushan?" he pointed up ahead.

"It looks like the walls of Weixian.

"If we keep going, we'll be there just before dark."

"Great!" he shook his spear.

"It is now the eighth hour and all is well!" the crier yelled as the group walked through the city's main gate.

"Let's stop over in that open space.

"We can stay there for the night." Shoushan pointed.

"Wow, this city sure is big!" Yangban looked around.

"Tomorrow we'll rest for the morning before we start out again, so you can look around a little."

As they were resting against the wall and waiting on the water to heat up for their tea, the driver rushed up and said, "Hey I just talked to my friend and he said there is going to be a fight tomorrow between two Kung fu masters!" He pointed behind him.

"Really, where?" Yangban asked.

"A few streets that way."

"Hmm, sounds like a good way to spend the morning." Shoushan raised his thumb.

"Did your friend tell you who they were?" Yangban stood up.

"Yes.

"One is a White Crane teacher and the other is an Eagle Claw teacher.

"My friend said the Eagle Claw teacher is trying to take over the area because the other guy is getting old."

"Oh, oh sounds like trouble for the eagle." Shoushan shook his head.

"Why?

"My friend says the White Crane teacher doesn't have a chance." The driver sat down.

"Oh, just a hunch.

"But let's all get some rest and go over and watch tomorrow." Shoushan laid down next to the wagon wheel.

"Erh, erh, erh!" A distant rooster crowed.

After the morning meal was finished, everyone helped to secure all their belongings in the cart while the driver obtained the location of the fight from his friend. The moment he returned he jumped up into his seat on the cart and waited.

"You know the way, so you can lead." Shoushan pointed forward.

"This way." He turned the horse.

Slowly the group headed further into the city, passing numerous street vendors setting up their small tables for the new day; barbers, fortune tellers, tool repair and dentists all struggling to survive the day by finding a few customers. Meanwhile, the store owners quietly began tying back the shutters on their businesses and sweeping away the dirt from the worn wooden walkway.

Children began dashing back and forth across the street while chasing a small dog, as their mothers stopped to look at the items hanging in the doorway of different shops.

Yangban continually glanced from one side of the street to the other in amazement at the activities of this large city.

"Ow, ow!" the dental patient grabbed his jaw.

"If I don't pull this tooth today, it will hurt you for another two years." The dentist continued pulling.

"Shoushan, look!" Yangban pointed at the dentist.

Out of the corner of his eye he noticed a formal carriage about to enter the main street as he walked by the extraction. "Hmm, it looks like a wedding." He turned to watch.

The groom, wearing a traditional long red robe, walked in front of the sedan chair carrying his wife to his family's compound where she would be formally welcomed into the family.

"Pop, pop, pop!" the firecrackers were thrown next to the groom and scared away any evil spirits while announcing the joyous occasion.

Yangban stepped back as the procession passed by and then turned to continue down the street.

As he passed the next intersection, he looked down the alley and was intrigued by the number of people standing at the entrance of a small inconspicuous storefront. "Hey Shoushan what's that all about?" he pointed down the alley.

"Oh, that's one of those opium dens.

"Stay away from those places." He shook his finger.

"Why?"

"They all go in there to smoke the opium."

"What is opium?" He stood and looked down the alley.

"It's a drug made from poppy seeds and it does strange things to your mind.

"And after you've done it several times you become addicted and keep going back."

"Wow!

"Where does it come from?" He scratched his head.

"I heard the foreign devils smuggle it into Guangzhou from India and then it is sent to all the big cities."

"Really?

"I think I'll take your advice and avoid it." He turned and continued walking.

"Yangban, look!

"That must be the school our driver was talking about."

"Yeah, it looks like some people are already gathering for the match." Yangban pointed towards the group.

"Let's stand over there near the school. We should be able to see everything from there." Shoushan walked to the side of the street.

Moments later a middle-aged man stepped out the door of the Kung Fu school and walked to the middle of the street, removed his jacket and began loosening up his joints. After several minutes he turned and watched as another man walked into the street.

"I'm Master Zhou Xiangxi. They call me Agitated Crane. I moved here several years ago from Yunnan Province and I have been teaching my White Crane Kung Fu across town since my arrival.

"Recently, I have been hearing from reliable sources that Master Tang Fendu from the Eagle Claw Kung Fu school has been telling everyone that my Kung Fu is terrible and I should go home.

"I have done nothing to harm him or his school and I have nothing against him.

"So today I came here to prove how good my Kung Fu is so that my reputation stays strong." He bowed to everyone in the audience.

"I am Master Tang Fendu, Soaring Eagle, from the Eagle Claw Kung Fu School. I have been teaching in this city for many years.

"My friends have told me they heard from reliable sources that Master Zhou has been telling everyone that I should be cutting hair instead of teaching Kung Fu. So, I have accepted his challenge to prove that my Eagle Claw is strong." He turned to bow to everyone.

As he finished his formal salute to the audience, he turned and bowed to Master Zhou who respectfully returned the salute. Slowly Zhou unbuttoned his jacket and placed it on the ground next to a spectator, walked back to the middle of the street and instantly began a prearranged series of movements from his style to loosen up his joints.

Tang stood motionless and watched while his opponent prepared himself for the fight.

"So, Yangban, who do you think will win?" Shoushan whispered.

"Hmm, I'm not sure. I've never seen that White Crane style of Kung Fu before so I don't know." He rubbed his chin.

As Zhou finished his routine and stood motionless, Tang suddenly attacked. Instantly, Zhou's eyes opened wide as he momentarily appeared surprised; causing him to quickly step back. When he stopped, he exhaled deeply and slowly shook his head. Slowly he raised his arms and stretched them out until they were almost fully extended and then began circling his opponent.

With each step he took, Tang slowly stepped to continue facing him. Zhou quickly turned around began, circling in the opposite direction and suddenly charged forward with a continual barrage of punches, first vertical, then horizontal, and then a combination of both. As he moved forward, Tang stepped back to avoid the punches and tried to attack, but each attempt was cut short by Zhou's next attack. As Tang began to stumble, Zhou suddenly stopped his attack, waited for his opponent to stand up, and then backed up to the middle of the street.

"Wow, that's an interesting fighting style." Yangban whispered.

"Yes, it is." Shoushan smiled.

Tang cautiously followed and rolled up his shirt sleeves. "Ahh!" He rushed forward while kicking and punching. But with each kick Zhou simply turned his body, outstretched his arms and deflected each punch. Suddenly, Tang jumped up and kicked three times in succession. As he did, Zhou slid his front foot forward and dropped under the attacks followed by a rising technique which spun Tang's body in midair and forced him to land face down. "Thud!" his forehead hit the hard ground followed by his body.

Zhou immediately stepped back and waited for Tang to prepare for the next exchange. "You got lucky with that throw, but it won't happen again." Tang shook his fist as he stood back up.

The two fighters stood and stared at each other for several seconds, and as Tang raised his hands before settling into a typical Eagle Claw fighting position, Zhou slowly stepped to the side with his right foot and stretched out his arms to imitate a crane's wings. Cautiously Tang stepped forward as if to close the distance. Immediately, Zhou began stepping in a semi-circle with his arms still outstretched. As Tang stepped in again, Zhou quickly turned and stepped in the opposite direction. Suddenly, Tang's facial expression changed as his opponent circled around him.

"If you think all that circling is going to help, you're wrong. It doesn't scare me in the least!" He turned again to face his opponent.

Meanwhile, Zhou continued his circling without saying a word. As Tang shifted his hand position and stepped to the side, Zhou charged forward with a continual barrage of punches, striking to the sides then up and down, followed by angular strikes from each side while driving Tang backwards. Soon Tang was backing into the crowd surrounding the fight and immediately charged forward towards his opponent. As he threw his first series of punches, Zhou quickly jumped to the side in a single leg stance and rebounded

*back towards Tang while punching at the back of his ribs. "Crack!"
echoed through the crowd as Zhou impacted the ribcage.*

*"Ai-yaa!" Tang stopped his punches and grabbed his side. "Cough,
cough, you'll pay for that" he said while rubbing the swollen area.*

"Wow, did you see that?" Yangban whispered to Shoushan.

"Yes, I did.

*"That was quite an interesting way of avoiding a kick." He rubbed
his chin.*

*"I've never seen anything like that before." Yangban stared at the
fighters. "I'm going to have to talk to him after this is over about
his style." Shoushan nodded his head.*

"Me too!" he placed his hand on his friend's shoulder.

"Are we finished?" Zhou stood and bowed to his opponent.

*"No! I've fought with much worse scratches and won, so don't even
consider stopping until I say so." Tang pointed his finger at Zhou
with a furious glare.*

"Are you sure?"

"Yes! And don't try to make me feel like I can't fight."

"Oo-kayy.." Zhou settled back into his previous stepping stance with his arms outstretched.

Tang immediately began breathing very deeply and forcefully and appeared to be gathering his energy. "Thud!" echoed across the ground as he stomped on the ground. "Thud, thud!" echoed again as he began charging forward. Within seconds he was within range of his opponent and began swinging his arms at various targets on Zhou's body. As Zhou retreated to defend the punches, Tang increased the speed of each attack, driving him back. Tang abruptly changed from punching to kicking and as the first kick raced towards Zhou's side, he instinctively jumped to the side to avoid the impact. As he did Tang turned and kicked; catching Zhou in mid jump and sending him rolling backwards.

"Nice kick, not too powerful, but a nice kick." Zhou stood up and brushed off the loose dirt.

"What… not very powerful? That was one of my best kicks." Tang placed his hand on his forehead.

"I guess I'll have to quit being nice by holding back my power."

"Don't hold back on my account. I can take it." Zhou settled back into his fighting position while leaning his head from side to side as if to stretch the neck muscles.

Again, Tang began breathing deeply but this time he tensed his hands and fingers while opening and closing his fists. "Thud" his foot hit the ground and he quickly rushed forward to close the distance. When his fist neared Zhou's face, he quickly leaned back and grabbed Tang's arm, pulling him forward and off balance. Immediately, Zhou sprung forward as if being launched from a slingshot and hit Tang in the chest with a double palm strike. "Thwump!" Instantly Tang's upper body was driven backwards while his feet lagged behind.

"Cough, cough, cough." Not bad, not bad. There wasn't much power in it, but it wasn't too bad." He leaned forward, rubbed his chest, and brushed off the dust.

The moment Tang started to prepare for another exchange, Zhou rushed forward and attacked. Kick, kick, kick, punch, twist kick, and punch. This time Tang stood his ground and never retreated. As Zhou continued to attack, Tang stepped in even closer and stopped the techniques before they could accumulate full speed and power. Without slowing down Zhou began a series of elbow attacks and effortlessly slipped inside each of Tang's defenses. "Thud, thud," the first two techniques hit Zhou's opponent in the chest. "Thud, thud, thud," the next three found the ribcage near the spot where the previous punch landed.

"Ai-yaa!" Tang stepped back and placed his hand on the injured ribs. "Lucky shot." He said while waving his other hand at his opponent.

"Really?

"Which one of those that hit you was the lucky one?" Zhou asked while maintaining his fighting stance with his arms outstretched.

"What? They were all lucky."

"Maybe we should stop so you can go home and rest and recuperate."

"No!

"You're the one who is going to need to go home and rest!

"Aii-yaa!" Tang rushed forward and began punching and kicking with even more intensity. Again, Zhou stepped backwards to avoid the attacks and the moment he saw Tang begin to tire, he slipped inside the first arm and grabbed the elbow. As Tang reached over to try and release the grab, Zhou quickly grabbed the other elbow. Instantly Zhou turned and swept Tang's feet out from under him, forcing his body to turn in mid-air until his head was the lowest point. Momentarily Tang appeared to hang in space with his feet pointing straight upward while his head began to race towards the hard ground. "Thud, thump!" His head hit the dirt and was immediately followed by his back.

"Ahhh…" Tang rolled over and grabbed the back of his head. "Cough, cough, spit."

"I think we're done here today." Zhou stepped back and saluted his fallen opponent.

"No! cough, cough." Tang struggled to sit up.

"I don't want to kill you. So, I think this fight is over." He walked over to pick up his jacket, slowly put it on while watching his opponent sit on the ground, turned, and walked back to his school while shaking his head.

"Yangban, let's go inside and ask him about his style." Shoushan tapped his friend's shoulder.

"Good idea, I'd like to hear about his fighting strategy," Yangban said as they stepped inside the doorway of the small training hall.

Standing just inside the doorway, as their eyes gradually adjusted, they noticed a small table at the far side of the room. Hanging above the table at each corner were two vertical placards with Chinese calligraphy artistically painted in gold paint. Each placard expressed specific Kung Fu – Codes of Ethics. The right sign said: Zun zu, zun shi, zun jiao zun (respect the ancestors, respect the teacher, respect the teachings being taught), and the left sign said: xue ren, xue yi, xue kung fu (learn kindness, learn fellowship, learn kung fu - or hard work) In the center of the table was a large single character (huo – or fire) that had been intentionally turned upside down and meant "to control the inner fire."

Centered on the table was a simple incense urn surrounded by several small drawings of Master Zhou's deceased teachers. Hanging on the wall on each side of the table were numerous well-worn long and short weapons.

"Excuse me, Master Zhou.

"I am Li Shoushan and this is my friend Cheng Yangban and we are from Pingdu city.

"We watched your fight outside and were curious about your unique style." The two simultaneously bowed.

"Pingdu, where is that?" Zhou asked while lighting several sticks of incense before ceremoniously moving them up and down in front of each drawing and then placing each stick carefully into the urn.

"It's over on the east side of Shandong Province and we are here for the day escorting some cargo for my father."

"Ahh, so you are practitioners as well?" he turned to look at them.

"Yes, I train in the Tam Tui style and Yangban practices the long-fist style."

"I see. How can I help you?"

"We were wondering if you would allow us to ask you some questions about your style?"

"Sure, sure, come in and sit down while I make some tea." He said while pointing at the small wooden stools near the wall.

"Your style of Kung Fu, what do you call it?" Yangban asked as he sat on the worn stool.

"It's called White Crane and it comes from the Sungzan Temple in the western province of Sichuan near the border with Tibet."

"Sungzan, that sounds similar to Songshan in Henan where the Shaolin temple is located." Shoushan pointed to the south towards the distant province.

"Yes, it should, because that's what it means."

"Really, I didn't know they had a temple that far to the west." Yangban softly scratched his chin.

"Yes, when we were forced to leave our original temple, we found this Shaolin Temple that had been abandoned, so we repaired the buildings and put the Shaolin Temple sign back up."

"Your White Crane, I've never heard of this style." Shoushan blew across the top of the steaming liquid in the small porcelain cup.

"It has been passed down in the western province for many generations. I'm the first to leave the area.

"It's based on the movements of a White Crane as far as attacking and defending." Zhou walked to the door and looked out towards the area where the fight had occurred.

"We imitate the actions of a crane when it's attacked.

"Patience is the first rule of our crane style.

"Wait until your opponent has totally committed himself to attacking and then evade and counter."

"Hmm, interesting." Shoushan looked up out of the corner of his eye.

"Our original style was based on more of a defensive attitude, but I am working on an alternative theory where the crane is more aggressive.

"Ahh, that's why I saw you charging forward with a crane technique, but usually cranes will wait before they attack." Shoushan stood up and imitated several movements.

"Exactly."

"That is such an ingenious improvement! I'm going to have to go back home and re-think all the training I learned when I was young." Yangban said as he sat and shook his head.

"That's good, that means your family style will now improve because of the new thinking."

"Wow!"

"Ha! Yangban you seem to be at a loss for words." Shoushan pointed at his friend while laughing.

"Cousin Zhou, cousin Zhou, are you alright? I just heard from my sister that you were in a fight." The man rushed in the school and looked Master Zhou over for injuries.

"Yes, yes, I'm all right, so you can calm down now.

"Excuse my cousin. He gets excited easily.

"Cousin, these are my two friends from Pingdu, Li Shoushan and Cheng Yangban. They are escorts and here to deliver some cargo.

"This is my cousin Wan Tingwei from Anqiu City. He is here visiting his sister who is my wife."

"Hello, we're glad to meet you." Shoushan and Yangban bowed.

"So, you're escorts for a cargo wagon, then you must be fighters as well." Wan bowed.

"Did you see his fight?"

"Yes, we did and it was quite impressive." Shoushan saluted Master Zhou as a sign of respect for his fighting ability.

"Yes, that's what I hear from my sister, too.

"Well, I have to go and help my sister. I'm glad to meet you gentlemen and I'll see you later tonight, Zhou." Wan turned and headed out the door.

For several hours the trio sat and discussed their individual styles of training and the fighting applications. Eventually, as the sun slowly began to set behind the distant treetops and the shadows in the street grew longer, the two visitors decided to begin their walk back to where their cargo was located. Goodbyes were exchanged and in departing, an obvious friendship was now established between the three.

"Goodbye, Zhou!" Yangban yelled as he waved to his new friend before turning the corner.

Days after the group returned to Pingdu, Yangban quietly strolled into the Li family compound.

"Hey Shoushan, how's your wife?" he asked as he saw Shoushan while walking across the compound.

"Better now, she had a baby boy a couple days ago and is resting."

"Congratulations, have you chosen a name yet?"

"Yes, we decided to name him Li Zhizhan."

"Wow, that's a great name for 1810 and the year of the horse. He should do really well in life with a name like that." He patted his friend on the shoulder.

7. DELICATE FIRE

"Hey Yangban, come up here!" Shoushan yelled as he waved his arm.

Yangban ran up ahead of the cart with a nervous expression on his face.

"Is something wrong?" He asked while stopping next to his friend.

"No, nothing is wrong. I just had a question that I was curious about.

"Remember two years ago, when we went to Weixian and saw Master Zhou from the White Crane School beat the Eagle Claw master?" Shoushan imitated the Eagle and White Crane techniques.

"Yeah, that was quite an interesting fight." Yangban shook his head and looked at the sky.

"What new theories have you come up with for your family style since seeing that fight and talking to our friend Zhou?" he tapped his friend on the back as they walked.

"Well, I've been thinking about how to include some of his techniques into the forms of our family style. We have some movements that are supposed to be defensive but seem to lack power. Now if I use Zhou's White Crane blocking ideas, they would definitely enhance the techniques. So, I'm putting together a list and when I get through, I'll show them to my father." Yangban tried to imitate the Crane hand positions.

"Yes, I've been working on some ideas for our Tam Tui techniques as well. The concept of making the White Crane more aggressive still has me in awe and I think about it every day." Shoushan said.

For the next hour the two walked and continued to discuss their ideas and impressions about the unique style they witnessed. As the sun began to sink behind the trees, Yangban ran up ahead to find a suitable spot to camp for the night. Soon everyone arrived and helped to build a campfire and erect a covering to protect them from the cool night air. One by one the distant stars began to appear in the black sky as the sun was replaced by the thin slice of the moon. The continual chatter from the birds gave way to the silence of the deep dark sky, and now the only sound was the occasional crackle from the small fire.

The next morning before the sun began sending its first rays over the horizon, Yangban and Shoushan rose early to spend two hours practicing their family arts, followed by research into the White Crane theories. The temperature during the night had dropped considerably and even now showed no signs of relenting, so with each exhale the two made during their work-out their breath remained clearly visible.

Soon the distant sun began to lighten the dark and it was time to begin another segment of the trip. The ropes were adjusted and now securely held the crates as the horse was nudged to begin pulling the aged cart. The narrow dirt path was still damp from the overnight cold air, so each step of the horse did nothing to raise a dust cloud. Off in the distance a lone farmer could be seen slowly making his way out to the field and beginning the long arduous task of harvesting the crop.

Hours later as the sun climbed high in the clear sky, the temperature remained as cold as when the group first woke up, so walking helped to keep everyone warm. The fields that just a few short weeks ago were bright and beaming with life were now all turning brown and patiently waiting to be harvested before the cold winter arrived. The trees continued to drop their leaves, creating a soft blanket of multi-colored patchwork.

Anqiu City, a small quiet farming community, yet the birthplace of "The Great Wall of Qi." The residents here have survived completely from the yearly harvests and their profits at the market in neighboring Gaomi city, for centuries. At the edge of town, on the road leading to Gaomi, the local barber and tailor struggle to maintain their professions as the remaining residents toil in the fields.

"Wan Tingwei, when will your daughter be getting married?" Jin Fengshu the barber yelled across the street as he carefully trimmed the customer's queue.

"Ohh…, I hope soon."

"She's been talking about it for months now and I'm starting to worry." Wan the tailor replied as he sat sewing a patch on the worn jacket.

"Hey did you see the notice on the wall down the street about the fight?" Jin stood up and walked across the street.

"No. What did it say?"

"Well, it looks like someone is challenging Master Zhi to a fight."

"Really, someone thinks they can beat his powerful Cha style? When?" Jin said as he finished braiding the queue.

"In three days."

"Where?"

"Out at the edge of town where that big tree is leaning over towards the road." Wan pointed down the street.

"I'll have to make sure and set up my chair near where the fight is on that day." Jin finished braiding the hair and tied a short string to the last braid.

"Me too!"

"The notice said it was someone called Delicate Fire who was challenging Master Zhi."

"Delicate Fire? I've never heard of her."

"Hey look, here comes another delivery. I wonder where they're coming from?" Jin said, as he pointed at the cart coming into town.

"I've seen that one guy before." Wan said as he turned to walk back to his cart.

Slowly the cart made its way down the dirt street with Yangban and Shoushan leading the way. After several weeks on the road, the cart and all its coverings were covered with a thick coating of fine dust. Each time the wheel sunk into a hole in the ground, a small amount of the dust shook loose, fell to the ground and disappeared.

All the members of the troupe were tired and dusty with an expression of just trying to get to their destination on their faces. As they continued further down the street, none of them looked anywhere but straight ahead, while Jin and Wan stood and stared just a few feet away.

"Squeak, squeak, squeak," the worn wooden wheel announced to everyone it was not happy about the dust covering the axle and causing friction, while the tired-looking horse steadily moved forward.

"Hey mister, do I know you?" Wan said as he waved his arm and stepped forward.

Unfortunately, no one in the troupe turned to acknowledge the question, so Wan dropped his arm and stood watching as the group passed by in silence. Moments later, the horse turned down a side street and the group disappeared.

"Hey Jin, could you watch my cart for a short while? I want to go find out who that guy is." Wan walked up to his friend and pointed at his cart across the street.

"Sure, sure, but don't be gone too long." Jin said without looking up from his newest customer's hair.

Wan quickly turned and headed in the direction of the cart and its escorts. Moments later he turned down the side street and saw the group stopped at a supply store. As he walked up to the cart, he saw the occupants all inside talking with the owner.

"Hello Lou." He said as he stepped inside and waved at his friend behind the counter.

"Hey Wan, what brings you in here?"

"I saw this group come into town and thought I knew two of them."

"Which ones?"

"These two here." Wan pointed at Yangban and Shoushan.

"Do we know you?" Yangban asked as he turned around.

"I think so, my name is Wan Tingwei and a while back I went to Weixian to see my sister and her husband, Master Zhou Xiangxi."

"Yes, yes I remember you." Yangban said as he bowed.

"How is our friend Zhou? We haven't seen him since that time."

"He is doing really well and his school is thriving." Wan bowed.

"What ever happened to the Eagle Claw Master?"

"Oh… he moved out of town several months after that fight. Speaking of fighting, did you see the notice on the wall down there?"

"No, we didn't stop to look at anything, we just wanted to get here and deliver the cargo."

"Well, in two days there is going to be a fight out at the edge of town between Master Zhi Fenwei from the local Cha style school and someone called Fan Xuedu."

"Really? Maybe we'll have to stay and see who this stranger is and if she is any good."

"Okay. Wan, we need to get this cart unloaded so it can be checked." Lou said as he walked towards the door.

"Come down and see me when you're done." Wan turned and headed outside.

"We will." Yangban *said as he arranged the paperwork on the counter.*

One by one the boxes were carefully removed from the cart and carried inside to be opened. As Yangban and the helpers carried the crates inside, Shoushan and Mr. Lou carefully opened each one and unwrapped the delicate porcelain before examining it and placing it back in the container.

As the sun quietly slipped behind the rooftops and the group finished with the last box, Mr. Lou offered the group a space on the floor near the crates to sleep while they were in town.

Within minutes the exhausted group was asleep. After what appeared like mere seconds, the first sounds from a neighborhood rooster, "Erh, erh, erh," announced the start of another day. Slowly the two fighters gathered their weapons, walked out to a secluded spot at the edge of town and began their morning training rituals. Two hours later as the sun began to look over the horizon and shine through the trees, Yangban and Shoushan finished their practice and headed back into the city. As they neared the first buildings, several locals were heading out with their small carts filled with tools necessary to till the awaiting soil. Ahead, the first store was opening its doors, carrying out some of the decorations from inside and arranging them along the wall for their customers.

"Let's walk down and read the sign about the challenge match." Shoushan *said as they neared the store of their friend.*

"Hmm, it says she's from Hebei Province and is traveling through this province to find a comparable practitioner for her straight sword techniques. "Yangban said while rubbing his chin.

"Look, down here it says she's killed several challengers." Shoushan pointed at the bottom of the sign.

"Wow, now I know we'll be staying another day to see that fight!" Yangban patted his friend on the shoulder.

"Definitely, I want to see how good this woman is, if she has killed several fighters during her challenges." Shoushan turned and began walking back to the store.

"If she's anywhere near as good as she says then Master Zhi better bring every ounce of his Cha style." Yangban finally turned to catch up to his friend.

Early the following morning as the fighters began walking back to the city, they heard the town crier in the distance, "it's the seventh hour and all is well" and decided to walk directly over to the area where the fight would be conducted. As they neared the site, several spectators were already sitting along the road waiting for the event.

"I wonder if that is Delicate Fire over there." Yangban pointed at the woman practicing in the nearby trees.

"Probably, she moves way too fluidly for a beginner and no one is talking to her, so she probably isn't from this city." Shoushan stopped to watch her techniques.

Thirty minutes later while they stood near the growing crowd, Yangban turned and saw a man walking towards the area. "It looks like Master Zhi is coming this way and he's carrying a broadsword," he said.

"There's the city official," Yangban pointed behind Master Zhi at the man with the traditional uniform and small round hat with the square side extensions slowly being carried by four servants on a sedan chair. Eventually they walked up to the edge of the growing crowd, lowered the chair to the ground and stepped to the side, as the official stood up and climbed down. As he walked towards the open area, everyone quietly stepped back and allowed him a clear path to the center, while his servants carried a small table and chair, placing them near the center. Instantly the official sat down, opened a large scroll and waited for the fighters to present themselves before his table and announce their challenge. As he waited, Mr. Jin and Mr. Wan arrived and instantly immersed themselves in an animated personal conversation.

Soon, Master Zhi stepped through the crowd that by now had surrounded the entire area and walked up to the table. "I am Master Zhi Fenwei. I'm also called "The Cha Fist Mountain." I've come here today to accept a challenge and am prepared to sign this waiver releasing my opponent from any damages or responsibility if I die." He said while turning to address the official and then the crowd.

"Good, sign your name here." The official pointed at the scroll.

"You may step back." He said after Master Zhi signed the scroll.

Several minutes later the crowd began to separate on the opposite side and a woman stepped through while carrying a straight sword. The moment she passed the inner edge of the crowd, the opening closed and everyone began whispering to each other while pointing at the stranger. Shoushan and Yangban stood silently watching the two fighters in the center.

"Who are you thinking will win?" Shoushan leaned over and softly asked his friend.

"Judging by the way they each carry themselves, I'm not sure. This fight should prove to be very interesting," he said without turning his head.

"My thoughts exactly."

The woman walked up to the table and said, "I'm Fan Xuedu, also called "Delicate Fire." I've come here today to extend a formal challenge against Zhi Fenwei. I'm willing to sign the official document releasing my opponent from any damages or responsibility if I die." She bowed to the official.

"Good, sign your name here." He pointed at the bottom of the scroll.

"You may step back." The official pointed towards the opposite side of the area and then returned to concentrating on the document. After several minutes the official stood up, walked around the table and announced to the crowd, "I have examined the signatures on this document and pronounce them official. Each fighter has agreed to release his opponent from harm if he is injured or dies. I will now affix my signature and seal to the bottom," he said while

moving his exquisite brush across the delicate fabric. As he finished, the servants cautiously picked up the table and chairs and carried them back to the sedan chair, while the official walked over and stood at the edge of the circle.

"You may begin." The official yelled as he pointed at each fighter and motioned for them to step into the center.

Simultaneously, each of the fighters began walking towards the center and stopped when they were within striking distance. Without saying a word, they stood and looked at each other as a soft breeze crept down the street. Then as if on command, they extended a formal salute to each other, and stepped back into a traditional stance from their respective styles. Again, both stood motionless while gazing at the fighter across the open area. Suddenly, the two charged forward and attacked with only one arm. Punch, punch, block, block, kick, block, punch, kick, block, the scenario continued until they each stepped in to block "thud" the arms slammed into each other and stopped while the fighters stared at each other. Seconds seemed to stretch into hours while the crowd anxiously waited for the fight to continue. Suddenly, both fighters jumped back while turning and drawing their swords.

"Now it's starting, and it appears she may be as good as she claims," Shoushan said without turning his head.

Yangban remained silent while nodding his head in agreement.

"See how she strategically places her steps as she walks around the circle. Her weapon remains completely hidden behind her back so Master Zhi can't see it." Shoushan pointed.

"Yes, that's true, but Master Zhi seems to be very proficient at keeping his sword invisible behind his leg, and he moves across the ground as if he's floating on a cloud." Yangban moved his hand to imitate a cloud.

"That's a good observation and it'll make this fight even more interesting."

Across the open area Mr. Jin and Mr. Wan continued their excited conversation while pointing at the fighters.

"What do you mean Master Zhi doesn't have a chance?" Jin inquired while holding his arms out to the sides.

"Do you see how good Delicate Fire is?" Wan questioned.

"But Master Zhi is just as good." Jin reasoned.

As the gentle breeze continued to drift across the open area, several small clouds dashed across the barren sky and pushed a shadow temporarily over the two fighters. Seconds later, as the clouds rushed off to the horizon while dragging their shadow across the ground, the fighters began to carefully circle each other. Step by step they continually matched each other's movements without closing the distance. When one fighter stepped, the other instantly followed and when one of them stopped, the other immediately froze his motions.

Slowly Master Zhi stood straight up and circled his sword around his body before raising it over his head, while closing the extended hand into a fist. As he stood with his feet together and the sword pointing at his opponent, Delicate Fire remained motionless, with her gaze fixed on the man across the open space holding the sword.

Suddenly, Master Zhi charged forward with the sharp blade strategically positioned over his head. Delicate Fire waited until her opponent was almost upon her before she spun to the side, withdrew her straight sword from its protective rosewood sleeve and hit Master Zhi in the back with the case, while striking at his heel with the sword. Fortunately, Master Zhi lifted his leg, spun around as she hit his back and swung his sword in a large circle, which caused Delicate Fire to lower her head to avoid the sharp blade. As she dropped her head Delicate Fire instantly swung her leg up behind her in a circle like a scorpion tail before bringing it down in front and barely grazing Master Zhi's extended arm.

As the speeding foot passed his arm, Master Zhi instantly lunged forward with his sword towards his opponent's stomach. Fortunately, Delicate Fire twisted her body to avoid the sword which then slid across her stomach and cut off a frog button from her jacket. Before Master Zhi could retract his weapon, Delicate Fire jumped up and kicked his chest, forcing him to abandon his attack and avoid falling.

"Good kick. Unfortunately, it wasn't very powerful," he said while brushing the dust from his shirt.

"Hmmph," she scoffed while checking the condition of her jacket.

While Master Zhi was busy removing the dust from his shirt, Delicate Fire jumped forward and thrust her thin straight sword at his throat. Master Zhi leaned back just enough to allow the sword to stop only inches from his skin and kicked upwards at her wrist holding the weapon. "Thud," the hand instantly released the sword and the weapon sped upward. Delicate Fire instantly jumped and grabbed the sword's tassel, pulling it back down. She rolled away from her opponent before standing up, while pointing her first two fingers at Master Zhi. "Hmmph," she scowled as she turned her head slightly away.

Master Zhi slowly began walking in another circle while spinning his sword in a circle in his hand. Delicate Fire shrugged her shoulders and instantly circled directly opposite her opponent.

Again, moments seemed to stretch into forever as the fighters circled each other with their weapons pointing directly behind and their open hands extended towards their opponent. After several circles Delicate Fire charged forward and swung her thin blade upwards at the elbow of Master Zhi, then turned the blade to cut down at his leg. Master Zhi moved his arm slightly to allow the weapon to pass and then swung his leg up in an outward semi-circle; sending it crashing into Delicate Fire's shoulder. "Thud!" the shoulder instantly dropped and forced her to once again roll away from her opponent. As she began to stand up, she spun around and cut at

Master Zhi's ankle, "Phfft," the fabric on the pants released and exposed a small thin line of blood beginning to stream towards the foot.

"Ah-ha, good cut." Master Zhi responded as he looked down at the red stream. Suddenly he jumped forward and swung the sword over his head and down at Delicate Fire's head. "Clang!" the two weapons met above her and continued down until her sharp sword hit her own forehead from the force. The moment the swords stopped, Master Zhi kicked her in the chest; sending her flying backwards before landing on her back and rolling over. "Hmmph!" she scoffed again as she jumped up and brushed the foot print from her jacket before wiping the blood from her eyes.

"He's starting to bother her!" Shoushan whispered to Yangban.

"Yes, I noticed she isn't as confident as when she started. It's like she's realizing she has finally found someone worthy of her abilities." Yangban rubbed his chin and smiled.

Delicate Fire slowly tilted her head slightly down and rushed forward with her gaze still pointed at the ground. As she neared her opponent, she began swinging her sword in a large reverse direction circle while continuing forward. "Clang, clang, clang!"

the weapons met as Master Zhi backed up and defended each circling attack. Finally, as they neared the crowd, Master Zhi blocked a forward thrust from the straight sword, as Delicate Fire dropped to the ground, spun her leg backwards in a circle and swept the feet out from under her opponent. Instantly Master Zhi's legs rocketed backwards faster than his body could keep up with, causing him to become horizontal in the air just prior to landing face first on the ground. His feet came to rest on top of a spectator's shoe.

"Thud!" his face caused the dust to puff up and float temporarily before gently settling back to the ground. "Pffth," Master Zhi began spitting out the fine soil which gathered in his mouth. "Hmm, not bad, not bad at all." He said when he finally stood up and wiped the dirt from his face.

"Hmmph!" Delicate Fire responded as she watched her opponent regain his composure.

Master Zhi exhaled deeply, gripped his sword tighter and began slowly stepping forward towards his delicate opponent. As he neared her position he suddenly jumped up and kicked three times while continuing forward, sending her frantically backwards while trying to avoid the attacks. As Master Zhi landed from the kicks he instantly dropped down and began spinning forward with his leg extended. First a front sweep, then back, front, back and finally he jumped up and kicked her directly in the chest, sending her falling backwards before landing on her head and rolling over. "Hmmph, hmmph!" she scoffed as she knelt on the ground and punched the earth.

"Enough of this friendly fighting. Now I'm going to show you the power of my family style!" she yelled as she stood up and pointed at the fighter in front of her.

"Are you sure?" Master Zhi asked.

"YES!" she charged forward and swung her sword wildly over her head until Master Zhi was within striking range. "Clang, clang, clang!" the sharp edges of the two weapons clashed as the fighters moved in response. As she chopped at his side, Master Zhi spun his sword and blocked the path. As he cut at her shoulder, she instantly twisted and deflected the sword's heavy momentum. Move after move they danced as if choreographed in the open area with neither fighter winning the advantage.

Sixty minutes after the challenge began, both fighters stood drenched in sweat but still moving as though they had just begun. Gradually the sun crept ever closer to its highpoint before drifting towards the distant horizon. The city official vigorously fanned himself in an attempt to keep pace with the rising temperature while numerous spectators moved back to the thin shade of the surrounding trees.

Again, the seasoned fighters began circling, Delicate Fire quickly charged forward and stabbed at each side of Master Zhi's head. Immediately he slipped the sword inside her weapon and neutralized each attack before circling his sword to defend his head and then cut at her feet, forcing her to jump after each successive attack to avoid the incoming sword. As she jumped the final time, Master Zhi kicked her legs and forced her body to spin in mid-air before driving her face into the loose soil. "Thud!" she hit the ground and dropped her trusted ally. "Cough, cough, pfft." Master Zhi watched as she tried to breathe and spit out the dirt.

"He's slowly wearing her down and clouding her mind with doubt," Shoushan flatly said.

"It was only a matter of time." Yangban said.

"Do you want to continue?" he asked as she struggled to her feet.

"YES!" instantly she charged without her sword and began wildly punching and kicking. As she attacked Master Zhi used the back of his sword to defend each technique, leaving visible bumps and welts on Delicate Fire's arms. Master Zhi slowly walked over to her sword lying in the dirt, picked it up and tossed it in front of her. "Try using this." He waited for her to pick it up.

"Hmmph." She struggled to say while coughing and trying to grip the handle. Each time she squeezed her hand to grip the weapon her face grimaced from the pain of the welts. Finally, she inhaled and then exhaled deeply several times before grabbing the handle tightly and lifting her head to stare straight ahead at Master Zhi, preparing for another exchange with her opponent.

"Ehrr ahh!" she yelled while rushing forward as Master Zhi stood motionless. The moment she drew near Master Zhi charged forward and thrust his sword at her chest, forcing Delicate Fire to abandon her attack. Fortunately, she avoided the sword's full force by turning. Unfortunately, her timing was late and the sword sliced into her shoulder. "Ai-ya!" she yelled as Master Zhi withdrew his weapon and swung it around towards her leg. "Thud," his sword caught her shin before she could defend the blade. "Ahh!" she looked down at the blood streaming from the fresh wound. "Thud" Master Zhi kicked her directly in the chest, as she looked down, sending her stumbling backwards before rolling over.

Master Zhi slowly stepped back and watched as his opponent desperately tried to stand. "Cough, cough, huuuh, huuuh" she struggled to get fresh air into her lungs.

After several minutes Master Zhi asked, "Do you want to continue?" as Delicate Fire was still trying to stand. "Y... cough, cough, Y....cough, cough" she attempted to answer.

"I think we should end this, because I don't want to kill you." He began walking over to the local official.

"Y... you think I'm through?" she yelled while struggling to maintain standing.

"I think if we continue, you will end up dead, and I have no interest in making that happen." He turned to face his opponent.

"I... can't let you stop."

"This fight is not worth dying over. All you wanted to achieve is another victory to appease your ego, and that is not an acceptable reason." He pointed at the sky while slowly moving closer to his opponent.

"If you are unwilling to accept defeat today, then you will torment yourself for years over the outcome, but either way I will not allow you to make me kill you without a proper cause."

For several minutes the two fighters stood only feet apart while the sweat poured down their backs. The sun continued to throw its rays of heat towards the ground as the shadows crawled further into the recesses to hide.

"If I lose today, who will believe me when I say my technique is superior?" she fell to her knees and leaned on the sword.

"Anyone who saw your techniques today, will believe they are superior."

"But they will find out that I lost one of my fights."

"Everyone loses a fight at some time in their career. It's inevitable." Master Zhi stepped closer and held out his hand to help his opponent to her feet.

"Come, let's go inside so I can work on those injuries." Carefully he helped Delicate Fire to her feet.

"That was quite a challenge match!" Yangban said as he shook his head and turned towards his friend.

"She has some excellent techniques, but now she has to fight to gain control of her ego over the loss," Shoushan said as he turned towards the city.

"And that fight will be even harder to conquer if she's not careful." Yangban placed his hand on Shoushan's shoulder.

8. OPIUM WAR

China, 1839, was a time of immense struggle for the Middle Kingdom, not only for the general population then but also for their government as well. For over one hundred years, the leaders had been forced to combat the continual smuggling of opium into its southern port of Guangzhou. Initially, the trade of opium with the English was based on China's use of the addictive substance for specific medicinal purposes. Severe cases of pain from injury or specific disability oftentimes necessitated the administering of highly addictive substances to alleviate a fraction of the pain. Unfortunately, the level of addiction created by the use of this substance became a financial attraction to the underworld.

As the first medical practitioners became addicted to their own curative drug, they quickly transitioned into the first black market dealers to the general public. Day by day, their illegal market grew one client at a time, until the demand required more than the physician could supply. Soon, back-alley opium dens began to flourish in the impoverished areas of Guangzhou, and year after year their popularity grew. Other cities surrounding this seaport, soon became infected with the addiction and its profits, causing the importation of higher quantities, which fueled the market and perpetuated the vicious cycle.

As the expansion of the illegal market spread further and further from the coast, its pressure soon became a burden on the productivity and economy in the area to the point that the rulers far to the north in the Forbidden City became aware and took notice. Initially, the emperor sent officials to investigate the growing problem, to determine an effective strategy for control. Unfortunately, this took years to investigate and even longer to attempt to implement. Meanwhile the demand was rapidly spreading north until even Yangban was hearing whispers of its arrival in numerous cities they visited while delivering cargo or rebelling against the corrupt officials.

At first, he began seeing strange complexions and abnormal actions, from seemingly normal acquaintances. People he had known throughout the years slowly became more distant and withdrawn, while their bodies continually wasted away. Consequently, people he once trusted and relied upon were now dead or had become untrustworthy due to their addiction to the black cloud creeping across the country. Furthermore, he began seeing more and more opium dens on the back streets of the larger cities, and the number of individuals entering and exiting the houses steadily grew while their overall appearance continued to drift closer and closer towards death.

Numerous businesses, that for generations had survived during harsh conditions and actually prospered, were beginning to show signs of the strains from the loss of revenue because of the effects of the drug on their workers. Everywhere he walked the signs were becoming more numerous and increasingly obvious of the stranglehold this cloud was gaining over the Middle Kingdom.

Now the Imperial Palace and all its officials, were feverously scrambling to devise an effective solution. Their initial attempts at appealing to the foreign devils with the rationale of how the illegal smuggling of the drug into the country was undermining and eroding the fabric of the Middle Kingdom's economy were left officially unanswered. A response by the British began to raise its ugly head, when the emperor received notices of an increase in the amount of opium being smuggled into Guangzhou and feeling its effects on the economy.

"Zhufei, did you see someone opened another opium house since we were here last?" Yangban asked, while pointing at the small dilapidated house hidden at the end of the narrow alley.

"Yes, I talked to my friend who recently returned from Nansha near Guangzhou, and he told me the foreigners are importing more

opium than ever before." he looked down the alley and shook his head.

"Really, and now it's found its way into Taizhou?"

"My friend said he couldn't believe how many ships were bringing the drug into the city."

"Ai-yaa! The more our people get addicted to that deadly flower, the worse it'll be for the country. It won't take long and we'll be unable to keep the foreigners out."

"Exactly."

"Your highness, I've just received word that the foreigners are increasing the amount of opium they're smuggling into Guangzhou," the eunuch bowed.

"Send in my viceroy, Lin Zexu!" the emperor yelled as he pounded on the arms of his ornately carved throne. Two hours later the viceroy humbly approached the impatient ruler.

"Lin Zexu, I want you to go directly to Guangzhou and end this smuggling disease on our country." He walked to the edge of his raised platform and shook his finger at his servant.

"Yes, oh Great Ruler under Heaven. I will not fail you." He bowed.

As soon as Viceroy Lin arrived in the port city, he immediately began investigating the local officials to determine their level of involvement. Consequently, numerous officials were arrested and replaced with trustworthy allies while Lin focused his attention on uncovering the locations of the smuggling transfers. Meanwhile, Lin sent a letter to the rulers of England to appeal to their sense of dignity and moral compass. Months passed, and soon turned into two years without a response, so Lin began implementing steps to strategically limit the influx of the flower of death. Initially, he focused on surveilling the ports where the British docked their ships to offload the crates of opium balls. Unfortunately, the foreigners quickly retreated To Lintin Island which was beyond Lin's jurisdiction.

For months Lin worked to uncover more and more of the smuggling underworld while simultaneously working to limit the sale of the deadly drug.

"Hey Mister Lok, bring me some more of your wine!" the sailor struggled to yell through his intense state of inebriation.

"No! you've had enough. The last time you were in here and got drunk you broke six of my tables. So, you need to go home and rest."

"No! I'm not going home until I get more wine!"

"Sorry, but I'm finished serving you, so go home." Lok said as he turned his back and continued cleaning the small bowls.

"Hey, I said I want more wine!" he threw his bowl at the man behind the small makeshift bar.

"Ouch! I said you need to go home!"

"Give me some more wine or I'll come back there and beat you!" the sailor struggled to say while swaying back and forth near his friends.

"No!"

"Excuse me sir, but I've been watching and I think you should be careful how much you drink, because you might fall and get hurt when you leave," the local said as he stepped up and placed his hand on the seamen's shoulder.

"Get away from me you little peasant!"

"But sir, I'm only trying to help you."

"Don't!" he pushed the man backwards; causing him to fall on the table in the corner and break the legs.

"Hey! I told you to leave and now look what you've done!" Lok said as he walked over to inspect his friend and the damage to the table.

"Ah shut up. I told you to give me some wine." He fell against his shipmate.

"*You need to leave now!*" *Lok yelled as he walked over to the drunken sailor, leaning against his friends.*

"*No! I want more wine.*" *He staggered forward and fell on Mister Lok.*

"*Get out!*" *Lok pushed the sailor away and pointed at the door.*

"*Gimme some wine!*" *he turned and pulled out his knife.*

"*No, you need to leave! See what you did to my friend?*" *Lok stood his ground and again pointed towards the open door.*

"*He deserved to get hit. Now give me some wine.*"

"*What did I do? I was trying to keep you from hurting yourself.*" *The injured man yelled as he stepped in front of the sailor.*

"*Get away from me, you peasant!*" *the sailor yelled as he pointed the knife at the injured patron.*

"*Ha! You're too drunk to hurt anyone!*" *the patron yelled.*

"*I'll show you!*" *the sailor lunged forward and thrust his knife into the patron's upper stomach.*

"*Ai-yaa!*" *Mister Lok yelled, as he watched his friend collapse and begin bleeding on the dirt floor.*

"*Let's go, let's go!*" *the sailor's friends yelled in panic while trying to pull their drunk friend towards the door.*

"*Get some rags to stop the bleeding!*" *Lok yelled as he frantically tried to help his friend.*

"Lok, cough, cough, how is it?" the patron struggled to ask.

"Shh, shh, don't talk." He patted his shoulder.

"Go get the police." Lok whispered to another patron who was helping stop the bleeding.

"Okay, I'll go as fast as I can." The man jumped up and ran out the opening.

Twenty minutes later the patron returned with a local officer and said, "Here he is, Lok."

"What happened?" the official asked as he looked down at the injured local.

"It was a drunk sailor from the ship that stabbed him." Lok said as he stood up.

"Where is the sailor?"

"I think his friends took him back to their ship."

"How's our friend doing?"

"I'm sorry officer, but he just died several minutes ago." Lok said as he slowly stood up and bowed towards his friend.

"Where is the ship this guy came from!" the officer yelled as he looked down at the lifeless corpse lying in the dried blood near his feet.

"I'm not sure, but there aren't too many of them out in the water."

"Okay, I'll go right now and find which ship he's from." The officer turned and began walking towards the door.

"Good, he needs to be punished for his actions," Lok said as he stood up and wiped the dried blood from his hands.

Two hours later the officer located the ship, ordered a local fisherman to ferry him to the ship and slowly floated along the still channel waters towards the large wooden cargo ship.

"Captain, a boat is coming up on the starboard side!" the landsman said as he looked over the railing.

"Bring them aboard." The captain yelled.

Minutes later the small junk was pulled in tight to the side of the British ship. The guests climbed the rope ladder and stepped on to the large wooden deck.

"I'm officer Gao from the local police station. I would like to speak to your captain," he said as he scanned the deck.

"Wait here." The senior sailor replied.

"Knock, knock." The sailor lightly tapped on the captain's cabin door.

"Come in."

"Captain, there is someone here from the local police station who wants to talk to you." The sailor said as he stood just inside the door.

"Okay, escort him in."

"Captain, this is Officer Gao from the local police station," the sailor said as he escorted the guest into the quarters.

"I'm Captain Webb, how can I help you?"

"I'm looking for one of your men who recently returned from the bar." He bowed.

"Why do you need to speak with him?"

"He got drunk and killed someone."

"Well, before I allow you to arrest him, I want to do an investigation. So, if you'll give me until tomorrow, I'll then send someone to inform you of my findings."

The following day the captain sent a messenger to deliver a response to officer Gao. "Officer Gao, Captain Webb sent me to inform you of the findings of his investigation," the ship's officer said as he walked into the small police station.

"And what did he conclude?" Officer Gao asked as he stood up and bowed.

"He says he couldn't find enough evidence to warrant releasing custody of his worker to the local authorities."

"What? I have numerous eye witnesses to the crime and he says he is unable to find enough evidence? I don't believe it!"

"Sorry, but that is his message." The officer turned and headed towards the doorway.

"I'll have my superior contact him about this matter," Gao said as he bowed.

The next morning after the sun cleared the trees and shone directly on the still water's surface, officer Gao's superior, Officer Mak, stepped into the small junk boat and said, "Push off and take me to the foreigner's ship."

Twenty minutes later he grabbed the rope swinging from the side of the large wooden ship and secured his small junk to the side before climbing up the rope ladder and stepping on to the deck.

"I'm here to see your captain," he said to the sailor washing the deck.

"I'll take you to see him," another sailor said as he walked up to the visitor.

"Knock, knock, knock," the sailor lightly tapped on the cabin door.

"Enter."

"Captain, this is Officer Mak from the local police station." The sailor pointed at the visitor." Thank you. You can leave now," he said without looking up from his papers.

"Officer Mak, how can I help you?" he asked as he stood up, walked around the desk and sat in the chair next to his guest.

"*I came to talk to you about the investigation you conducted regarding your sailor and the death of one of my local residents.*"

"*Yes, I did an investigation and could not find enough evidence to warrant handing him over to your office.*"

"*Really? what about all the patrons who were in the bar when it happened and witnessed the attack?*" he leaned forward.

"*Well, I interviewed all the men who went into town on that day and none of them remember seeing anything.*"

"*What, are you saying all the locals are lying and that the man who died isn't real?*"

"*I don't know what actually happened, but my men don't remember seeing any killing. I'm not going to be able to release any of my men so you can arrest them.*"

"*Ai-yaa! I now only have one choice and that is to report this to the Viceroy from the Imperial Palace in Beijing.*"

"*If that's what you choose to do, then we have nothing else to discuss.*" He stood up, walked back behind his desk before sitting down and waved his hand as if signaling to his guest it was time to leave.

Officer Mak walked back into his station an hour later and said, "I'll be leaving for the Viceroy's office in thirty minutes. I want you to continue gathering evidence regarding the killing," he pointed at his subordinate.

"The foreigners are lying about their involvement. I'm handing this case over to Viceroy Lin, and I know he'll be coming by to interview everyone, so make sure you have everything in order," he said as he walked into his office to change into his formal uniform. Minutes later he returned and headed towards the door while signaling for his carriage to be brought out front. Soon the two men arrived with the small single-seat enclosed carriage, carefully lowered it to the ground and stepped back as Officer Mak entered and closed the ornately carved door. "Let's go." he said while waving his hand at the two men to pick up the vehicle and begin carrying him along the dirt path towards the city.

As the carriage continued deeper into the city, it soon arrived at the government office near the port. "Set me down here," Mak said as he pointed to the space near the front door of the tall building. Slowly he exited the vehicle, arranged his uniform, brushed away the dust that collected on his cloud boots and positioned his headpiece before walking into the building.

"I have come to seek an audience with Viceroy Lin," he said as he stepped up to the desk centered in the entrance hall.

"One moment. I'll ask his secretary if he is available." The young man turned and shuffled down the long hallway and disappeared around the corner. Thirty minutes later he shuffled back to the desk and said, "Please, please follow me." He gestured with his hand for Mak to follow.

After turning the corner, they stopped at the first door and stepped inside, where a man signaled for him to sit and gestured to keep quiet.

Mak eventually heard a small bell ring and suddenly the man at the desk jumped up and disappeared inside the interior door. Moments later he returned and said, "Please follow me. The Viceroy will see you now." He gestured for Mak to follow.

"Viceroy Lin, this is Officer Mak from the local police station." The man and Officer Mak bowed.

"Officer Mak, how can I help you?" Lin raised his head and looked at his guest.

"I have come to report that a local man has been killed by a sailor from the foreigner's ship." He bowed.

"Have you talked to the ship's captain?"

"Yes, your Excellency, I have, and he told me he was not going to allow any of his men to be interrogated or arrested."

"Really?"

"Yes, your Excellency."

"Very well, I'll take charge of this matter from here on out. Thank you for bringing this to my attention." He stood up and bowed.

"Thank you, your Excellence." Mak bowed, stepped backwards towards the door, and then exited the room. As he stepped outside into the bright sun and walked over to his carriage, he said, "let's

go back to my office," before stepping inside. Slowly the two men raised the vehicle and began the long trip home.

Hours later when he arrived at his office, he stepped inside the door and said, "I've handed the case over to Viceroy Lin. I know he'll be arriving in the next couple days to interrogate everyone, so get all your information together for his arrival."

Two days later as Officer Mak sat in his office, he heard a subordinate yell, "Officer Mak, Viceroy Lin is here!" Quickly Mak shuffled outside to meet his superior.

"Viceroy Lin, it's good to see you again." Mak stood in front of all his workers as they bowed together.

"Officer Mak, tell me where this ship is you told me about the other day." Lin walked inside to avoid the hot sun.

"It's out near Lintin Island, your Excellency. They moved out there some time ago to avoid our jurisdiction."

"Okay, then tomorrow morning I'll go out to talk with the captain, but for today, I want to see all the evidence that everyone has collected about the case." He sat down and began to fan his face with a small silk fan.

The next morning, Lin arrived just after the sun began to creep over the tops of the trees, and headed directly for the dock. "Viceroy Lin, I have taken the liberty to arrange a special boat for your trip today," Mak said as he bowed.

"Good, good. I'll stop by your office when I return." He said, as he stepped into the large junk boat.

Thirty minutes later the junk floated next to the large British ship and Lin climbed the rope ladder and stepped on to the main deck. "I'm Viceroy Lin. I would like to see the captain," he bowed to the deckhands.

"I'm Captain Webb and welcome aboard." He climbed down the steps from the upper observatory.

"Let's go inside my private office and we can talk." He gestured for his guest to follow.

"Please, sit down," Captain Webb said as he gestured to Lin.

"How may I help you?" Webb asked as he walked behind the desk.

"I've come here today to discuss the murder of a local resident." Lin slowly sat down and placed his palm on his knees.

"Yes, one of your subordinates came by days ago."

"He told me you did an investigation."

"Yes, and I couldn't find enough evidence to warrant sending him ashore for you to arrest."

"Really, did you interview all the witnesses at the bar?"

"No, I couldn't find anyone on board the ship who remembered being in that establishment on the day in question."

"Really?"

"Yes."

"I think your subordinates are lying to avoid prosecution for their involvement in the crime."

"I'd be careful about accusing any of my men for a crime."

"I'd be careful about aiding or allowing a murder to go unprosecuted." Lin stood up and pointed his finger at the captain.

"I think we're done here. You can find your own way off my ship." Webb turned and looked out the porthole.

Lin turned, and walked out the door and quickly climbed back into the junk. As the small boat began crawling back towards the shore, Lin stood at the bow and looked back at the foreign vessel. The moment the junk arrived at the dock, Lin jumped off and stormed over to his carriage, climbed inside and said, "Let's go... Now!"

Later when he arrived at his office, he walked inside and said, "I need all the military commanders in my office at first light!" Suddenly everyone in the building sprang to life and began feverously working to arrange the couriers necessary to notify the officers. One by one, a courier arrived and moments later dashed out the door with a delicate scroll in his hand. Later, as the sun melted into the trees and fell behind the horizon, the last courier left the building and frantically hurried down the dirt street, before turning the corner and disappearing.

The next morning before the sun awoke from its nighttime slumber, several men in military uniforms stood waiting near the main entrance to the government building. Suddenly an office worker turned the corner and began running towards the building with a key in his hand. "Good morning, General Yao, good morning, Captain." He continued until he addressed everyone.

"I'll open the door so you can come inside and rest," he said, while trying to unlock the door through the shaking of his hands.

Viceroy Lin soon arrived and immediately went into his office while saying, "Bring me some tea."

As the worker returned from delivering the tea he said, "Gentlemen, the Viceroy will see you now, could you follow me?"

"I called all of you here to discuss a military solution to a situation with the foreigners," Lin said as the last officer sat down.

"May we ask what the problem is?" General Yao asked.

"Yesterday I went out to the British ship and questioned the captain about the involvement of some of his men in a murder. All he said was that he couldn't find enough evidence."

"I want to know your suggestions for forcing him to comply with the investigation." Lin sat down and sipped his tea.

"I think we should close off the harbor so that the ships cannot enter or exit the bay. Then we can order him to comply or suffer the consequences of being arrested for their involvement." General Yao said.

"Hmm, sounds like a good strategy," Lin said as he leaned back in his chair and began looking upward at the ceiling.

"Okay, I think we should plan on implementing this maneuver in two days, at first light." Lin stood up, bowed to everyone and then turned to leave the room.

"General Yao, please follow me." Lin said as he stepped through the door.

"General, I want you to take charge of this operation and as I said, I want this in place in two days." He turned and looked directly at the officer.

"Yes, Viceroy, I'll begin immediately." He bowed.

Two days later, as the silent pelicans effortlessly floated within inches of the water's edge while searching for a morning meal, the dock was abuzz with activity. Up and down the water's edge military personnel scrambled back and forth, as the junk boat owners hurriedly readied their boats for a launch. Up on the horizon the sun illuminated the skyline until the dark blue night veil had been saturated with the bright light of the morning sun, creating a pale blue painting of a horizon seen in ancient artwork.

The junks with their large canvas sails, sewn together and supported by a series of wooden ribs imitating the bones and scales on a sailfish, sat with their decks just above the water's edge. Other canvases were arched across the deck from side to side like the backs of a whale and covered precious supplies or cargo underneath. The ribs and side planks were roughly hewn timbers, soaked and forced to curve to a prescribed shape. Maneuvering this archaic vessel, was accomplished by a single rudder and the courtesy of the wind gods. Since the depth of the channel was quite shallow, the use of oars was limited and reliance on the wind became even more precious, so the sails slowly grew larger until their size was restricted by the size of the junk.

"Everyone ready?" General Yao asked as he stepped on to his boat.

"Yes sir!" he heard repeatedly as each boat readied itself for launch.

"Go now, to your designated positions and wait for my orders!" Yao gestured to his oarsmen to begin rowing.

An hour later all the boats were in position and had sealed off the mouth of the bay to all traffic.

"Captain, I'm seeing a group of junk boats trying to seal off the entrance to the bay," the deckhand yelled as the captain stepped up on to the observation deck.

"What?"

"Yes, they have barricaded us inside."

For several days the junks sat motionless while blocking the movement of all traffic. Finally, Lin sent a messenger to Captain Webb's ship and demanded all cargo be offloaded immediately into the boats supplied by his military. Over the next several weeks every ship was emptied of its smuggled cargo and loaded into the appropriate boats. Afterwards, the cargo was transported to a secure location, piled in the center of an open field and set on fire.

Suddenly, the smoke turned thick and black while rising straight up into the clear sky, allowing it to be seen for miles.

"Captain, I'm seeing a serious fire in the direction of where the junks took our opium!" the deckhand pointed with a panicked expression.

"Hand me my eyeglass!" Webb said excitedly.

"Here, sir."

Webb pulled the long lens up to his eye, and swung it around until he found the area of the rising smoke. Slowly he twisted the end that focused the glass on a specific area and held the long tube motionless. "Hmm," he said, as he watched the smoke rise higher and higher. "Lieutenant, send my scribe up here now." He dropped the lens and looked blankly in the direction of the smoke.

"I'm here captain," the scribe said as he stepped on to the upper deck.

"Take this note and it's to be sent immediately to the king."

"Yes sir." The scribe said while looking at the other occupants on the upper deck with a surprised look on his face.

"Your majesty, I regret to inform you that our cargo which we carried from India to the port of Guangzhou, has been seized and burned. I estimate that the total loss is approximately 2.6 million

pounds of raw opium pods. I await your further instructions, signed Captain Webb." He looked back into his lens while saying, "I want that to go out today."

Quickly the message was transported to a ship outside the barricade and relayed to an awaiting ally.

Meanwhile, over the next number of months, Captain Webb repeatedly attempted to resolve the issue with Viceroy Lin by demanding a reimbursement of all lost cargo. Unfortunately, Viceroy Lin countered with a demand that the guilty seaman be handed over to the local authorities for investigation.

Eventually, the British government replied and their steel warship slowly inched its way closer to the attempted barricade and quietly arrived in the channel along with several other warships.

"Captain, I think you need to see this," the seaman in the crows-nest yelled down to the observation deck as he pointed further out into the still water towards the sea.

Captain Webb silently raised his lens to his eye and looked in the direction the subordinate was pointing. "Well, well, well," he said as he continued looking into the lens. "I think we just received an answer from the king." He lowered the lens and smiled. "Send me my scribe." He again raised the lens and scanned the area.

"Sir, your scribe has arrived," his lieutenant said as the scribe stepped on to the deck.

"Write this down."

"Viceroy Lin, I have repeatedly tried to resolve this situation peacefully and it has continually become obvious that your only answer is for my seamen to be arrested and tried as criminals. The cargo that we carried from India to be sold in your port of Guangzhou has been seized and burned. I am requesting for the last time that you reimburse us for our losses or we will be forced to use military action to resolve the situation. Our military ships have arrived and are awaiting my instructions. If you refuse to comply, we will be forced to destroy your junk boats, sail up the channel and seize your port of Guangzhou." He dropped the lens. "Send it by boat now." He raised the lens back to his eye.

Several hours later his small boat returned. The deckhand climbed up the rope ladder and delivered the response to the captain who was still standing on the upper deck. "Hmm, it seems Lin feels he has no need to comply with my offer." He stood for several minutes looking out at the horizon broken up by the thick layer of trees standing high upon the top of the hills.

"Send this reply." He said as he sat on the railing. "Viceroy Lin, if you do not comply to my demand and reimburse my king for the loss of his goods, I will destroy every junk boat in this harbor and sail northward until I reach Guangzhou. Then I will burn down

the city and seize the port in the name of the king of England." He stopped and continued looking through the lens. "Send it now."

"Lieutenant, I need a courier to sail out to the Nemesis with this message. Tell them to ready themselves to destroy every junk boat in our path."

"Yes sir, I'll send someone immediately," the lieutenant said as he smiled.

Two hours later the small boat returned and the seaman stepped up on to the upper deck and said, "Captain, the Nemesis captain said he will be ready at first light."

"Good." Webb slowly lowered his lens, slid it back into its leather sheath and carried it on his shoulder as he walked back to his cabin.

Early the next morning, a lone eagle confidently dropped from a high branch in a tall pine tree overlooking the point of land extended out into the bay and soared along the surface of the still water, occasionally flapping its large wings to maintain its speed and height while scanning the smooth surface for a tender morning meal. Suddenly, its sharp claws dropped from its underbelly and grabbed a small minnow floating near the surface. Instantly the majestic bird began to climb away from the mirrored surface and return to its nest. In the distance, several black crows hurriedly tried to catch the eagle in an attempt to steal its catch.

"Flagman, signal the Nemesis to begin its mission and remove these pests from our path." Captain Webb said as he walked to the edge

of the platform and stopped near the railing while removing his lens from its case.

"*Boom, boom, boom, boom, boom!*" The big guns shook the ship and the sound echoed across the smooth water's surface as the big guns sent their initial rounds speeding towards the unsuspecting wooden boats. A large dark cloud of smoke lingered near the side of the ship and partially cloaked the iron dragon. "*Splash, splash, boom, splash!*" A junk in the center of the bay exploded into a cloud of wood splinters before the fire erupted and turned the small craft into a raging inferno.

"*Boom, boom, boom, boom, boom!*" Again, the sound of the big cannons echoed through the bay and rushed up the hillside through the trees.

"*Boom, boom, splash, boom!*" three more vulnerable junks fell victim to the thunder from the iron ship.

Soon the entire bay was ablaze with the thick smoke and fire from the burning junks while the locals ran desperately along the coastline.

"*Boom, boom, boom, boom, boom!*" again the iron dragon spit its fire towards the defenseless Chinese junks. "*Crash, boom, Ai-yaa!*" another junk fell victim to its wrath while the men on board yelled and could be seen jumping into the channel.

Hours later, all that remained was the iron beast and the jubilant British cargo ships. Every Chinese junk that was positioned to barricade the bay from sea travel had been reduced to a burning *pile of waste lumber and charcoal, while numerous fires raged on, and sent large plumes of smoke straight up into the still air like tall pillars supporting the dark blue sky. The inhabitants and owners had long ago jumped into the bay, swam ashore, only to stand in horror and observe their boat being reduced to ashes.*

Slowly the menacing iron dragon began creeping forward with several accompanying warships following close behind towards the city of Guangzhou. Meanwhile, Captain Webb and his crew raised their large sails, which slowly turned their ship and began sailing out of the channel towards the open sea.

9. LIGHTNING STRIKES THE DRAGON

1845. The Qing government three years earlier had been dealt another blow to their struggling economy, when the foreign devils from England forced them to pay an indemnity of millions of dollars for their losses in the first Opium war. Additionally, the devils then began importing even more of the "flower of death" into the newly expanded ports of access. Poverty was rampant throughout the Middle Kingdom, opium dens began sprouting up everywhere, and the population was becoming more and more disillusioned by the government.

Pingdu was still a small quiet settlement of only a handful of family compounds, with a total population of approximately 500. Life was simple and the days passed by slowly in this farming village. This was not a booming metropolis with numerous occupations, nor a port city where ships could dock and deliver foreign goods. This was a secluded, rural, and struggling village, one of the many in China.

Old Li had passed on years earlier and now Shoushan was sitting in the old worn wooden office chair. Yangban had been gone for several years through his association with the Yi Hua Tuan rebels, but had recently returned to rest and avoid prosecution due to his rebel associations.

"Hey Shoushan, how are you doing?" Yangban said as he stepped through the old familiar creaky door and into the small office.

"Hey Yangban! I don't believe it! It's been a long time since I have seen you." He stood up and bowed to his old friend.

"Yes, it has, and I thought about our many trips every day.

How are you and your family doing?"

"Oh, everyone is just fine. My son Zhizhan has grown." Shoushan sat back down.

"How is your business going?"

"Oh, it's going good, and now Zhizhan is escorting the cargo."

"Ai-yaa, has it been that many years?

"I remember when he was born." He put his hand on his forehead and looked at the ceiling.

"Yes, it has".

"When he returns in a couple weeks, I'll have him show you his new Kung Fu style he learned on one of his trips. It's called Praying Mantis." Shoushan imitated a hand gesture.

"Praying Mantis? I've never heard of it." Yangban tried to imitate the hand gesture Shoushan just showed him.

"He says he learned it from a monk named Sheng Xiao Daoren while he was over near Qingdao delivering an order."

"Have you seen any of the techniques?

"Yes, a few. I watched him several times while he was training, and it looks like it is quite effective. It does have some strange motions and movements, but once we talk to him, we can find out their meaning."

"Interesting, I definitely want to see this new style. Make sure and let me know so I can stop by and ask him about it."

"How's Xiaoshu been doing?"

"Oh, he's doing okay. He works here and maintains all the buildings in the compound and the equipment. That way he doesn't have to go along to escort the cargo."

"He doesn't want to help with any escorting of the cargo?"

"Ohh… no…he tried it once several years ago and swore he would never do it again."

"*Really, what happened?*"

They had some trouble on the way to Qufu with a couple of bandits thinking they were going to steal everything, and fortunately Zhizhan and Lauwei went along and had no trouble teaching the pair a deadly lesson. Later when they returned Zhizhan said that Xiaoshu completely froze like a stone during the encounter, and afterwards he shook the whole way to Qufu!" Shoushan walked back to his chair while shaking his head.

"*Really? I figured he would grow out of his fear of fighting as he got older. I guess not.*"

"*But he really enjoys working with wood and stone.*" He sat down and leaned back in his chair.

"*Well, that's good. Okay, I need to go and practice for a while, but I wanted to come by and see you first. When Zhizhan returns, send someone over to let me know.*" He stood up and headed towards the door.

"*Sure will. See you then.*"

"*Master Cheng, Master Cheng, my uncle said to let you know Zhizhan has returned from his trip,*" the young boy said as he saw Yangban walking through the Cheng family compound.

"*Okay, thank you and tell Shoushan I'll come by tomorrow morning.*" He patted the boy on the shoulder.

The next morning Yangban walked out of the compound, glanced at the aged characters on the wall and then reached up to brush away the layers of dust. Slowly he walked down the quiet dirt path, turned the corner and headed towards the Li compound archway before stepping into the small office he had known so well over the years. Sitting in the comfortable office, he talked with Shoushan while they waited for his son to arrive. Soon the back door opened and as Zhizhan walked into the office he said, "Father, here is the list of crates we brought back yesterday from our trip to Ankiu."

"Yangban, do you recognize who this is?" Shoushan pointed at his son while looking at his friend.

"Wow! He looks like someone I knew many years ago, but he was much smaller and younger." Yangban put his hands on his face.

"Zhizhan, you've grown quite a bit since the last time I saw you training out in the yard." He stood up and put his hand on the young man's shoulder.

"How have you been, Uncle Yangban? It's been such a long time." The young man bowed to his elder.

"I'm doing well. I've been traveling. Your father tells me you're guarding the cargo now."

"Yes, I started a few years ago and I like the traveling and people I meet."

"What about the thieves who are always trying to steal your cargo?"

191

"Oh yeah, well I guess all the training I did when I was young and all the teaching from you and my father has paid off, because they haven't been able to steal anything." He clinched his fist.

"Good, good that's the way it should be." Yangban raised his thumb in approval.

"Your father also told me that you learned a new style of kung fu."

"Yes, I was over near Qingdao, and met a monk and after several hours of talking about Kung Fu, he said he really liked me, and asked if I wanted to learn his special style." He sat down near the desk.

"He said it was a very effective fighting style and since I was escorting cargo, it might be very useful. So, I stayed for a few months and he taught me everything he knew. So far it has helped me a lot with defending the shipments."

"Would you care to demonstrate some of this style?" Yangban asked as he sat next to his friend.

"Sure." He stood up and walked to the middle of the office.

"The first set is called Beng Bo (crushing step)."

Zhizhan slowly began the series and then suddenly burst into a series of strong stomps, shuffles, grabs and punches before kicking several times in succession. As he turned, he kicked behind his front leg towards the knee of his opponent, grabbed, and pulled back. Next, he shuffled forward with a series of quick blocks and punches all while executing a strange series of foot stomps and advancing shuffles.

"That was very impressive." Yangban stood up and saluted his young nephew.

"I really like how it moves and those attacks are quite unique." He tried to imitate the movements he just witnessed.

"Would you care to show that style to me?"

"Sure, sure I'd be happy to teach you, uncle." Zhizhan bowed.

"Tomorrow morning let's go out near the big leaning tree. It's always been a good place to practice." He pointed towards the location while sitting down.

"Great, great I can tell that style will be a great asset to what I already know."

For hours the three sat in the small office and talked. Eventually the sun slipped behind the tree. The long shadows had already crept up the back wall of the office, signaling the closing of another day. Eventually Yangban said goodbye and headed home while his friends finished up their daily chores.

Early the next morning, as the sun finally began to light up the distant horizon, Yangban finished his personal training and gathered his weapons before heading out of the compound to meet with Zhizhan. The dark sky was beginning to lose its blackness while allowing a pale blue veil to begin growing above the horizon. Far off in the distance, a few solitary clouds continued to multiply while several birds began a deep conversation, while the faint sound of a clattering wagon carrying tools could be heard between the chirps from the birds.

"Good morning, Uncle." Zhizhan saluted as he walked up to the tree.

"Good morning."

"I think I'll stretch first before we begin."

"Okay, I've already finished my training, so while you're stretching, I'll practice some of my energy exercises." Yangban walked out into the open area.

For thirty minutes Zhizhan used the tree to assist in stretching his arms and legs, followed by slowly practicing numerous hand routines to help loosen the joints and circulate the blood.

"I see you're finished with your energy training, so we can start whenever you're ready."

"I'm ready." Yangban raised his thumb while smiling excitedly.

"Now, this new system has three prearranged sets (forms) so far. Beng Bo (crush step), Lan Jie (chaotically connected), and Ba Jiao (eight elbows). Each one teaches some very important principles for this system," Zhizhan said, as he walked out to the open area and began to demonstrate several movements from each.

"Let's start with Beng Bo. It utilizes this crushing type of stomp to help accelerate the technique, advance forward quickly, and

confuse the opponent about our intentions." He demonstrated the first section of the form.

"Ready? The opening starts like this." He demonstrated and Yangban imitated his movements.

Eventually they completed the prearranged series of movements and then began breaking down the form into small sections in order to research the individual techniques more precisely. Before long the afternoon sun had slipped behind the large trees. All the birds finished their conversations and settled into the trees, signaling the closing of another day. The fighters walked back towards the office, and agreed to meet early the next day to continue their research.

The village began to slowly awaken for another day as the two fighters reviewed the series the following morning. Afterwards they broke it down movement by movement.

"My teacher said that Praying Mantis has twelve different fighting concepts: hook, grab, strike, block up, mantis hook followed by a grab, advance, recede, strike first, contact, cling, tag, and lean. He said that each one is very unique, and to make this style effective, each one needs to be perfected." Zhizhan demonstrated each concept on his friend.

"Hmm, those are going to take some time to understand and to utilize correctly in each technique," Yangban shook his head while looking at his nephew.

"I know, it's been several years since I learned them and I'm still trying to make them a natural movement with each technique. But each time I gain understanding about a specific concept, I find it opens a door to a different concept, so it makes me research that one. And then that leads me to another concept, so it's a continual circle of understanding, research, and improvement."

"Great! That means I'll be continually improving these concepts for many years and my techniques in all my forms will always be improving." He raised his thumb in approval.

"Yes, that's also what Sheng Xiao Daoren said."

"Speaking of him, have you seen him since he taught you the praying mantis style?"

"Unfortunately, he told me he was going south towards Huainan after he left Qingdao. And when I got home, I immediately had to deliver an order to Yantai, so we never saw each other again." He looked at the ground and shook his head.

"That's too bad. It would have been nice to talk to him about this style, find out his insights about the applications and discuss the praying mantis theories."

"Yes, that's true. I know that since I learned this style, the more I practice, the more questions I have to answer. But what I rely upon then is the understanding I have from when my father taught me my family's long-fist."

"That's good because everything he taught you is extremely valuable and so many aspects of each different style are duplicated

in other systems. Blocking is blocking and punching is punching. All you need to do is figure out how this particular style relates to each other style and how it executes its unique theories while fighting." He walked over to drink some water.

"I realize that, but at times there are still so many areas where I don't have an answer."

"Keep researching, keep researching and eventually insights will come to you about every question that has stirred your mind. The key is, don't stop searching and don't stop training. Otherwise, the day you stop training, is the first day of your slow degrading of your techniques. Also, remember that just because he taught you this unique style, that doesn't mean you can elevate yourself above others and stop your own personal growth and understanding. On the contrary, now is the time for you to become even more humble because of all the special knowledge that you have acquired. It's now your responsibility to pass it on to the next generation correctly and educate everyone about what the founder Wang Lang intended when he developed the style and passed it to Sheng Xiao Daoren."

"That's a good point."

"When he developed the system, he envisioned and incorporated certain aspects, theories and principles unique from the other training he had acquired. Now, when we learn this style, we need to keep those in mind, because they are our access into Wang Lang's mind and what he was thinking while he developed the concepts. Yes, even he used other ideas from different styles, which is how we

got the eighteen styles that comprise the praying mantis style. No system is totally pure. They all have aspects from other systems incorporated into them, but it's the fundamental idea of how the techniques apply that make each system unique."

"Wow, I thought I was teaching you about praying mantis and here you are teaching me!"

"No, we are teaching each other, as in all kung fu systems, and that's the way it was meant to be, since we are all in this together." Yangban stood up and headed back towards the open area.

"Let's get back to our training and see what we can figure out."

"Agreed." Zhizhan followed him out to the area.

"See, how when you said Sheng Xiao Daoren told you that your grab should have this idea of pulling connected to it when you finish? Well, that's just like in the other kung fu that I know, and I'm sure it's in your father's long-fist."

"Hmm, you're right but I never thought of it like that. The movements look so different. But now that I think about it, it does work the same way!" he saluted his friend.

"I have an idea for our training this afternoon, why don't we see which movements and theories are identical to the ones we know from our family styles!"

"I was wondering when you would suggest that."

For the next several weeks they spent many hours each day practicing and researching this new style's twelve concepts for application, seven long ways to attack, eight short ways, eight hard ways, twelve soft ways to attack, and the eighteen various styles used to develop the praying mantis system, all in relation to their previous training.

Eventually, Zhizhan had to return to the road with another delivery. So, the last few days of training he ensured his uncle had learned the entire system along with all the fighting theories before he said goodbye.

"Zhizhan, this new style is going to keep me busy for quite a while trying to understand all the concepts, develop the applications, and then incorporate the theories into my family style." He placed his hand on Zhizhan's shoulder as they walked back to the office.

"And me too, with all the insights you gave me.

"Hopefully, when I return, we can spend more time together researching the style."

"That is an excellent idea." Yangban turned to bow before heading back home.

"Erh, erh, erh!" the lone rooster announced to the compound the ending of another night, and the eventual arrival of the warm sun.

Inside, Yangban finished cleaning his morning teacup and gathered his weapons before leaving. A light fog hung gently in the air and wrapped the aged pine sentries standing in the courtyard, while a single flame flickered in the window of the stable. As the lone fighter slowly walked towards the main archway, a neighborhood dog walked up to greet him in hopes of a moment of his attention.

"Hello there." He reached down to pat the companion on the head several times, and rub his side before continuing.

As he stood in the main opening, he turned to look in both directions. Hmm, nobody's up yet, so maybe I'll go out near the grove of trees to practice. Silently he adjusted the large weapons on his shoulder, turned to look at the then aged symbols on the side of the arch, and headed down the small dirt path. As he walked, he observed how the walls had aged over the years since his childhood. I remember when these walls looked so tall and like they were new, he thought.

Minutes later as he reached the grove, he leaned his weapons against the largest tree and lifted his leg high on the trunk to begin stretching. Twelve fighting principles of praying mantis, he thought while leaning forward against his leg. After several minutes of stretching, he stepped back, opened into a basic stance in order to sit and focus on breathing for thirty minutes. Afterwards he began to slowly perform each hand form and weapon and use the slow movement to warm up his muscles.

I want to investigate those twelve principles and see how they work. Kick, block punch, punch, grab, kick. These praying mantis theories are so intriguing. Sweep, sweep, jump kick, punch. Two hours later the sun slowly rose above the trees and tried to warm the cool morning air; Yangban sat against the old tree and analyzed the newly acquired principles while resting his tired muscles. *If I can adjust my family's style of fighting to include these, it should make some great improvements. We have some strong fighting concepts already, but these new ones will really enhance the basics.* He slowly stood up and grabbed his sharp spear. *It's time to begin working on my weapons and their applications.*

Looking around he walked over to a nearby tree and began thrusting his trusty ally at a specific crease in the bark on the trunk. *Spear forward, pull back and block the foot, block high overhead, pull back, and spear the bark again, walk back and forth while blocking, turn spear the bark, pull back and spin around to hit with the butt end. Kick, kick, swing the spear overhead and strike sideways.* For two hours he continued using the tree as an opponent with each of his various weapons to maintain a high degree of accuracy with each attack. *It's time to go back and eat. Afterwards I'll practice my slow-moving routines in the courtyard.*

"Hey, Uncle, what are you doing?" a boy asked as Yangban walked into the compound.

"I'm going inside to eat before I continue my training."

"Can I watch when you train later?"

"When I come out, why don't you practice what you know while I'm training?'

"Okay, great! I'll come back in a little while." The boy turned and ran across the open space.

Quietly the hungry fighter walked inside his small dwelling and prepared a simple meal of rice and vegetables before heating a pot of water for tea. The room had warmed from the cool overnight air and was beginning to ask for the windows and doors to be opened to relieve the accumulation of excess warmth. Slowly he opened the worn window shutters and stood in the opening basking in the cool breeze. Afterwards, he rested for an hour before returning to the open courtyard to resume his training.

Gradually, he began moving through a form designed to be practiced at a slow speed to help develop and perfect specific principles of movement. Step forward while sinking into a low stance, move your arms forward and imitate a tiger's claws, pull down and back and change your hand position to imitate a praying mantis grabbing its prey, then return to the forward position.

"Hey, Uncle, I came back!" the boy said as he ran through the archway, threw a rock up on the tile roof and watched it bounce and roll back down to the ground.

"Good, I'm curious to see what you're learning." Yangban said without looking as he continued his practice.

"I just started learning the single sword and I'm still on the basics."
He showed his senior the small worn sword.

"What movements are you working on?"

"The flowers and circling the body."

"Ah-ha! Two of the more important ones since they are harder to
perfect and execute when you're fighting.

"Show me." Yangban stopped his slow practice and stepped back.

The boy firmly grabbed the handle of the weapon and stepped out
into a wide stance and then began to slowly move the sword around
his body in a figure eight pattern. "Thud, thwack!" "Ouch! "Thud,
thwack! Ouch!"

"Hmm, I see that you and your sword are not getting along very
well.

"Try going slower and don't be afraid to get hit."

"But it'll hurt."

"If you are so afraid of hitting yourself, you will not move the sword
correctly and then you hit yourself. Also, the pain from hitting
yourself is not going to last very long and you need to accept it and
understand that pain is what you decide it is. If you think it hurts
really bad, it always will. But if you believe that it's only a
sensation and will go away soon, then that is what it'll do. It's all
up to you and your belief." Yangban picked up his sword and
demonstrated how to properly move the weapon.

"See how close I keep the sword to my body as I flower?

"Now try again and keep the sword closer to your body. It is supposed to be defending and attacking using one smooth motion."

Circle, circle, "thud, thwack, ouch!"

"Keep going and don't stop if you hit yourself. If it hurts keep going." Yangban said as he smiled.

Now let me get back to my research of the twelve soft attacks while he's wildly swinging that sword. For the next hour he worked on this strange fighting concept while occasionally observing the young child struggle with the sword and trying to avoid hitting himself.

"Uncle, can you explain about the circling around the body movement?" the boy asked when he saw his elder stop temporarily during his training.

"What is it you don't understand?"

"What's it used for?"

"When you swing the sword in front, you are cutting an opponent and when you swing it behind you, you are cutting to the back, after that you draw it in close and defend your entire body as it circles the body."

"Oh, okay I think I understand." The boy began to scratch his head as he looked up at the sky.

"Keep trying and eventually you'll figure it out." He turned and walked back to where he was practicing.

As the light slowly began to change color, and the shadows climbed higher up into the trees, the boy heard his mother calling and without warning, turned and ran back across the compound towards the main archway. "Bye, Uncle," he yelled just before turning the corner.

For months Yangban practiced daily to improve this new system and develop a sound understanding of its fighting principles. Eventually, he received information about a situation in Qingdao that the Yi Hua team was attempting to stop.

"Shoushan, I'm leaving for Qingdao tomorrow. It seems the officials are trying to exploit the local farmers again, so some friends from the Yi Hua Team are going to go over to try and help stop them."

"Okay, but be careful."

Seven days later Yangban arrived at the port village and went directly to see his friends in the group.

"Shinwu, I heard there was some trouble with the officials and the farmers." He walked into the small room and sat down.

"Yes, they are trying to make the poor farmers give up most of their crops to help some people down south.

"But we talked to some of the farmers and found out the local officials have been stealing the food and selling it on the black market." Shinwu shook his head, pounding his fist on the table.

"And as they continue, the farmers are starving and losing money, just so the officials can cheat them and make money." He leaned back and looked at the ceiling.

"If we find enough proof of their stealing, we can then report them to an official high enough to be willing to listen."

"How much evidence do you already have?" Yangban picked up his cup of tea and blew across the steaming liquid.

"Only a few of the farmers we talked to showed us the paperwork they received when they delivered their produce to the officials. The rest didn't have anything."

"Tomorrow we'll go out and talk to some more people and see if we can get any more solid proof." Yangban leaned back and rested his elbow on the table while sipping the tea.

Over the next several weeks, members of the group continually searched for documents while talking to people who witnessed the crimes. Unfortunately, most of the farmers were never given any paperwork so their task became even harder. Eventually, they were able to uncover enough evidence to be able to present it to the county magistrate.

Initially the county officials were unwilling to listen to the case due to the criminal's long standing in the village as an official. After repeated attempts and additional evidence, he agreed to review the incident. Months later the county official determined there was sufficient evidence presented against the village official and had him arrested.

During the trial, the village official reluctantly admitted to stealing from the farmers over a period of years while blaming them for holding back their crops. Afterwards the county official sentenced the local to jail in addition to being required to wear a large wooden neck lock that was tied to a post in the middle of the village for six months with a sign proclaiming his crimes.

Hmm, twelve fighting theories. I'm going to need a partner to help me with those, he thought as he walked outside weeks later, sat down next to a large tree and began imitating the hand techniques his nephew taught him. Minutes later as he sat contemplating the concepts, he saw his friend walking towards him.

"Shinwu, I learned this new Kung Fu style called Praying Mantis and I'd like to discuss its fighting strategies with you." Yangban stood up and demonstrated a hand technique.

"Praying Mantis? I've never heard of it." Shinwu looked up at the hand technique from the corner of his eye.

"It has these fighting theories and I need a partner to help so I can figure them out."

"Sure, I'd love to help. Maybe I can use some of them in my Ancient Fist Style." He stepped closer.

"The first four are called block, hook, grapple, and pluck.

"Now extend your arm like when you punch."

Shinwu extended his right arm towards Yangban and as soon as it neared his chest, Yangban reached out and applied the four techniques. "Whoa!" Shinwu exclaimed as his arm was snatched forward, causing his head and neck to experience a sense of whiplash.

"I need to learn more of that!"

"It has to do with how a praying mantis seizes its prey when it attacks. As it reaches out his first instinct is to block his opponent's attack and then seize the arms while pulling back all in one smooth motion." He demonstrated the technique.

"This pulling causes his opponent to lose his footing and leverage to the ground while giving the mantis more strength from pulling the arms in close."

"As soon as I figure it out better, I'll be happy to teach it to you, since you're willing to help me with my research."

"Great. It appears to be a very effective fighting style." He rubbed his arm.

"Some of the concepts are unique, so it might take me a little while to make them effective, but when I'm ready, I'll let you know."

"Good. When will you be going back to Pingdu?"

"Probably tomorrow. I need to go back and see how my mother is doing."

"Oh, okay, I need to walk over to Yantai, so I won't see you when I get back."

"Well then, I guess this is a good time to say goodbye." Yangban *turned and extended his friend a formal salute.*

"Goodbye, my friend." Shinwu *returned a salute and turned to slowly begin his journey.*

10. WHISPERS OF LIGHT

"Zhufei, did I tell you what I heard yesterday about our countrymen when we stopped in the city to sleep?" Yangban said as he looked down at the dusty road.

"No, you didn't."

"I was talking to the hardware store owner while you were getting your hair and braid trimmed, and he showed me an article saying a lot of men were leaving the country and going across the ocean to dig for gold in a place called America."

"What? you're saying our citizens are getting on a ship and crossing the ocean just to dig for gold?"

"Yes."

"When was that article written? It must be old."

"No, it's recent. The date said May 1849."

"Wow, that's only two months ago."

"Rumble, rumble," the sound raced across the barren fields, up the hillside and into the trees where the two solitary fighters were busily training. As the alarm moved through the trees neither fighter released his focus, so the sound continued up over the hilltop and disappeared in the valley below. The distant squadron of storm clouds marched forward from behind the horizon and soon closed ranks to become a united front line without a single soldier out of position. Suddenly, the initial shots were fired from their electrical guns as the lightning flashed, sending a warning shot downward towards a dead tree and exploding in a cloud of wood fibers "Crack!" the soldier in the sky announced to Yangban and Zhufei of their impending attack. "Crack, crack, crack!" three more soldiers released their enthusiasm at joining the march.

After several minutes, the trees and bushes began to lean abruptly while their leaves fluttered wildly from the strong wind racing up the hill. This momentarily stirred Zhufei to stop his training and observe the commotion.

"Yangban, I think we need to stop for now and find some shelter."
He turned and headed for his belongings.

212

"Wow, it looks like it's going to be a serious storm in about two hours." Yangban turned and looked at the army in the sky heading towards them.

"There were some caves in the side of the hill we passed late yesterday. If we hurry, we should be able to get there before the storm catches us." He pointed back down the dusty path.

Quickly they gathered everything and began jogging back around the hill to the steep slope with the multitude of holes in the face and giving the appearance of a honeycomb. As they neared the first opening, they suddenly stopped as someone from inside casually stepped out.

"Oh… hello, we were trying to find some shelter from the big storm heading this way and thought these were empty."

"No, many of the farmers live in them with their families, but there are several further back on the slope, that are still vacant." The woman pointed towards an area of smaller caves off in the distance.

"Thank you," the strangers said as they bowed and turned away. Instantly they began jogging in the direction the woman specified. Thirty minutes later they reached the area of smaller openings and quickly inspected the first caves to verify if they were occupied.

"Hmm, I see why no one uses this one, the floor slopes downward towards the back so any water will always run inside." Zhufei pointed at the floor.

"Let's try the next one." He turned away from the opening. Walking up the steep incline Yangban noticed an opening that was overgrown with numerous small flat stones piled in the center as if they had slid down the slope and landed abruptly in front of the opening.

"Look in here." Zhufei said as he stepped next to Yangban and pointed inside.

"It's pretty dark back there, but the floor in the front seems to be flat so the rain won't run in." Yangban said as he leaned forward to peer inside, while squinting his eyes and shielding his forehead.

"There's some dry twigs over there we can use for a fire," Zhufei pointed down below the opening. Minutes later they returned with their arms full of small twigs and dried leaves, walked around the pile of rubble and dropped the bundles close to the opening. "Thud!" the sticks and larger limbs hit the ground and echoed through the cave.

"Hey, what do you think you're doing?" a voice in the thick blackness of the cave yelled.

"What?" Yangban and Zhufei said as they jumped back and landed in a fighting pose. "Who's back there?" Yangban yelled as he strained to try and see where the voice came from.

"I'm Liu Dongxu, "Whispers of light," and I was meditating peacefully until you came in and made all that noise."

"We were just bringing in some wood for a fire." Zhufei said as he scanned the darkness.

"Fire, why do you need a fire in my space?"

"We thought we'd stay here for the night." Yangban replied.

"Really, I prefer being alone, so maybe you should find another place to stay."

"We won't bother…"

"Boom!" the stranger landed within several feet of Yangban and pointed his finger at the unwanted guests with his eyes almost closed. Instantly Yangban and Zhufei stepped back with a shocked expression, raised their arms to defend themselves and gasped.

"You're starting to bother me." He suddenly rushed forward and stopped just inches from his startled intruders.

"Do I have to throw you out? Maybe you should get on a boat eastward and go to the land of the white devils and help them dig up all the gold they recently found!"

"Hey, we're not trying to bother you, we just want to get out of the storm!" Zhufei stood up and yelled while placing one hand on his hip, and pointing with the other hand. Meanwhile, Liu turned and stepped closer to the extended hand.

"Don't point at me!" he slapped the hand away, as his eyes remained almost closed.

"Hey, don't be so rude or I'll kick you!"

"I doubt that." He turned back towards Yangban.

"What? Ai-yaa!" Zhufei jumped forward while thrusting his foot forward towards the stranger's back. As the foot neared its target, Liu turned and casually slapped the foot to the side before kicking Zhufei in the side, sending him stumbling into the dark.

"Why did you do that?" Yangban stepped forward and pointed at Liu.

"I said don't point at me!" he slapped Yangban's hand.

"Are you going to kick me also?"

"If you point at me again, I definitely will."

"Arghh!" the sound echoed through the cave and suddenly Zhufei appeared, charging forward towards Liu. Initially, Zhufei swung his arms in large circles as if to strike the sides of the head followed by a jump kick to the chest. As he continued, Liu swatted each fist away as casually as chasing away a pesky fly. The moment the kick neared his chest, Liu stepped back while grabbing the foot and pulling forward. Immediately Zhufei's body began to sink towards the soil and as he landed, the impact jarred his momentum and forced him to swing his arms wildly at his opponent.

Liu waited until Zhufei landed and quickly stepped inside the ineffective strikes, grabbed his opponent's arm and threw him against Yangban; causing them both to collapse on the ground in a pile.

"Hey, you'll pay for that!" Yangban said.

As Zhufei rolled to the side, Yangban jumped up and rushed forward. Instantly, Liu stepped backwards into the thick darkness and disappeared as Yangban kept charging.

"Thud, thud, boom!" suddenly Yangban flew backwards out of the darkness and back into the light, and then landed in the same spot where he fell earlier.

"What happened?" Zhufei asked as he watched his friend stand back up and rub his side.

"I charged him but then everything went black," he said as he turned and watched Liu slowly step into the light.

"Boom, crack!" the lightning outside attacked an ancient tree near the mouth of the cave. "Crack, crash!" a large branch hit the ground. Suddenly the army of storm clouds that had joined forces earlier, arrived over the caves and withdrew the sun. Instantly the few rays of sunlight creeping into the cave disappeared and left the three fighters standing in darkness.

"So now how are you going to fight?" Liu asked.

"I can see you enough to fight." Yangban stepped forward and rushed Liu with a series of kicks to the chest. As the first kick neared Liu, he twisted his body and grabbed the leg as it sped by, before turning and throwing his opponent into the thick blackness again.

"Thud, ughh," the invisible victim exclaimed.

Zhufei stood and watched his friend disappear, before crashing against the wall. Suddenly, his friend charged forward, while punching at the stranger standing at the edge of the complete darkness. Unfortunately, the cave's interior was blanketed with a thick veil of dark gray, creating an illusion of everything appearing to be closer than usual.

"Whoosh, whoosh," each of Zhufei's punches missed their target and rushed off into the darkness. "Thud, thud, thud," Liu stepped in and hit Zhufei in the chest with his palms then jumped forward and kicked him three times as he stumbled backwards before disappearing into the darkness. Liu quickly turned around and saw Yangban shuffle forward with a combination of kicks and punches. Unfortunately, as he neared his target and was on the verge of making contact, Liu suddenly dropped down to the ground, swung his leg around in a large circle and swept both feet out from under Yangban. Instantly his body began to spin in mid-air until his feet were above his head, just before landing on his shoulders and head in the thick layer of dust. "Thud."

"Are you done playing yet...Ha!" Liu stepped back into the grey veil until his body was almost invisible. Meanwhile, Zhufei scrambled forward into the dim light and reached down to help his friend back to his feet. As Yangban brushed off the layer of dust, Zhufei scanned the area to try and locate their opponent. "You'll pay for that!" he yelled while looking around.

"Oh really?" Liu replied as he stepped forward, barely enough to become a faint silhouette.

"Yes." Zhufei jumped forward while kicking, and again the grey veil cast an illusion of distance, causing the techniques to only attack the thick expanse. Meanwhile, Yangban circled around to the side and stepped forward to attack as Liu was focused on Zhufei's kicks.

"Thud, thud!" Yangban kicked and punched Liu; sending him rolling towards the mouth of the cave.

"Ah, so you can kick." Liu said as he stood in the light, brushing off the dust before leaning forward and rushing back towards the two strangers.

"Watch out, Yangban, I see he fights with the "faint light" technique I've heard about from my friends," Zhufei yelled as their opponent drew near. Quickly Yangban stepped sideways and closer to the light while watching Liu move forward. Soon the two fighters had their opponent directly between them and slowly began to close the distance.

"Ah, so you're going to try and attack me at the same time." Liu stood straight up, placed one arm behind his back and extended the other arm forward.

"Very well, let's see how your strategy works." He settled into a strong fighting stance and positioned himself so he was able to see both opponents.

Suddenly, as if on cue, Yangban and Zhufei stepped in to punch. As they did Liu jumped up and kicked them both at the same time.

Outside the army of storm clouds began throwing their arsenal of lightning bolts at the ground below. "Crack, crack, crack, rumble, rumble, rumble, crack!" With each attack the flashes of light momentarily illuminated the small cave and exposed the barren walls hidden deep within the darkness. Yangban and Zhufei flinched as the light raced through the dwelling, Liu never reacted and stood motionless.

"Well, are you done already?" Liu asked.

"No!" Zhufei said as he dropped down and swung his foot around in a circle towards Liu's leg. Instantly Liu jumped up and kicked Yangban in the chest, while simultaneously hitting Zhufei in the head. "Thud, thud," the two fighters fell backwards as Liu landed. Instantly Liu stepped forward and kicked Zhufei again as he tried to stand up, sending him once again into the darkness.

"Crack, flash." The storm outside continued sending its charges downward and the momentary flashes began to appear more frequently. Now each loud rumble in the sky was accompanied by a series of flashes and several "Crack, crack" booms. Meanwhile, the rain which had been trying to hold back, now turned into a torrential downpour. At the mouth of the cave the water dropped as though it were a solid sheet and hit the pile of rubble before splashing menacingly away from the opening. As it did, the overspray slowly began creeping down the back of the pile and seeping into the cave, causing the area to turn into a growth of dark brown mud.

Inside, the battle raged on with each new encounter sending someone into the dark recesses, only to return and watch their friend fall victim to the same scenario while Liu "Whispers of light" stood waiting for their return.

"How long are you two planning on continuing this game?" Liu finally asked.

"Game?" Zhufei said as he stood rubbing his ribs.

"Yes, game. It's obvious that you're not getting anywhere with your attempts to scare or intimidate me, so it must be some sort of game."

"No this is not a game!" Yangban said as he stumbled out of the dark.

"So, then what are you trying to accomplish with your so-so techniques?"

"So-so techniques?"

"I've lived on Wudang Mountain for over forty years and seen many fighters who thought they had expert techniques only to find out, there are those who are much more advanced. I hope you didn't view your abilities as extremely high, because you'll need to practice more to get there." Liu waved his finger in the air.

"I knew my techniques weren't the best in the world, but I didn't think they were that bad." Zhufei scratched his head.

"So, you're saying that we are only mediocre practitioners?" Yangban asked with his eyes wide open.

"Actually, I'd say your kung fu is way above average and if you diligently practice, you'll get to the point where you're really good. But today you're not at that level, and neither am I."

"You're not at that level? You just beat us without any struggle, and you're not really good? I think you need to give yourself more credit for your abilities." Zhufei sat on the ground and leaned against the wall.

"I know how good my abilities are. I just choose not to elevate myself. I'd rather just keep training and learning."

"I like that mindset. It reminds me of all the times my father told me to be careful about how I allowed my mind to convince me about the level of my abilities." Yangban reached down and dusted off his pants.

Okay, so are we done trying to fight?" Liu asked as he walked over to a smooth rock protruding from the side of the cave wall and sat down.

"Yes, and it's about time, because I was beginning to get tired of walking around in the dark back there in the corner." Yangban smiled.

"So, can we start a small fire now? That way I can finally see my way around in here." Zhufei stood up and walked towards the mouth of the cave.

"Sure, sure." Liu waved his hand.

"Crack!" the clouds attacked again.

"You lived on Wudang Mountain for forty years?" Yangban began building a small circle of stones for the fire.

"Yes, I was asked by my teacher to go out and see the world for a while and decide if I liked what I saw and wanted to stay, or come to back to the temple."

"Hmm, interesting." Zhufei stopped momentarily to reflect on what he just heard.

"So where have you traveled since leaving?"

"Oh, I've been as far west as India and as far east as Shanghai. I went to Vietnam and then over to Guangzhou, but I haven't gone too far north yet." Liu carefully drew a map in the soft dust.

"Thwack, thwack, thwack!" Zhufei began striking several rocks together to create a spark for the fire.

"That's quite a distance, Yangban said.

"I guess so, but with all the traveling I still know what I want to do," Liu said as he dropped several small twigs and leaves on to the pile.

"I remember one time when I was young, I needed to make a decision about my future and could not decide what I wanted to do." Yangban began as he sat down near the circle of rocks. "After several weeks of continually jumping from decision to decision but not getting any closer to a final choice, my mother told me to leave it alone for a while and an answer will eventually present itself." He began breaking the sticks in half and stacking them next to the

rocks. "And so, I did what she suggested. After a few more weeks, I was sitting under a tree after training all morning and just looking up at the trees but not thinking about anything, and the thought of working as an escort entered my mind as clear as the empty sky. As I sat there the thought just seemed to absorb into every cell and fill my entire mind with complete clarity." He looked up at the ceiling as if he was reliving the moment.

"Yes, my teacher said the same thing before I left the temple, but it hasn't happened yet. I guess I'm still thinking about it too much," Lin said as he looked outside and watched the sun begin to slip between the army of clouds and cast several thin rays of light into the mouth of the cave.

"Looks like the storm is beginning to pass by and let the sun come back out," Zhufei said as he stood up, walked over to the opening and looked out at the sky.

"So, Liu, can I ask you about your special technique of fighting?" Zhufei asked when he turned around and faced the small pile of sticks which were beginning to grow red at the ends from the heat.

"Sure."

"Where did you learn that "whisper of light" technique?" he sat down.

"It was something I learned specially from my teacher at the temple years ago. He said I had the right fighting style, which would allow me to use it effectively."

"Well, it looks like you've mastered it, after the way you threw us around," Yangban said as he shook his head and smiled.

"Oh, the light in here earlier was no problem at all. Usually, my teacher made me train in a cave that was completely dark." He waved his arm at the walls and ceiling.

"Wow, no wonder," Zhufei said.

"So how did you train for that art?" Zhufei asked as he threw several more sticks into the growing fire.

"Well, when I first started, I had a lot of trouble with holding my eyes almost closed. My teacher took a cloth, cut a small slit in the middle and tied it around my head so I couldn't see anything except for the faint images in the slit. After several years of training with the cloth, he finally had me remove the cloth and begin training in the dark."

"How could you train in the dark if you couldn't see anything?" Yangban asked.

"Usually what my teacher did was to light a single candle and place it in the center of the cave. Then he would attack me. He said it helped to teach me how not to focus on the light but look around it for my opponent while learning how to keep my eyes almost closed."

"How did having your eyes almost closed help?" Zhufei asked.

"He explained that when your eyes are open, you get too much light and too many distractions into your mind. But when they are *almost closed, your mind will stop looking in all directions and focus in one area. Also, it helps to allow your mind to relax and soften its focus, which helps to enhance your intuition and sensitivity."*

"That's interesting, but how did you learn to decipher distances and reach when you were fighting?" Yangban said as he stirred the burning embers, which were now burning with a bright red glow.

"Yeah, that took a while and I received quite a few bruises from my teacher while he was teaching me." Liu rubbed the side of his head.

"Initially I had such a hard time figuring out how far away he was when he attacked that I always missed when I blocked or attacked. Consequently, he would repeatedly hit me and yell at me for not paying attention to what he told me to do. Eventually I began to figure out how to adjust for the low light and could occasionally defend against his strikes."

"Occasionally?" Yangban asked.

"Yeah, I never progressed to where I could defend against all of them because once I was able to defend some techniques, he blew out the candle and made me start over. And then he hit me all over again until I could defend against him, which was several more years." He smiled while looking outside.

"That was some serious daily training." Yangban said.

"Yes, and when I was finally able to defend his attacks, he then began attacking at full speed, and I received even more bruises,

because his kicks usually knocked me back against the walls of the cave!" his eyes widened as he explained the situation.

"So now that you've mastered the technique, it must be really easy to fight someone in the light." Zhufei asked.

"The art makes my sight extremely sensitive to any movement when I'm fighting and allows me to react even earlier to my opponent's techniques. Also, with my eyes almost shut, my opponents aren't able to watch my eyes to interpret my next movement, so it delays their reactions."

"That is a really great deception!" Yangban exclaimed while tapping his forehead with his fingertips.

"Would you ever teach anyone the art?" Yangban asked as he leaned his head forward to bow politely while sitting.

"Sure, I'd be happy to help my kung fu brothers increase their fighting abilities and arsenal."

"Great!" Zhufei raised his hand and extended his thumb in approval.

"If we start now, I can show you some of the basics before the sun goes down later, and then we can practice when it begins to get dark in here." Liu stood up.

"Sounds good to me!" Yangban raised his thumb.

"The first exercise we need to practice is how to keep your eyes almost closed while you're walking around. And the key is to relax your eyelids as you practice, otherwise it will only take a few

minutes before your eyes and face begin to strain, which will then force you to stop." Liu demonstrated how to properly position the eyes.

"It takes some practice to be able to hold the eyelids in that position. Every time I think I have it, my eyes either close completely or they open wide," Zhufei said as he stood motionless trying to develop the technique.

"Keep holding them in the exact position. It takes a while to develop the habit of not opening them all the way."

"I can feel my forehead beginning to tighten up and it's getting harder to hold my eyelids still." Yangban said as he stopped to rub his eyes.

"Yes, this is harder than it looks but it's like any other practice. The more you train at it the quicker you can ingrain a new habit and the better your technique gets." Liu stepped back to watch.

After an hour of training, the three stopped to drink some tea and give their eyes a rest. "Okay, now that we've rested, it's time to adjust your training." Liu stood up and walked over to the open area.

"The technique you just learned needs to be practiced until you can comfortably sit or stand with your eyes in that position for long periods of time without any strain whatsoever. If you notice any strain after an hour of practice, it means you need to train more because the practice has not become a natural habit. Eventually, you'll be able to keep them in that position all day and it won't bother you." He looked at his students.

"The next phase of your training is to be able to walk around while keeping them in that position and not hit anything or fall."

"Thud." Yangban hit his foot against the rocks surrounding the fire.

"See, it takes some practice."

"Yes, with my eyes almost closed it's harder to be able to judge the distance of everything." Yangban stopped, opened his eyes, looked around the cave and then outside before beginning again.

"Keep moving around. You need to get a good feel for what everything looks like from that perspective. And don't stare at your eyelashes, you need to look past them and out into the room so that you can forget they're there. If not, they will always be a hinderance and restrict your progress." Liu began walking around with them to assist their practice.

"Try walking up to something and stop when you think you're about to hit it. Then open your eyes and see if the distance is what you thought it was."

"Thud." Zhufei hit his head against the cave wall.

"Your mind needs to recalculate everything it thought was real." Liu stopped within inches of Yangban.

"This too must be practiced until you know precisely how far everything is from your body. Otherwise, when you're fighting, *you'll always miss your opponent because you'll think they're closer than they actually are."*

As they continued their training the sun slowly continued its journey towards the distant horizon while pushing the shadows further and further across the floor and up the walls of the cave. Meanwhile, the remnants of the recent storm occasionally dripped from the cave opening and splashed on the rocks, causing the faint sound to echo through the room.

"I'm starting to get a basic sense of judgement about the distances." Zhufei said.

"Keep moving and keep practicing. It must become completely natural if you want to use it at all."

"As I move in and out of the light by the opening, I notice how much harder it is to gauge the distances." Yangban said as he stepped away from the mouth of the cave.

"Good, keep trying and make your mind work it out.

"Now we're going to change the practice again, so start moving slightly faster." Liu said.

"Thud, ouch! I hit the wall again." Yangban said as he stopped to rub his forehead.

"Ha!" I remember hitting everything in the room many times when my teacher first told me to speed up." Liu laughed.

"Crash. Hmph, I just hit the rocks and fell," Zhufei said as he slowly stood up.

Over and over, they continued to run into the wall or trip over something on the ground before falling, only to stand up and repeat the drill. Gradually the sun sank behind the hilltop and the light in the cave slowly sank into the walls and let the darkness surround the small fire.

"Good, now it's time to experiment with using the technique in its most advantageous setting." Liu began walking directly towards his new students and extending his hand at their face.

"Thud." Yangban walked into Liu's fist, which was stopped in front of his face.

"I guess I should have blocked that."

"Probably." Liu stepped back.

"Now start moving even faster, but be careful, because your depth perception is going to be way off at first." Liu said as he stopped by the fire, lifted a small branch with his foot and tossed it into the fire.

Soon, the light from the sun totally disappeared and relinquished its authority to the small fire. Now flickers of light jumping occasionally from within the circle of stones barely escaped the pile of rocks quietly soaking up all the moisture falling from above. Outside the owls continued their conversation as the earlier storm occasionally flashed its march forward in the sky by lighting the tops of the storm clouds and sending streaks of light through the cloud's interior.

"I think we should slow our steps again, so that you can give your eyes and minds some rest." Liu stopped by the fire and watched Yangban and Zhufei begin to slow their movements, trying to acclimate.

"Observe how much effort you need to exert now that you've slowed down in relation to moments ago. How well can you interpret distances and surfaces? How does it feel as you move in and out of the darkness in the cave? Does your mind seem calmer now that you've slowed down? Can you sense objects in the cave better? Sensitivity, feeling, intuition, motion and distance are some of the concepts that you need to master even when you're moving at full speed.

"Cats and tigers can see very well in dim light, or no light at all. Why? They have specially designed eyes for low-light hunting, and they are able to detect the slightest movement, which you will eventually develop through years of training."

"I think we should stop for the night before your brains explode with all this new information." Liu sat down near the fire.

"Agreed." Yangban said as he stopped and rubbed his eyes.

"Agreed." Zhufei walked over to the fire.

"Tomorrow we'll practice again." Liu stirred the red embers before throwing another stick into the pile.

After several minutes of quiet reflection Yangban walked over to a secluded area and went to sleep. Zhufei sat near the fire and stared aimlessly into the reddened sticks, as Liu sat in a lotus position with *his eyes closed. Eventually, they both retired to a private area and fell asleep, as the glow from the burning wood slowly diminished.*

Early the next morning, as fog blanketed the valley below, Yangban stepped outside, looked around at the tops of the hills hovering above the thick air and walked over to a small flat area to begin his morning energy training. Two hours later, as several birds began calling to their neighbors, he finished his exercises and walked back towards the cave.

"Liu, I saw you meditating when I went out to train. Did you meditate all night?" he said as he stepped around the pile of rocks and stirred the burnt twigs.

"No, I usually arise at four and sit for about three hours." He sat down near the circle of stones next to Zhufei.

"It helps me train my mind for when I'm using the whispers of light technique."

"Hmm." Yangban said.

"Today when we practice, I want to work on your individual fighting styles and show you how to use the "whispers of light" technique when you're fighting."

"Great. I was wondering yesterday about how this technique would incorporate into my family's style of fighting." Zhufei grabbed several twigs and placed them directly on to the remaining red embers.

"First let's talk about the strategies of your family's kung fu. From your individual perspectives, would you say your style is more offensive or defensive in nature?" Liu gestured with his hands a moving forward and a moving backward motion with his hands.

"I think we'd both have to say they are more offensive in nature." Zhufei nodded his head as Yangban replied.

"Okay, then you need to always remember that when you fight while using the "whispers" technique. Your focus must be on the speed of your hands and feet in relation to their retreating motions."

"What?" Zhufei asked.

"What happens when you're attacking, is that your movements are moving away from you and so is your opponent. So, you need to become very proficient at determining the outward speed of techniques and the speed your opponent reacts with as he retreats. Why? Because motion moving away from you is different from motion moving towards you. Moving away from you appears slower than motion moving towards you." Liu looked at both of his students.

"When you're using the "whispers" technique, all movement will change its appearance of speed, especially when your opponent is attacking."

"Pop, pop, crack!" The small fire awakened from the long night and announced its readiness at warming whatever was placed in its vicinity. Meanwhile, out beyond the accumulation of fallen

shards of stone, the early morning birds happily continued their conversations.

"Techniques that you think will be fast enough to stop their attack, may not be effective, unless you can adjust your speed, and that only arises after many hours of training. Consequently, in your personal family styles, you need to spend many hours of research to figure out how to use the "whispers" technique, and as you use it, when to move while using it." He lightly tapped his temple.

"In your long-fist style, there is an attitude towards bombarding the opponent with numerous long punches. But if you don't keep in mind the timing, as to when your fist will arrive in relation to their defensive motions, will you be effective? You may have an advantage because you're using the "whispers" technique, but then lose it due to your lack of training and understanding about timing while using it.

"Each opponent will have a unique style or interpretation of his style, and you must be capable of adjusting your "whispers" technique to their specific talents. Now, practice what we researched yesterday and visualize an opponent from every style that you know of or have heard about." Liu stood up and stepped back from the growing fire.

For two hours the fighters continued practicing trying to utilize the "whispers" technique against an array of unique styles. Each time they began to understand how to use the technique, Liu would change the style they were opposing and force them to learn a completely new approach.

Day after day they trained, and Liu continued explaining more and more in-depth theories and concepts about the special art in order to more fully acclimate the two fighters to the new fighting strategy. Each day when they began to grasp the art, Liu changed their practice in order to expand their understanding.

For weeks the two remained with the Wudang monk and trained daily in the new secret art. Eventually, they decided it was time to continue their journey northward and bid their new friend goodbye. As they slowly walked around the jagged pile of rocks with their sharp edges glistening in the early light, Yangban turned and politely bowed one last time. Unfortunately, Liu had already turned towards the wall and returned to his meditation. Yangban stood for a moment, smiled and turned to walk out into the morning sun gradually climbing over the far horizon.

"That was quite an adventure over the past weeks," Zhufei said as Yangban walked up.

"Yes, it truly was."

11. MIST IN THE TREES

An hour after the sun crept above the treetops, as the morning dew and faint mist hanging between the trees finally disappeared, Yangban and Zhufei were finishing their training. The birds excitedly chirped another group conversation, while below the squirrels dashed from tree to tree and numerous butterflies fluttered in the sun. The cool night air struggled to survive but gradually surrendered to the sun's downpour of rays.

Walking through the gates and into Taizhou, they noticed that one by one, the shopkeepers began to open their doors and arranged their wares against the wall for another day of haggling over the price. On the corner post supporting the overhang of a small tool repair store across the street, Zhufei stopped to read a notice about the recent invasion of Wuhan and Nanjing by the rebels from

Taiping. "Hmm, it looks like there's another fight building against the government," he said while reading the worn notice before turning to continue into the city. "Yes, it seems there are quite a few revolts going on all over the country lately." Yangban yelled over his shoulder as he looked back at his friend. "Yes, but I figured the loss to the foreign devils thirteen years ago would have been enough fighting for a while. I guess not." He turned and followed his friend down the street.

Several blocks down the street a group of men feverishly worked to finish assembling a small stage started the day before. Poles had been raised to create the back which allowed for personal banners (triangular flags tied to poles) to be hung announcing the performer. A long canvas was draped across the front of the stage to hide the platform's framing and give the illusion of a cloud. Musicians eventually walked up, huddled together and appeared to be discussing their setup location. Minutes later a woman and her daughter arrived carrying a large overstuffed bag. Carefully she opened the top and pulled out a long scroll and began tying it to the backdrop.

"Hey Yangban, do you see what that banner says?" Zhufei pointed at the woman tying up the scroll.

"Yes, interesting, it says they moved from Hefei last year at the beginning of the year of the Ox – 1853 – and their kung fu balancing art has been passed down in their family for ten generations." Yangban rubbed his chin.

"Great, I like watching a skilled performer balance and walk on top of porcelain teacups." Zhufei raised his thumb.

"We've got time before we leave for Pingdu. Let's stay and watch for a while, and see what she performs." Yangban looked around to find a vacant seat.

The woman and her daughter meticulously arranged the first bowls on the stage floor in a specific pattern and then placed another bowl on top of several on the bottom row.

"Wow, did you see that? I've never seen anyone try to balance on top of two bowls." Zhufei scratched his head.

Curiously, they watched as the woman pulled several long strips of cloth from the bag before handing one to the young girl. After inspecting the bowl arrangement, the woman glanced at the girl and nodded. Instantly the girl tied the cloth over her eyes and stood motionless.

The moment the older woman finished tying the cloth over her eyes, she began a series of slow movements while cautiously stepping between the delicate bowls. Her routine appeared to follow a specific pattern, two steps forward past the bowls then one step sideways between the bowls arranged in the center, followed by two steps forward, reach out with the toe over a single bowl as if sensing its existence, turn around and begin again. Several minutes later, she paused while standing in the center of the arrangement and spoke to the young girl, who nodded and immediately began the same stepping routine between the bowls while the musicians quietly began playing in rhythm with her steps. As the two silently *moved throughout the arrangement, the anticipation from the crowd seemed to build as they watched the performers effortlessly move but never touch a bowl or each other. Soon, as if on cue, they stopped and turned towards each other, nodded and carefully stepped up onto a single bowl. For several seconds they stood motionless with their arms extended to the sides.*

"Wow!" a child in the audience explained while pointing at the stage.

"It looks like it's now going to get interesting," Yangban leaned over and whispered in Zhufei's ear. Without saying a word, he responded by nodding his head, as the musicians continued to play. Suddenly, the music paused for a note, and the two performers slowly began stepping from one bowl to another. First, two steps forward, swing the toe sideways as if sensing a bowl to the left and carefully place the foot on the bowl. One step forward, turn and jump back to the previous bowl. Again, this routine continued for several minutes and then suddenly without warning, the woman jumped and landed on the stacked bowls.

"Huh" a man sitting in front of Zhufei gasped as he watched the performer balance on top of the stacked bowls.

"Wow, it's hard enough to balance on one bowl without falling or breaking it, but now she's up on two bowls." Yangban said without turning his head.

As they watched, the young girl suddenly swung her leg up behind her back and caught her foot as it touched her head, while the other woman began jumping from one set of bowls to another. Finally, the two performers removed the cloths in unison, from their eyes, and began quickly stepping from bowl to bowl before transitioning into a two-person sparring routine. Kick, Kick, block, jump, punch, jump, the performers launched at each other, as they gradually stepped faster and faster across the bowls.

Suddenly, they stopped all movement, turned and faced the center, raised one leg and pointed the toe at each other before throwing the leg over their head and arching backwards off the bowls.

"Great, great!" the two fighters standing in the back heard the crowd yell.

"I wonder what style of kung fu they practice?" Zhufei said while clapping his hands and watching the performers bow to the crowd and quickly remove their props from the stage.

As the woman and young girl stepped down from the platform, a young man dressed in a traditional Taoist uniform jumped up on the stage and walked to the center.

"Hello, I'm Lao Yunma, I'm called 'Mist in the Trees' and I will demonstrate some of my Taoist Kung Fu from Wudang Mountain." He raised his hands together and saluted everyone.

"Boom!" He stomped the floor and stepped out into a low stance, separating his hands. While looking across the stage, he suddenly kicked at an imaginary opponent, dropped down and swung one leg around to sweep the legs before jumping up and kicking three times. As he landed from the kicks his elbow came crashing down as if breaking an arm. Turning backwards, he simultaneously

241

kicked and punched, stepped down and rapidly swung his foot backwards and up over his head like a scorpion's tail, before continuing the leg around to the stage while punching forward.

"He's pretty good." Yangban whispered.

"Yes, and I like that kick he just did," Zhufei nodded while raising his thumb in approval.

"Now I will show you one of our weapons forms," he said while saluting the crowd.

"Ahh, save us from the torture and just go home!" A man in the front of the crowd yelled as he pointed at the distant horizon.

"Excuse me sir, have I offended you?" Yunma asked as he turned towards the stranger.

"That little children's dance you claim is kung fu is what is offensive."

"Little children's dance?" Yunma grinned and turned away.

"Don't turn your back on me!" The stranger instantly jumped up on the stage and pointed at the performer. Suddenly the musicians stopped.

'I'm Hui Zhigao, the Thundering Lion. I teach the invincible Shaolin Fist here in town, and I am insulted by your bold claims of being from Wudang Mountain."

"But sir, I am from Wudang." Yunma politely bowed.

"Liar I have seen true Wudang style and your bad attempts are insulting."

"Oh, oh, I think there is going to be trouble!" Yangban whispered to Zhufei, who just stood silently while smiling and nodding his head.

"Sir, I don't want any trouble, but I am from Wudang and I would appreciate it if you wouldn't call me a liar."

"With techniques as poor as yours, you are definitely not from Wudang. Maybe you just made it all up." He put his hands on his hips and looked away.

"Made it up? Ahhh..!" Yunma clenched his fists and rushed forward, but Zhigao just stood motionless. As Yunma jumped up and kicked his opponent twice in the chest, Zhigao exhaled deeply and pushed the Taoist backwards. "Ha! As I told you, definitely not Wudang."

"I am from Wudang and I'm now going to show you!" Yunma rushed forward again, but this time he used a zigzag stepping pattern. As he drew close, Zhigao swung his arm in a circle and blocked his path. Yunma effortlessly slipped under the large barrier, stepped up behind Zhigao and swung his foot up past his head; kicking his opponent in the back of the head. Instantly Zhigao's head propelled forward and hit the stage floor before his hands could stop the impact.

"Thud, ahh...." He laid on the floor holding his face.

"You, you'll pay for that!" he yelled from between his hands. Slowly he staggered to his feet while holding his face in one hand and said, "Today is going to be your last." while shaking his fist.

"Who do you think will win?" Zhufei asked.

"I'm thinking it will be the Taoist." Yangban replied as he stepped forward.

"Really?'

"Yes, he seems to have better self-control."

"I don't know, Thundering Lion is pretty big."

Zhigao straightened up and began exhaling heavily while tensing his forearms. Suddenly a strong breeze blew across the stage and caused the bamboo poles holding the large flags to bend seriously while the fringe on the flags fluttered wildly. As all the spectators shielded their faces from the dust with their hands, Yunma stood motionless.

Soon, Zhigao slowly lowered his arms and stepped back into a low stance and stared at his opponent, while the bump on his forehead grew larger. His front hand was open and pointing across the stage at Yunma. As he stood up, he slowly closed his hand into a fist and began stepping forward. One step, stop, another step, stop. Then suddenly he rushed while shaking his fist and yelling, "Ai-yah!" Yunma silently stood watching the large man approach and when Zhigao's fist was nearing his head, he instantly dropped down into a split with his arms extended to the sides. As Zhigao appeared to look down, his momentum carried him forward into Yunma's extended arms, tripping him and sending him face first into the stage floor. "Boom!" He hit the platform and skidded until his head and arms were off the stage.

Yunma quickly jumped up and stood watching as the large man frantically avoided falling off the stage in front of the crowd.

"Ha! child's play!" Zhigao shrugged his shoulders. Again, he charged forward. As he neared the Taoist, his leg shot forward to kick. Yunma reached out to block the technique, but before he could grab the foot, Zhigao stepped down and grabbed Yunma's arm. Instantly he spun around, causing Yunma to swing wildly in the air before being thrown across the stage.

"Boom," he hit the wooden floor and slid on his back, but before his body stopped, he quickly jumped up, turned around and saluted his opponent. As he did the breeze completely stopped and the large flags fell limp on the bamboo poles.

"What? I throw you to the ground and all you do is stand up and bow?"

"Nice move, I like how he used his momentum to disperse the throw and then stand up" Yangban said as he nodded his head.

"Yeah, I'll bet Thundering Lion didn't expect that!" Zhufei gestured the technique with his hands.

"So, do you still think Thundering Lion will win?"

"Hmm, Mist in the Trees is definitely no beginner, so I'm not sure." Zhufei scratched his chin.

"Zhigao extended his arm, aimed his open palm at Yunma and slowly began walking in a circle around his opponent. Yunma stood still and only moved to continue facing Zhigao. After several circles Zhigao charged forward with a series of kicks and punches. As each combination neared its target, Yunma either leaned back or to the side sufficiently, to barely avoid the techniques.

Suddenly, without warning Yunma stopped defending each combination and began charging forward, forcing Zhigao to stop attacking and begin defending while backing up.

"Ahh ha! I see why he's called "Mist in the Trees." Yangban said as he placed his palm on his forehead.

"You do?"

"Yes, his fighting is like the trees in the dense fog. It's barely visible and seems to lack any strength or power. Then as you walk further in you realize the power goes on forever, but you are too far in to be able to turn around and escape. The Mist in the Trees has surrounded you and has you under its power. Brilliant!" Yangban smiled.

"Wow, truly amazing." Zhufei shook his head.

Move by move and moment by moment Yunma continued to surround Zhigao with his strategy and soon it seemed as if Zhigao's only escape would be to stop fighting. But he was too far embroiled in this fight to stop and escape the mist, so he desperately continued.

Kick, kick, punch, punch, Zhigao launched at Yunma. Unfortunately, each missed his target. Punch, punch, kick, he tried but Yunma slipped to the side, swung his foot back against Zhigao's leg while his palm slapped his chest. Instantly Zhigao's body spun in mid-air, "Thud!" he hit the stage floor and caused the bamboo poles to shake.

"Uggh!" he rolled over on to his hands and knees. "Cough, cough," he looked at the floor while trying to breathe. As he stood up and rubbed the back of his head, his eyes winced from the pain.

"You, you'll pay for that. Nobody throws me to the ground and walks away!"

He rushed forward while swinging his fists in a large circular motion. Yunma quickly began backing away at the same speed as his opponent charged forward. As Yunma neared the edge of the platform he planted his right foot on the stage floor, spun around backwards with his left foot and kicked Zhigao in between his shoulders, sending him off the stage and into the crowd. "Crash!" he landed on an empty chair between two elderly men. As they sat and clapped excitedly, Zhigao jumped up, grabbed the broken chair and threw it on the ground. "Slam!" "I've had enough of your silly little games." He stepped over the broken chair and jumped onto the stage. Yunma stood silently waiting without any expression on his face and instantly rushed forward in a zig-zag pattern as Zhigao readied himself by settling into another stance. "Boom!" Yunma stomped the stage, jumped up while spinning backwards and kicked at Zhigao's head. Instantly Zhigao dropped his head below the kick, grabbed the leg as it passed over his head and twisted around while throwing Yunma across the platform again. "Boom!" he hit the floor, rolled forward, quickly stood up, turned and bowed.

"Do you notice what he's doing?" Yangban leaned in and asked Zhufei.

"Not really." he whispered.

"He's drawing Thundering Lion further and further into the mist. First, he broke his confidence with the body throws, then he stirred up his emotions when he threw him off the stage. And now he confuses him by pretending to let him win."

"Wow, I never saw any of it that way." Zhufei placed his hand on his forehead.

"Yes, and now watch the next several exchanges and you'll see Mist in the trees totally confuse Thundering Lion."

"Again? I throw you to the ground and you turn and bow?" Zhigao scratched his head and immediately charged forward with one fist extended forward and the other on his hip. Meanwhile, Yunma stood motionless with his salute still extended. As Zhigao drew near, he suddenly spun around and allowed his opponent's momentum to continue forward. "Thwack!" Yunma slapped Zhigao in the back as he passed by. Instantly Zhigao turned around and attacked with a long-extended punch at Yunma's head. Yunma leaned back to avoid the punch, kicked the armpit of his opponent with his toe, grabbed the fist and pulled before throwing Zhigao to the floor.

"Boom!" he landed face first. As he stood up, the blood had already begun dripping off the end of his chin from the split in the large bump on his forehead.

"See, he's toying with him like a cat playing with an injured mouse. And the more Mist in the Trees plays with him, the more confused and frustrated Thundering Lion becomes." Yangban said while smiling.

"How long do you think he'll toy with him?"

"Hmm, that depends upon how much Mist in the Trees wants to torture his opponent. And whether Thundering Lion is willing to quit and accept defeat."

Zhigao stood back up, and silently stared at the fighter in front of him, while breathing heavily and squinting from the stream of blood dripping off his eyebrows. Seconds seemed to stretch into forever as Yangban and Zhufei anxiously waited for the next encounter. No one in the crowd moved or said a word as the two fighters stood facing each other. Suddenly, a gentle breeze began to slowly push open the large flags and drive away the tension building in the crowd. Overhead, a small dark cloud quickly dashed in front of the sun and threw a moment of darkness across the stage, beginning at Yunma and rushing towards Zhigao. And then, it was gone and instantly the crowd softly stirred in anticipation of the inevitable moment that was soon to arrive.

"Ai-yaa!" Zhigao stormed across the stage. Instantly Yunma charged towards his opponent and as he did, the crowd gasped loudly. In a moment the two fighters were only feet apart and Zhigao lunged forward with a long straight punch. Simultaneously, Yunma drove an open palm directly at the incoming fist. "Thud!" the two forces met and momentarily froze while collecting every ounce of the crowd's anticipation into a single point in time. Again, time stretched into eternity as the two stood locked together by a single point. Suddenly, the two opposing arms began to shake, subtly at first but then quickly becoming more noticeable.

"Oh, this is going to be good," Yangban whispered to Zhufei while grinning widely.

"Oh, oh," Zhufei said as he leaned forward.

The blood continued to stream down Zhigao's face and was now drying on his jacket and turning it a dark crimson color further and further down the front. Meanwhile, the fierce expression on his face began to slowly disappear as if it was running away with the shadow from the previous cloud. Now, his face began to grimace as his body shifted subtly from side to side. As he moved, Yunma remained still with an intense stare on his face. Suddenly, Yunma grabbed the fist, pulled hard while kicking Zhigao in the chest. "Thud. Ahh!" he stumbled backwards and held his chest.

"I've been patient with you and said nothing so far, but I suggest you quit because I don't want to kill you." Yunma pointed at his opponent.

"Leave now and you can go back to your school and continue teaching. If you stay, I cannot guarantee if you'll survive."

"Cough, cough, what makes you so sure you're going to win?"

"So far you haven't been able to stop me with your best techniques."

Zhigao charged forward and said, "You're going to see my best techniques right now!!" swinging both arms in a large circle, he quickly closed the gap and accelerated as he drew near. Unfortunately, Yunma remained still and as the first fist neared his head, he casually leaned back and allowed the arm to pass. As the next fist approached, he quickly stepped in and chopped hard at his opponent's exposed bicep. Immediately the fist relaxed and the arm began to shake uncontrollably. Zhigao's face grimaced from the pain as he reached down to raise the injured limb. As he did Yunma slipped in closer, turned and drove his elbow directly into his opponent's solar plexus, followed by a side kick to the exposed stomach. "Ughh!" Zhigao said as he stumbled backwards before falling and rolling over on to his face.

"I think we should end this." Yunma said as he watched his opponent struggle to lift himself to his knees. Finally, Zhigao raised his upper body, slowly sat back on his heels and offered a struggled salute to his opponent; signaling he agreed with the suggestion. Yunma returned a salute, turned towards the crowd and saluted everyone before picking up his weapons and walking off the stage.

"Let's go talk to him." Yangban said as he placed his hand on Zhufei's shoulder. As they walked around the crowd, Yangban kept watching to see which direction Mist in the Trees was heading. "Good, he's heading to the north also," he said to Zhufei as he pointed.

Minutes later as they neared the edge of town, they saw Mist in the Trees enter a small teahouse.

"Good, we can sit and talk to him while we drink some tea." Yangban pointed at the door.

As they stepped up to the open doorway Yangban looked inside and was surprised by the size of the stage at the opposite end of the large open room. Above the stage platform was an intricately carved landing with a rosewood railing supporting an ornately carved placard with large brass characters welcoming all visitors to the family business. Supporting the elaborate roof over the stage were four wooden columns carved with dragons wrapping their way to the top and painted in bright colors of green, blue, red and gold. On each side of the large open room were second-floor walkways looking out over the numerous tables and stools precisely situated in rows for the daily flow of customers. At regular intervals the detailed railing was attached to carved posts extending up into the ceiling before continuing on around the corner to the opposite side of the room.

Below the overlooking landing, the quaint tables were busy with small groups all leaning in to keep their conversations somewhat private. The chatter from the many tables was steadily growing as each new group of arrivals quickly searched for an open table and instantly settled into an intense conversation.

"Excuse me," an elderly gentleman said as he pushed his way through the doorway.

"Sorry, we were looking for someone." Zhufei replied.

"Hmmph."

"Ahh, there he is." Yangban said as he pointed towards the far corner table.

"Good." Zhufei started walking into the room and meandered past the numerous noisily chattering groups of patrons. As they neared the fighter sitting quietly alone, Yangban said, "Mist in the Trees,

I'm Cheng Yangban and this is my friend Lai Zhufei. We watched you fight with Thundering Lion earlier and were wondering if we could sit and talk to you?" he bowed while extending a formal salute.

"Sure, sure please sit down." Mist in the Trees gestured for them to sit, "I'll tell them to bring two more cups and another pot of tea."

"That's okay, I'll go get some." Zhufei turned and walked towards the kitchen.

"Yangban, where are you two from?" he picked up the small cup and gently blew across the leaves floating on the top and forcing them to one side before slowly sipping the hot liquid.

"I'm from Pingdu on the eastern side of Shandong Province and Zhufei is from Jinan. I train in the long-fist Cha Quan style along with Shuia Jiao Shou Praying Mantis, and Zhufei trains in the Hua Style." Again, he saluted his new acquaintance.

"Praying Mantis, I've heard of that style." He sipped from the cup again and then looked at the ceiling out of the corner of his eye.

"I learned it from Li Zhizhan and he was taught by a Taoist called Sheng Xiao Daoren." Yangban leaned back on his small stool.

"I heard you tell Thundering Lion that you lived at Wudang Mountain. How long did you live there?"

"Thirty years, and last year my master told me I needed to go out and experience living in the world."

"Praying Mantis, hmm, my teacher on Wudang knew something he called "secret style" and also "soft style" that had hand positions like those. I wonder if they are related?"

"If you ever come to Pingdu I'll gladly teach you the style that I know." Yangban saluted his new friend.

"I'll do that, but first I need to travel west to Xian," Mist in the Trees said as he returned the salute.

Zhufei soon returned from the kitchen with two cups and a steaming pot, set everything on the table and sat down. "Would you like some more tea?" he asked.

"Yes, please," Mist in the Trees said as he lightly tapped on the table to signify his appreciation.

"Can I ask you about your name?" Yangban asked as Zhufei sat down after pouring the tea.

"Sure, what would you like to know?"

"I noticed when you were fighting that you incorporated numerous levels of psychology regarding your name. Was that a unique style that you learned while on Wudang?"

"No, it wasn't an actual style but it was an aspect that my teacher taught me specifically because of the mental qualities he noticed that I displayed throughout my time there. He told me that as he watched me fight, he could see that I liked to employ very subtle psychological attacks, so he taught me ways to improve on my basic techniques."

"I could see that you were very proficient at your ability to disrupt and confuse Thundering Lion mentally, but not in an extremely obvious manner so that he would notice. And I liked how you kept drawing him further and further into the mist in the forest until before long he was so far into the veil that he couldn't escape even if he wanted to." Yangban raised his thumb in approval.

For the next several hours the three fighters sat and discussed the fight with Thundering Lion, all of their individual exploits while traveling and the underlying theories of their personal kung fu styles. Eventually, the afternoon sun caused the long shadows to creep across the street and up the buildings before it reached the trees on the horizon. Many of the customers had long since finished their intense conversations and returned to their businesses. Meanwhile, the workers in the teahouse were busily cleaning the tables and floor in preparation for the evening influx of fresh topics and familiar faces.

Slowly the three stood up from their table and walked out the door, turned and headed towards the north down the narrow dirt path. An hour later as they neared a small path lazily meandering up a steep hill Mist in the Trees said, "Well my friends, this is where I must leave you and begin my journey to Xian."

"It sure has been an eventful day. We arrived in time to see you fight Thundering Lion, use your expert psychological skills and then have the honor to sit and talk with you all afternoon," Zhufei said as he politely bowed while saluting his new friend.

"I agree with everything he just said, and as I told you earlier, if you ever make it to Pingdu, please stop in and I'll teach you my praying mantis style." Yangban bowed.

"I'll do that, I can't say exactly when I'll be there, but I will make a point to go there after I'm finished in Xian." Mist in the Trees politely bowed, then saluted each of his new friends and turned to walk up the hill.

Yangban stood and watched as his friend walked up the meandering path towards the horizon and slowly disappeared into the orange sunset.

"I really enjoyed talking with him," Yangban said as he turned towards the north and began walking on the road.

"I agree."

For the next week the two fighters continued on their journey and eventually arrived at the intersection where Zhufei would depart for Jinan.

"Okay my friend, I guess this is where we separate. It's been a very enjoyable journey and if you ever come to Pingdu, remember that my door is always open for you." Yangban saluted his friend.

"Thank you, and if you come to Jinan don't hesitate to come to my house, because you're always welcome. Zhufei saluted and then bowed.

Slowly they each turned and headed in their own directions while leaving behind one last set of footprints in the loose soil.

12. TOUCHING THE SUN

Several years had passed since Yangban had seen his friend Zhufei. Fortunately, they both arrived in Anqiu to help the starving locals by "procuring through subversive means" the grain in the government storage bins and secretly dispersing it to those most in need.

Afterwards, as they sat in a small teahouse on the outskirts of the city, Zhufei asked his friend, "Yangban, do you remember in 1849 when we went down to Tungping and had to help the farmers?" Zhufei sat down at the corner table in the teahouse.

"Yes, I remember how much they appreciated our efforts." He looked up at the ceiling.

"Well, I just heard from Chenhong, one of our members, that the Magistrate down there is now selling the Imperial horses." He placed his elbows on the table and leaned forward to speak softly.

"Are you serious? It's only been seven years! Wow, and I heard from a cousin that the government is fighting with the foreigners again over the opium. It seems to be a busy time for corruption."

"Yes, it sure is, and Chenhong told me this story about what is happening in Tungping."

"Magistrate Hui, I have finished counting the Imperial horses and their off-springs." Jiuting, the stable worker handed him the papers.

"Are you sure these numbers are correct?'

"Yes, Magistrate, I counted them three times."

Hmm, it looks like we have a nice surplus of foals. My cousin will be very excited to buy some of these royal horses.

"I need you to go over to Taotun and get my cousin Jinfa." Hui turned and poured the steaming tea into his porcelain cup.

"I want to see him tomorrow, so don't waste any time."

"Yes, Magistrate, I'll leave immediately." Jiuting walked outside and looked up at the dark sky.

"Rumble, rumble, crack!" the lightning hit a tree at the edge of the city.

Great, now I have to walk the next ten miles in the rain. Quickly he pulled his jacket closer and shifted his ragged bamboo hat to shield his eyes from the impending warm summer rain.

"Splat, splat, splat." The first drops of moisture hit the loose soil and created a small indentation while turning the surrounding soil dark. By the time Jiuting reached the city walls, the downfall of solitary droplets had turned into an army of invading soldiers all trying to find their own virgin spot in the soil and leave their imprint.

Standing in the large archway, Jiuting looked out in the direction of Taotun, and noticed the grey sky was being consumed by large black menacing clouds slowly swallowing the entire sky as they moved towards the horizon.

Great, just what I need. He shook his head. I guess I'll take my shoes off and walk in the mud barefoot.

For the next three hours he continued on his journey even though the rain steadily worsened. His body was totally soaked and every piece of clothing hung heavy on his body with each step while sticking tightly to his skin. Occasionally, he would stop and roll up his pants again because the mud continuously crept up his legs, caked on the fabric and steadily pulled downwards.

Ahh, finally. He began to see the first outline of the village through the rain and low hanging clouds. Thirty minutes later he walked *up to the edge of the small community and stood under the overhang of an abandoned building. Exhausted and drenched, he silently leaned against the wall while gathering his strength before venturing into town.*

"Hey, Jinfa, your cousin Magistrate Hui over in Tungping sent me here to tell you he wants to see you in the morning." He leaned on the stable fence under the roof to avoid the rain.

"Really, tell him I'll leave here at sunrise." Thank you for walking over to tell me, but for now I need to finish cleaning the manure from the stalls so it's done before I leave tomorrow. He grabbed his pitchfork and returned to his project.

As Jiuting walked past the abandoned house and began his trip home, the sun silently pushed its way through several clouds and signaled the retreat of the droplet army attacking the saturated soil.

The next morning, as the golden globe climbed out from behind the distant tree-line, Jinfa stepped outside and looked up to see a clear blue sky. Good, I'll have a much better trip than Jiuting's was yesterday. Later, he finally walked into the Magistrate's office and said, "Good morning, cousin Hui, Jiuting told me you wanted to see me. I hope it's not something bad?" He sat on the well-worn stool.

"Actually, I wanted to find out if you have any buyers for some Imperial foals," Hui leaned in close and whispered.

"How many?" he looked around to verify they were alone.

"Ten." Hui held out his hand and gestured the number with his fingers.

"When?"

"Come by next Monday afternoon, late, and bring your ropes."

"Great, I'll see you then." He stood up, and looked around the room again before walking out.

The following Monday Jinfa returned with a cart and sufficient halters for each foal, quietly walked down a dirt path towards the back of the stables, placed a halter on each foal and within minutes was headed back to Taotun.

"Do you want to leave tomorrow?" Yangban sat back in his chair.

"Yes, the sooner we get there, the quicker we can put an end to the corruption."

"I'll meet you here after my morning workout." Yangban stood up and walked towards the open doorway.

"Where are you going to practice?" Zhufei yelled just before his friend stepped through the opening.

"Out near the big dead tree."

"I'll see you there."

Early the next morning, Yangban was sitting motionless in a basic stance while his friend walked up and placed his belongings against the aged fallen wooden soldier. Casually he began stretching and when Yangban finished, he walked up and said, "Good morning, I was waiting until I saw enough of your Kung Fu and mental capabilities before I decided whether to teach you a secret Shaolin art."

"So, did I pass your evaluation?" he walked over, wiped the sweat from his forehead and leaned back against the smooth decayed bark-less tree trunk.

"Yes, and I'm glad I've found a potential student."

"What is this secret Shaolin art that you want to teach me?"

"The Shaolin "Touch of Death." He hit the tree trunk with two fingers and indented the surface.

"You mean Dian Xue, are you serious?" I've been hoping to learn more about that art for many years but I never knew anyone that practiced it!" He stood up and placed his hands on each side of his head with an expression of total amazement on his face.

"Do you want to start today?" Zhufei dropped his leg and stepped back from the fallen soldier.

"Absolutely! And we can practice all the way to Taotun."

"First you must agree to teach this art only to someone who has earned your trust and shown the proper mental capabilities to withstand the intense training along with only using it for self-

defense. This is not a type of training for those who want to use it to boost their ego by hurting others during a fight for no reason other than personal gain." He said with a stern tone in his voice while shaking his finger.

"I understand that idea completely. My father warned me about who I eventually teach and to make sure they are worthy of the training. And through our travels I've seen way too many fighters with the wrong attitude."

"Good, let's get started." He walked out into the morning sun.

For three hours Yangban learned a series of breathing and energy-building exercises unique to the art. Afterwards, he began to learn the acupuncture meridian and the specific points which correlated to the individual techniques.

"I see the sun is just beginning its descent, so let's get something to eat before we leave. We will have plenty of time while walking to discuss the vital points on the body." He gathered his belongings.

Throughout the afternoon the two fighters walked and discussed the earlier training. All the energy lines running throughout the body and which organs were affected by their flow. The primary points on each energy meridian and when the frequency cycles of the meridian dropped throughout the day, and caused the points the greatest susceptibility to an energy attack. Afterwards, Yangban learned the subtle art of how to generate different levels of energy into the fingertips, how much energy would be required on each point to create a specific physical or mental affect, and how much was required to cause permanent damage or death.

265

"When we stop tonight, I'll show you how to use a tree as a training partner. You'll need to develop a lot of strength and conditioning in your fingertips for this art."

Stopping along the dirt path as the sun finally sank further and further below the trees, the two warriors found an open area secluded from the passersby near the thick under-brush and slowly cleared a small area to build a campfire. The sky was now a bright orange as the sun cast its rays against the distant clouds, so Zhufei and Yangban walked over to a large tree and began discussing the advantages of training with a tree as a partner.

"As you practice, you'll need to develop the ability to repeatedly hit an exact spot, because as you're trying to hit your opponent with a deadly strike, he's trying to avoid the attack. Both of you are continuously moving around each other, which means your aim must be very, very precise." He pointed at a very small crease in the bark.

"Try and strike as small an area on the bark as possible, but don't let your fingertip hit outside a space the size of a small coin."

"This is similar to the training my father made me practice as a young boy." He began lightly tapping the surface of the tree trunk.

"He always had me practice trying to hit a smaller and smaller moving target while saying, "This will come in handy some day when you're in a fight."

"Later after you have developed the internal energy, I'll show you how to project your energy outward and into the tree or your

opponent. But first we need to focus on developing a very solid foundation."

Over the next several weeks the two fighters trained throughout the morning and usually finished just before the noon day sun began falling towards the horizon. Afterwards, they continued on their journey southwards while discussing the intricate details of the training.

"Now that you've been hitting a small spot with your fingertip, try hitting a larger area with your fist. You'll find the energy building exercises that I taught you will assist in directing your fist's punching power." He walked over and punched a nearby tree.

Eventually, they arrived in Tungping and sought out the relatives of Jiuting to begin collecting information about the circumstances of Jiuting's untimely death. Months earlier, Zhufei received word that Jiuting had been arrested and sentenced to jail for claiming that Magistrate Hui had been stealing from the emperor. Unfortunately, he had no evidence to support his claim and was jailed for the accusation. While incarcerated, he became sick from the poor conditions and died. Afterwards, his family began investigating the claims and consequently contacted Zhufei's friends to help with the investigation.

"Zhufei, I'm noticing a lot of strange sensations in my hands and fingertips whenever I practice those special energy building exercises. And sometimes it lingers into the afternoon."

"Have you been practicing the special energy releasing exercises when you are finished?"

"Yes, every day, but sometimes it doesn't relieve the sensation. On the days when the sensation vanishes, my fingertips get really, really hot, like they are on fire."

"I'm glad you explained everything the way you did, because I've been waiting for all those indications to manifest in your body. They are telling me you are ready for a more advanced level in your training."

Throughout the remainder of the morning, they practiced and refined numerous subtleties associated with the new routine. As Yangban practiced, he noticed the earlier sensations quickly vanished following the improvements. Now only the heat sensation remained during the time of intense focus and disappeared whenever he stopped.

"Wow, that feels like I have been touching the sun." He sat down and wiped the sweat from his forehead.

"Good, that's a sign that your training is developing in the correct direction. Soon that feeling about the sun will be a constant sensation." He smiled and put his hand on his friend's shoulder. "Tomorrow we'll walk over to Taotun and talk with Jinfa's son. Hopefully, he's willing to talk about his father's cousin."

Gradually the light from the distant star began to creep between the trees and illuminate the leaves and branches before dashing across the open fields and casting subtle shadows on the stone walls.

Suddenly a solitary cardinal began to sing to all its friends, announcing the beginning of another adventurous day. Quietly the seasoned fighters slipped through the wooden soldiers patiently standing at attention for years. As they reached their training area, the cardinal hopped down from the shaky branch to grab a small worm slithering through the grass and then returned to the tree.

For hours the two continued their training with intermittent sessions of attacking the bark on a tree.

"Yangban, you need to aim for a smaller target and start circling the tree while you hit. Your opponent isn't going to just stand still while you hit a vital point on his body."

The sun was about halfway through its climb when they finally finished their routines. As they gathered their belongings, Zhufei turned and looked down the dirt path before saying, "I think we should begin our trip now instead of later."

Without saying a word, they turned and began walking east towards the quiet farming village. The squirrels were busy scurrying across the path from tree to tree as the variety of birds chatted up a storm in the nearby trees. Meanwhile, a few solitary farmers toiled in their fields to diminish the continual multiplying of unwanted weeds.

Far off in the distance, someone from the neighboring village was busily trying to eradicate a pile of decayed logs with a blazing fire. The smoke continually pushed higher and higher as the bright orange flames raged.

As they walked, Zhufei curiously watched as Yangban repeatedly shook his hands in an effort to alleviate the intense heat.

"You seem preoccupied as we walk."

"Yes, my hands are continuing to get hotter the more we walk."

"Sounds like the internal exercises are doing their job and continuing to build more and more internal qi(energy).

"Soon it will be at a tipping point and you won't be able to turn it off." He smiled at his friend. "Always remember, once you master this act, a slight touch is powerful to most people and a gentle tap is very serious pain."

Eventually they arrived at the quiet village, and quickly located the Magistrate's cousin. "Are you Jinfa?" Yangban leaned on the worn wooden fence board.

"Yes, I am." He stopped cleaning the stalls.

"Jiuting's mother and sister asked us to come and talk to you about your father's cousin." Zhufei put his foot on the lower board.

"My father helped his cousin sell some of the emperor's horses. When my father tried to tell someone, they said it was all his fault and arrested him. Then he died in prison while his cousin kept his position. What else do you want to know?" he asked as he returned to his chores.

"We want to help charge him for the crimes he has committed."

"Good luck with that."

"Do you have anything that proves he sold the emperor's horses."

"I know someone he sold one to. He lives on the other side of town up on the hill. Look for the horse with two lines on the forehead." He walked away and climbed up onto the loaded cart.

Yangban and Zhufei questioned the owner of the horse who confirmed that Jinfa sold him the foal. After an hour of persuasion, the owner agreed to testify about the sale. Several weeks later, the fighters had a sufficient number of witnesses and evidence to submit everything to the regional magistrate. After several more weeks, the regional official interviewed all witnesses and concluded the local magistrate was guilty. Afterwards, he sentenced the criminal to several years in prison, after being chained to a post for three months in the middle of town with a sign-board tied to his neck about the crime. All horses belonging to the emperor were confiscated.

"Zhufei, months ago when we left Tungping, you said this feeling in my fingertips would go away, but now it stays all throughout the day." He rubbed his hands together the next morning following their training.

"Ahh, you are getting close, just keep practicing and don't ever skip the dispersing exercises."

He demonstrated the technique.

"I have noticed an incredible improvement in your accuracy and intensity when hitting a tree. Soon you'll be ready for another advanced technique."

The following morning the thick fog hung throughout the landscape and caressed every branch and leaf, signaling the changing season. The usual chatter from the residents in the trees remained silent with their wings pulled tightly to their bodies. Navigating to the usual training area was slow, and each step was carefully placed to avoid any holes or limbs.

Soon, the excess moisture saturated their clothes, causing them to hang heavily from the shoulders like weights. Each step through the heavily dampened grass caused their shoes to quickly absorb more moisture than they could hold. Consequently, each step forced the water to push out from the sides with a subtle squish, squish sound.

Later as they walked northward toward Shandong, the weather began to display more signs of the arrival of the harvest season. Occasionally, a lone red leaf could be seen hiding amongst the backdrop of green, while the fields continually displayed more and more signs of mature crops waiting to be harvested. At night the two rebels resorted to camping in a cave or under a growth of thick underbrush to ward off the cold. Day by day the terrain released the hills and mountains to allow the farmers a more suitable farming platform. The wheat had recently been plucked from its main artery to the soil and transported back to the village for the removal of the husks.

"Yangban, soon I'll be leaving you for Jinan, but before I go, I want to teach you the final part of the Dian Xue training." He walked out into a large open area. "As you practice, you need to constantly be aware and sensitive to subtle changes in your body technique and mental state. Otherwise, you'll gradually go over the edge and end up past the point of no return mentally or physically."

"This next exercise will demand an even greater level of focus, awareness, and control so be very, very careful as you practice." He squeezed his friend's shoulder.

"Dian Xue is a very ancient practice. There have been many who learned it but shouldn't have been taught the final stages, because their minds just weren't capable of the mental strains and demands. Consequently, they harmed others as well as themselves." He shook his head with a very saddened expression.

"Now follow me very closely and do exactly as I do during this routine. If you leave anything out it may cause you physical problems."

"What kind of problems? I'm asking so I know for future references."

"There are many illnesses it may cause and it all depends on what is left out, how long it's been neglected, and your overall energy level. So, don't forget anything!" He pointed at Yangban.

Zhufei began to move slowly and very precisely through a series of arm and hand gestures, first on one side of the body and then the exact same series on the opposite side. As each movement was

273

performed, a unique breathing pattern accompanied the motions, long slow inhalations that

gathered the body's energy at specific internal locations in order to stimulate its intensity. This was followed by long slow exhalations while mentally pushing all the intensified energy into an exact external body location.

"Use your mind more and to a higher level of concentration," Zhufei said between breaths. "See the energy from the sun pulse through your meridians and out to your fingertips."

For hours they stood motionless while internally forcing the energy to race through the meridians towards the fingers and then back to their core, only to begin the cycle again.

As they stood, the squirrels from the surrounding trees joyfully went about their morning racing back and forth from tree to tree. Occasionally, a single curious passerby would stop to observe the two tall strangers standing silently. After a few moments of cautious inspection, it would inch its way closer, stop and observe and then move in again, until it could lean forward and sniff the stranger's feet. Suddenly in a flash it would race across the wet ground and up a tree, before stopping on the trunk to turn and chirp wildly while wagging its tail.

Soon the furry residents relaxed to the strangers and no longer feared their presence. Now as they passed by the tall motionless fighters, they occasionally dashed between their feet on route to the next tree. Eventually the squirrels completed their morning ritual and rushed off to a high branch safe from predators.

The thick blanket of gray had finally released the local landscape and all occupants from its grasp and vanished before the bright morning sun. Now the clothes of the solitary figures once drenched from the wall of humidity began to dry. Unfortunately, with the bright sun shining down, they were soon drenched again, but now from sweat. This special routine demanded extreme patience and focus. Consequently, it resulted in profuse sweating throughout the duration of the exercise. The loose grey soil around their feet quickly turned to dark brown from the continual dripping of salty droplets from their elbows. Three hours later the fighters began to slowly move from their positions, first taking small steps to activate the muscles and finally regular movements once everything had agreed to the idea of motion.

"Wow, that was so intense and I loved every minute of it," Yangban softly said as he walked in several circles to acclimate back into reality.

"Yes, it sure does stimulate everything and magnify the sensations." He looked at his friend and grinned. "We only have several more weeks of walking before I say goodbye, so we need to spend all of our time practicing and discussing the art of Dian Xue." He turned and headed back toward the road.

"But for now, we should begin our journey."

Effortlessly, the droplets of sweat chased each other along the contours of the face, before reaching the jaw and dripping on to the moisture-soaked shirt tightly adhering to Yangban's shoulder. He quietly turned to gather all his belongings while the drip, drip, drip of salty sweat fell from his arms and hit the aged weapons lying on the ground just before he picked them up and secured a small string around the group. As they walked, Yangban remained silent for the next hour as he continued to reflect upon the training from earlier in the morning.

Meanwhile, Zhufei watched as the farmers steadily tilled the fields and turned the stalks from the recent crop into the soil to become fertilizer for the new seedlings in several months. Numerous birds followed behind the horse and plow and excitedly searched the fresh soil for bugs and worms. In the distance, other workers delivered the manure from the animals in the family compound and sparingly spread the waste throughout the turned ground.

Wow, that training session earlier sure opened up a number of meridians. I can now feel the energy and blood flow through the bottoms of my feet and back upwards, Yangban thought as he casually glanced at the dust rush away from his feet as he stepped in the loose soil.

The tips of my fingers are still tingling and I'm feeling this overall sensation of my body expanding while I walk. He looked up at the few solitary clouds trying to crawl their way across the open sky.

The gentle breeze began to increase and the distinct change in air temperature, quietly signaled that the impending winter's months of barren and solitude would be arriving soon. The trees held firmly to the last remnants of brightly colored foliage frantically clinging to the ends of their branches. Below, the squirrels scurried across the ground to gather as many seeds and nuts as they could hold in their cheeks before dashing up the nearest tree and depositing everything into a small hole in the trunk.

Hmm, the breeze seems to have minute changes in its temperature and it's quite subtle. I've never recognized sensation changes on such a scale before and they seem to last for a really long time. He extended his hand and allowed the wind to whisper to his palm.

"You seem lost in your thoughts since we began walking," Zhufei said as he put his hand on Yangban's shoulder.

"I've been contemplating about our training this morning and all the new sensations I've been experiencing."

"Really, like which ones?"

"Well, I'm now feeling the energy flow through the meridians on the bottom of my feet and the sensation of the blood rushing through my veins continues to feel like a raging river." He said while looking at his legs.

"Great, can you feel when the energy travels from one meridian point to another and begins to well up in the point like water from a waterfall gathering in a quiet pool?"

Suddenly, Yangban stopped and didn't say a word while looking directly forward. "Yes, now I can! I had to stop for a moment and focus on what you said. And now that I did, I can feel it really strongly." He smiled and slowly shook his head.

"Wait until the energy intensifies. Then you'll really feel some unique sensations, and they'll definitely make you stop and say Wow!" Zhufei said as he smiled and his eyes widened from the excitement.

"There's going to be more? I hope it isn't in the next few days because I'm still trying to get used to these."

Yangban turned his head to look up into the clear sky and watched as a large flock of geese flying southward maintained a precise V formation while calling out to each other. Nearby, another small group of geese frantically tried to catch the main flock and merge together to avoid making the 1000-mile journey alone. Off in the distance he could barely distinguish the outline of a group of ducks frantically flapping their small wings to move them further south and avoid the upcoming winter.

Each day the routine remained consistent, wake up and train for three hours, then throughout the day while walking, discuss the art in detail so that Yangban had all the knowledge his friend Zhufei had acquired. Day after day the landscape continued to remind everyone of the upcoming cold season; the early morning frost lingering longer and longer, the faint whispers of snowflakes delicately floating through the air in the early morning sunlight, and the appearance of more and more maple leaves blanketing the landscape in a myriad of color. Now, the soft white petals of snow began dancing through the air in the afternoon sunshine, then slowly touched the barren ground and softly rested on the bright leaves before hiding a solitary blade of brown grass that had succumbed to the change of seasons.

Meanwhile, the farmers that weeks earlier were out preparing the dormant soil for the next year's seedlings had abandoned their land and left only a few solitary birds to inspect the hardening ground for any signs of sustenance. Feverously scurrying across the field were a pair of young foxes trying in vain to catch the foraging birds, but each time the furry predator drew close and lunged at the feathered prey, the bird jumped high enough into the air to avoid the attack and flew away to another part of the field, only for the entire dramatic scene to begin again.

Within the small gathering of dwellings nestled securely inside the stone walls, the sounds of children playing mixed with puppies barking continued to race across the open expanse of barren land and echo back from the distant hill. The small stacks of bricks reaching out from the top of each roof sent the smoke slowly floating upwards before eventually disappearing into the dark blue sky.

Yangban quickly turned his attention back to the road ahead and pulled his jacket a little higher on his neck to keep the cold and moist flakes from entering. Looking ahead on the dirt road, he noticed that it was empty as far as he could see, leaving the two rebels completely alone. Several hours later after the sun slipped behind the hills and released the cold dark sky the fighters finished constructing a makeshift roof, covered the cold ground with leaves and twigs and then gathered stones for a small fire. With each passing moment the air continued to cool as the darkness grew closer and closer. Eventually, all that could be seen was the flickering light from the dancing fire and the twinkling of the distant stars dotting the silent sky.

"Have you thought of any other questions about your training? In a few days I'll be leaving for Jinan and I want to make sure you have all your answers," Zhufei said as he slowly turned the burning embers.

"I don't have any at the moment, but we'll see if any come to mind over the next couple days. "

Finally, the day arrived when the two seasoned fighters would separate and head down their own paths. The weather had unexpectedly warmed and the sky was completely barren of even the smallest cloud. Everywhere the birds chirped wildly in a chaotic conversation about the warmer weather, while squirrels and chipmunks joyfully scurried across fallen leaves.

"Okay, Yangban, it's time for me to take this path up here and head west." He pointed at the narrow road leading up over the small hill.

"Yes, I've been thinking about how long it will take me to get home to see my parents from here. It's been several years, so I'm really excited to see them again."

'I'm going to stay in Jinan for a while, so if you escort any cargo in that area, be sure to come by and visit. I'll be curious about how your Dian Xue is progressing." He bowed and turned towards the westward path.

"I definitely will!" Yangban bowed and waited while Zhufei climbed the hill and disappeared over the top."

The next several days he spent every moment while walking remembering everything that Zhufei taught him about the secret art. Consequently, the time seemed to race by and soon he was seeing the familiar signs of approaching Weifang.

Ahh yes, Weifang. Only a couple of more days until I get home so I think I'll walk a while longer before I stop.

Walking out the eastern gateway of the city walls, he headed down a familiar path and as he followed the road around several small knolls in the fields, he was quickly all alone. The farmers were all finished in the fields for the long day and at home preparing for the rising sun.

That looks like a quiet spot to spend the night.

Later, as he sat near a small fire and looked out at the barren fields resting before the arrival of the spring planting season, he saw a young man stop on the road and then turn and approach him.

"Hey, do you have any food you can give me?"

'No, sorry." He stirred the burning embers.

"Really, I don't believe you."

"I think maybe you should leave. I told you I don't have anything and you called me a liar."

"Give me what you have or I'll kill you and take it!"

"I think you should leave now, young boy."

"I'll leave when I am ready and don't call me a young boy!" He pointed his sword at the stranger sitting by the fire.

Yangban shook his head at the impetuous youth while sliding his hand closer to his spear.

Suddenly, the stranger stepped forward with his sword. As he did, Yangban quickly jumped up and pointed the sharp point at his face.

"Leave now if you want to live to see tomorrow." He yelled while glaring at the youth. Seconds drifted into forever as the two stood face to face on each side of the innocent fire burning at their feet.

Without warning the young man jumped over the fire and swung his sword over his head as if he wanted to chop down on his opponent. Yangban instantly stepped to the side of the hot coals, simultaneously turning and hitting the stranger in the ribs with a two-finger strike. As the stranger landed from the jump his left arm just swung uncontrollably by his side. Meanwhile, his left leg began to shake and lose strength, causing him to stumble and fall into a tree.

'I said leave!" Yangban pointed to the dimly lit road.

Slowly the stranger struggled to get to his feet and used his sword as a cane to assist in his efforts to get back to the road. After several minutes of watching to confirm that the injured stranger continued in his efforts to abandon the area, Yangban sat back down and again stirred the cooling twigs while shaking his head about the stranger.

Finally, after two more days, he saw the outline of Pingdu and increased his pace. When he arrived at the Li compound, he noticed the recently fallen leaves hadn't been cleaned off of the auspicious characters. After quickly brushing them free from the artistic protrusions he watched as the leaves gently floated downward to the ground.

I think I'll stop and say hello to Shoushan before going home.

"Creak," the old wooden door was still complaining about moving.

"Hey Shoushan! How are you?" He bowed enthusiastically and smiled.

"Wow, It's Yangban!" He walked over to place his hands on the shoulders of his old friend.

For the next two hours they sat and talked while drinking tea. It has been years so there was much to discuss and catch up on, where the shipments went, who was guarding each load, what kind of bandits they encountered?

"Okay Shoushan, I think it's time I went home to see my parents." He stood up and bowed.

"I guess you haven't heard" Shoushan looked away.

"Heard what?"

"Your father died several months ago."

"What! Really?" He fell back down in the chair and stared at the ceiling. Minutes passed without either one saying a word. All

Yangban could do was stare at the ceiling or look at the floor and shake his head. Moment by moment, the silence became increasingly stifling and soon reached the point of suffocation.

"I need to go." Yangban quickly stood up and headed for the door.

Minutes later he walked into his family compound and headed towards his parents' house. As he slowly opened the door he called out, "Mother, are you in here?" No response. After a few seconds he called for her again in a louder voice, "Mother, are you in here?"

"Yes, I'm here, who's calling?"

"It's me, Yangban, where are you?"

"Yangban! Is that really you? I'm in the kitchen"

He closed the door and rushed into the room at the back of the house and saw his mother squatting near a small fire, cutting a variety of vegetables into small pieces.

"Mother!" He walked over to her.

"Ahh, my son has come home!" She stood up and reached out to hug him.

"It has been too long," he said as he held her close.

She pointed at the small stool on the opposite side of the fire, and as he sat on the stool, she quickly poured all the finely chopped vegetables into the pot of boiling water. After stirring for several minutes, she scooped out a ladle full, poured it over a bowl of rice for each of them and then handed a bowlful to her son.

As they ate, they casually chatted about everything Yangban had done and seen in his time away from home.

Eventually, the stories about his life on the road began to slow down so he asked his mother, "Shoushan said that Father passed away several months ago. Did he suffer before he died?"

She placed her bowl on the small table, looked at the ceiling and then looked directly at her son, "No, he didn't. For several days he seemed to be a little tired, but nothing else. Then one morning he didn't wake up at his usual hour. When I checked on him later, he was gone." She looked at the fire and reached down to stir the reddened logs.

Suddenly, silence engulfed the entire house and effortlessly drove out even the faintest sounds. Outside, the compound seemed to freeze into the moment when she said he was gone. No birds chirped, no dogs barked, no children ran excitedly across the open courtyard while screaming for a friend.

Yangban continued to look at the floor and eventually said, "I sure do miss him. I wish I had spent more time with you two." His eyes began to fill with tears and were on the verge of overflowing.

"Yes, I know. Your father understood how important your choice to go and fight the government was to you." She put her hand on his shoulder.

"I never imagined when he had died, that it would leave me feeling so hollow and empty inside. I thought about it many times and was convinced I was ready for it and could handle the situation.

But now I'm finding out just how wrong I was in my thoughts."
He lowered his head and looked at the fire out of the corner of his
eye.

"It's okay. We all go through the same feelings when one of our
parents moves into their next life. But knowing you will see him
again will help to lessen the feelings of his loss."

"It may in a few days, but right now all I'm feeling is the loss of
someone who made me who I am."

"Tomorrow will be better, I promise." She lightly patted his knee.

For the next hour neither of them said a word. They just sat and
watched the burning embers gently flicker from bright to dim as a
soft breeze crept through the room from the open door. Occasionally
a solitary dog would bark once or twice off in the distance. Then
more silence signaled that darkness would soon surround
everything and consume the light.

13. CLOSING THE DOOR

"Yangban, now that we were successful in stopping the government from stealing from the farmers to support that second opium war, we need to go down to Qining and support those citizens in their efforts against the county magistrate," his friend Zhufei said as they sat drinking tea.

"I agree, after that war in 1839 against the dogs from England, I couldn't believe how much the government forced the people to struggle. And now twenty years later they think they can get away with it a second time."

"Qining, what's happening down there?"

"I found out that another local magistrate is selling off the food surplus on the black market and blaming the locals for the loss."

"Really?"

"Yes, so a good friend of mine asked if I could come down and help investigate."

"Okay, I think we should leave tomorrow." He finished his tea and stood up to leave.

"I'll meet you here in the morning."

Early the next morning the two rebels sat in the teahouse and developed a plan for their trip. Afterwards, they stepped out into the rising sun and began the long walk southward. The trip would be difficult for several weeks due to the mountainous region which required navigating through high and steep passes, in addition to encountering many large wild animals looking for an easy meal and starving bandits wanting to steal and kill.

Suddenly the steep terrain and rocky pathways gave way to the slowly leveling crop fields and smooth paths, while the trees began to dot the landscape along the edges of the patchwork of varying crops.

Months later as they crossed the Yun Ho River, they could see the outskirts of the walled city and knew they would be sleeping with friends later in the day.

This city was a hub for travel from west Shandong to the south along with numerous visitors from the western provinces. From here access to the coast was easily attainable through the great canal.

Walking through the main archway in the solid wall surrounding this ancient city gave the visitor a sense of travelling back in time to an era long since forgotten. The large bricks stacked precisely atop each other had created a formidable barrier to any invading foreigners, and stood ever so patiently over the centuries. High above the thick wall was a walkway for troops to defend the interior population during invasions. All this was constructed during a time when invasions were commonplace and the changing of rulers happened on a regular basis.

The large thick wooden gates filling the openings were built to withstand the most severe invasion. Menacing metal projectiles were attached to the outside to keep the invaders from pushing directly against the wooden frame and also helped to strengthen the wide framework.

Inside the opening numerous vendors sold their wares in small makeshift booths lining the walls in hopes of attracting the unsuspecting strangers. "Hey mister, do you want a haircut?" the first vendor yelled. Instantly several other vendors followed suit and began yelling for the two strangers to come to their booth and check out their wonderful products.

Slowly the rebels continued their direction forward and were soon forgotten by the vendors who had already moved on to the next visitors. Thirty minutes later they found the small house where their friends lived and stepped inside to the welcome greetings of mutual resistance fighters.

The following months were spent planning, coordinating, and executing all the covert attacks against the corrupt officials stealing from the starving farmers. Every member had a specific task to complete, from monitoring the grain being rationed out to the locals, to following the officials to track their whereabouts and activities throughout the day. Each detail was meticulously annotated in order to verify the actions when the evidence was submitted to the county magistrate.

Each time an official was replaced because of corruption, the next would quickly take up where the last one failed. The entire process would begin again. After several years of uncovering the corrupt officials, the government began to recognize numerous participants in the resistance movement and initiated steps towards arresting them.

"Hey Zhufei, I think I'm going to be retiring from the group." Yangban said as he stepped inside the doorway of the tearoom and sat next to his friend.

"Really?"

"Yes, with that last mission to stop the officials, I worry that they may be closing in on recognizing some of the members. Also, I think

I have been at it long enough and I don't want any officials arresting me for things we did years ago."

"Where will you go?"

"I'm planning to go to the temple not far from Pingdu."

"Which one?"

"The Hua Lin Temple."

"Oh, the one that took over after Shaolin was burned?"

"Yes. There are some good people living there and I think it would be a good place to retire."

"Agreed."

"If you ever decide to retire, you are always welcome to join me there."

"I'll keep that in mind."

"When do you plan on leaving?"

"Oh… maybe in a couple days, I want to rest up before the long journey north.

"Okay, at least we can spend some more time discussing and researching your praying mantis style."

"Good, I need someone to help me when I'm trying to practice the twelve different fighting techniques.

"Meet me tomorrow morning."

"Okay."

The next morning the two fighters met outside the walled city near an old tree. "I want to practice the various fighting techniques from this praying mantis style, and there are certain aspects that I cannot do by myself," he said while demonstrating several movements.

"The first ones are Gou, Lou, Cai, Gua (block, hook, grapple, and pluck.)

"I understand the first three, but the last two are still unclear."

"Let me play the attacker so you can try the movements on my arm." He extended his arm and waited for the application.

Yangban reached out, blocked, grabbed, hooked, and plucked, causing Zhufei's head to snap back and then forward. "Ouch!" he responded as Yangban released the arm. "Let me try it slowly so I can see better what I need to do. The action of plucking on the arm is still slightly unclear, but if we practice on it for the remainder of the day, I should be able to figure it out. Tomorrow we can work on some of the other principles." Zhufei said.

"Today I want to try and better understand the ideas of tag, lean, and stick," Yangban said as he walked up to the old tree the next morning just after the sun began to peek over the trees."

"Tag, lean, and stick?" Zhufei tilted his head back and looked up at the clouds.

"Yes, these three are somewhat illusive in nature but very essential in application.

"Punch with your right fist so I can show you the basic concept."

Zhufei reached out with his right arm as if punching. As he did, Yangban leaned slightly to the side to avoid the attack, grabbed the wrist and elbow, and then continued to move forward. Instantly Zhufei responded by trying to withdraw the arm, but Yangban moved with him and maintained control of the fist.

"Wow, that was interesting how you avoided my punch and then continued to control the arm even when I was pulling back."

"Like I said, it's illusive yet very essential."

Soon the shadows began to inform the fighters that the moon would be arriving in just a few minutes. They gathered their weapons and began to walk back inside the gates before they were shut for the night.

As Yangban was waking the next morning, he heard a lone rooster calling from off in the distance, "Erh, erh, erh!"

Time to gather everything and begin my journey, I should be able to make it to Tzuyang by tonight.

Thirty minutes later he was standing at the gates while watching the guards slowly push the aged timbers back against the thick stone wall. As they finished securing the gates he slowly walked past and turned towards the northeast and headed for Tzuyang. The first birds were just beginning to call to their neighboring friends about the new day, and only a solitary farm cart was meandering down the dirt path.

It was now early spring and the year of the horse was beginning to show signs of prosperity for 1858. The new sprouts of grass were reaching up through the hard soil while searching for the sunlight, as a gentle southern breeze softly moved northward across the fields.

Later in the morning as he was passing the small quiet village of Chuantung, he spotted a ragged looking stranger up ahead sitting along the roadside. His hand instinctively grabbed the spear slightly tighter and he carefully adjusted the backpack. As he approached the stranger the man jumped up and stood in the center of the road, turned and looked directly at Yangban.

"I need some food, so if you give me what you have in the bag, I'll spare your life."

"I'm sorry but I don't have any food in my bag." He turned to step around the stranger.

"I don't believe you, so give me your bag." The stranger stepped sideways to block the path.

"I told you I don't have any, so move out of my way."

"Ahh!" the stranger jumped at Yangban.

Instantly Yangban stepped back to avoid the attack while pointing his spear tip at the stranger.

"Move aside or I will use this spear to kill you."

"Ha, the rusty old thing doesn't scare me!" he shook his finger. "My nine-section chain will quickly take care of that old thing!"

"Step aside so I can pass."

"Ai-yaa!" the stranger rushed forward while swinging the chain from side to side.

As the large spike at the end of the chain neared Yangban, he used his spear and blocked the spike to the side followed by a slap to the owner's face, cutting a gash in his cheek.

"That's one move. Only a few more and you'll be dead, so move aside and let me pass."

"Ha, no one has ever gotten three moves past my chain."

Instantly he threw the spike at his opponent in an obvious attempt to drive the spike into his chest. Yangban again blocked the spike but this time he used the shaft of his spear to wrap the chain around and then stepped in and drove the butt end of the spear into the stranger's forehead three times in quick succession. "Thud, thud, thud" the stranger staggered backwards from the impact.

"Those three don't count. I just wanted to show you how weak your techniques are."

"What, weak?" he gathered his chain and began swinging it in a circular motion from one side of his body to the other while stepping forward. Yangban instinctively stepped backwards in time with his opponent's advancing steps and watched the chain, looking for any weakness. One, two, three circles all completely

defended the stranger. Suddenly the chain fluttered slightly and Yangban attacked by thrusting the sharp tip at his opponent's shoulder. "Fffttt," the tip hit the shoulder muscle just before sliding under the armpit; cutting through the tattered shirt and opening a deep slice in the muscles. As fast as the tip shot forward, Yangban retracted it and stood still with the point aimed at the stranger.

"That's two."

"You hardly touched me."

"Really, all the blood tells a different story."

"I'll survive long enough to kill you!" he said while walking in a semi-circle around his opponent.

"Really, the blood tells a different story."

Cautiously the stranger kept circling and trying to wrap his shirt around the wound. After several circles he stopped, grabbed the chain by the ends and rushed forward.

Yangban stood still and waited until his opponent drew near, then suddenly dropped down and swept his left leg in a semi-circle, hitting his opponent's ankles and sending him face first into the dirt. "Thud!" his face hit the ground followed by his chain.

"You'll pay for that!" he stumbled to his feet and spit out a mouthful of fine dirt.

Again, the stranger began to swing the chain over his head in a circle while stepping forward. As the chain passed in front of Yangban he jumped forward and kicked his opponent in the stomach and sent him stumbling backwards. Unfortunately, as he kicked, the chain continued around and hit him in the leg, cutting the fabric and opening a wound.

Quickly he tied a strip of cloth over the cut and stood waiting for his opponent's next attack.

"I told you my chain was superb." He said as he stood back up and pointed.

The stranger rushed forward again with his chain swinging side to side in front of him. Yangban waited for the chain to pass by and then quickly jumped over it, landing behind the stranger. As he landed Yangban turned and slammed the butt end of his spear down on his opponent's head. "Crack!" the stranger's legs buckled and he dropped to his knees and again falling on his face.

"Three."

"Uggh. Ch..ch..child's play." He said while kneeling on one knee and rubbing his head. Suddenly he rolled forward while swinging his chain at his opponent's leg, "crack!" the chain hit Yangban's spear as he planted the butt end into the dirt and raised his leg high into a single leg stance to avoid the attack.

Yangban quickly stepped backwards into a cross-legged stance and turned to swing the sharp tip at his opponent's neck. The stranger spun to face the spear tip while grabbing the chain at both ends and using it to block the razor-sharp edge. Immediately Yangban spun the spear vertically to drive the tip up under the chain and into his opponent's chin. As he did, the chain was twisted sideways to push the spear away from its target. Yangban instantly twisted backwards and kicked the stranger behind his ear, forcing him to fall on his side and hit his head on the ground.

"Cough, cough," the stranger crawled to his knees and finally up to his feet. "I'm tired of dealing with your mediocre skills, so now I'm going to end this and take all your food!" he shook his fist at the fighter in front of him and then charged forward while throwing the chain tip straight forward.

Yangban stepped to the side to avoid the point racing at his chest and swung his spear down hard on the chain just before pulling the tip backwards and into his opponent's face. "Thwack, crack!" the spear hit the nose and broke it; instantly causing the blood to stream down his face and drip from his chin.

"Four. Are you sure you want to continue?"

"Yes, I'm not done with you yet!" He spit out a mouthful of blood and charged forward again. As he drew near, he suddenly spun around and swung the chain around at waist height. Instinctively Yangban spun in the same direction and essentially neutralized the momentum of the chain and then swung his fist around and caught the stranger in the back of the head. "Thud!" the stranger leaned forward, dropped to his knees, as the chain fell in the dirt by his side.

"I'm done with you. You've wasted enough of my time." Yangban said as he turned to walk away and continue on his journey.

"Hey, get back here so I can finish with you!" he yelled as Yangban walked further and further down the road.

Some people just don't know when to quit, he thought while shaking his head.

I guess now I'll need to pick up my pace if I want to make it to Tzuyang tonight. Instantly he looked far off in the distance and focused on his next stopping point.

Several hours later he began to see the faint outline of the foreboding wall surrounding the ancient city. Numerous clouds were drifting over the distant horizon and obscuring the sun as the farmers all slowly began their long trip homeward for the night.

Good, I'll be able to make it to the city before the sun set, he thought as he shifted the spear from one hand to the other.

"It's the eighth hour and all is well." He heard as he walked through the large opening in the city wall.

Time to eat. All that walking has made me really hungry.

Later as he headed back towards the gate to find a place to sleep, he heard the crier in the distance, "It's the tenth hour and all is well.'

The next morning, he awoke to the sound of the large gates being pushed back, so he gathered his belongings and headed out to find a suitable training area.

I think today I'll focus on the techniques that idiot used yesterday.

"Circle, circle overhead, throw the spike forward," he saw in his mind as he began moving his spear. I need to watch for that "snake spitting its tongue" movement with the chain, he thought while swinging the spear tip towards the tree.

Circle left, circle right, swing the chain around to the side. Watch for the "hitting the large bell technique."

Two hours later he finally finished his training and walked out into the road and began another section of his journey home. He knew reaching the next city would be several days away, so he decided to walk at a steady pace and only stop when absolutely necessary. As he walked it became obvious that the terrain was changing quickly. The once flat open areas were giving way to the repeated areas of higher and steeper landscape. Walking the twisting, turning, steep pathways continually forced him to walk into the low clouds; slowing his pace.

Days later he reached the city of Shouchang and knew from here he could walk along the Yellow River, which would take him to Jinan in western Shandong Province.

I think I'll demonstrate some of my Kung Fu and try to make some money for my trip. He looked around the area and found a suitable spot next to several busy stores.

"Hello everyone, I am Ching Yangban and I'm called Rebellious Dragon. Today I am going to show you some of my family's unique Kung Fu style." He turned and saluted everyone listening.

"First I will start by showing some of our exercises to warm up the muscles." He said while leaning back until his hands touched the dirt; forming a bridge. Afterwards, he stood back up without using his hands and leaned forward to touch his elbow on his toe. "Wow," several people in the crowd said as he stood back up.

"Now I will show you our long-fist style." He turned and began an opening bow.

Stomp. Kick, kick, jump kick, sweep, punch, punch. "Excellent," an elderly man said while raising his thumb into the air. After several minutes he walked over and picked up his spear and said, "Now I'll show you my whirling spear techniques."

"Woosh!" he circled the spear over his head just before striking downwards. Strike, block, press, strike, block, press, jump back while blocking five times, then turn and thrust the tip forward. After thirty minutes of demonstrating, Yangban was drenched in sweat and ready to stop.

"Okay, I'd like to thank everyone for watching my techniques." He said while saluting everyone.

The next day he began walking north along the river road. Two weeks later as the sun reached its highest point, he walked around a small grove of trees where he saw the sign above the large gates telling him he was about to enter Jinan.

Ahh, my old friendly city, he thought while placing his hand on the walls of the opening.

I think I'll stop in and see how my old friend Master Jin is doing. He began walking towards the north side of the city.

This is quite a change from the last two weeks of walking. He looked at all the shops lining the street along with the steady stream of people walking on each side.

A blacksmith, maybe I'll ask him to sharpen my spear. He turned and walked inside the cluttered shop.

"Hello, would you mind sharpening my spear for me?"

"Sure, sure give me a few minutes to finish these straps."

"So, your weapon needs some attention?" *he asked several minutes later after flattening the long straps.*

"Yes, I was down near Chuantung and had to deal with a road bandit."

"Really, it doesn't look like you were injured, so it must have been his unlucky day."

"That's correct. Some people just don't know when to stop."

"I'll be right back." *He grabbed the spear and headed to the back of the shop. After a few minutes he returned.* "There you go, just like new."

"Thank you.

"Do you know Master Jin on the north side of the city?"

"From the Eagle Claw School?"

"Yes."

"Yes, he was married to my cousin."

"What happened?"

"He died about a year ago."

"Really, I hadn't seen him in a few years and was on my way to see him today. I'll make sure and tell his friend Old Li that he recently died because I'm sure he hasn't heard yet. Thank you for sharpening my spear and for the information about my friend. Good bye." He waved as he stepped through the opening.

Hmm… now what? He stood looking down the street while scratching his chin.

I guess I'll start walking towards Pingdu. I have plenty of daylight left so I should be able to reach Lichuan.

Street after street he walked down and recognized many stores and their owners from years earlier. Finally, he reached the east gates and decided to stop for the night before continuing eastward.

Early the next morning before the sun began to lighten the sky with its golden rays, Yangban walked out the gates and searched for a suitable training area.

Those "twelve praying mantis fighting techniques," are still not clear, so I'm going to focus on them today. He leaned his spear against the tree and began the warm up exercises.

An hour later as he began reviewing his forms, a young boy came running out through the gates and suddenly stopped. "Hey, mister, what are you practicing?" he asked as he slowly walked up.

"Good morning to you too."

"Oh, I'm sorry. Good morning master, what are you practicing?" he lowered his head and bowed.

"I'm practicing my family style of long-fist Kung Fu."

"Can I watch?"

"Okay, but no talking."

"Okay."

Ten seconds later the eternity overwhelmed the boy and he asked, "How long have you been doing that?"

"I thought you were only going to watch?"

"I was."

"I started this when I was your age."

"Wow!

"Okay I have to go before my mom comes looking for me, bye." He turned and ran back through the large opening.

Hmm... kids. Now back to my research. Cling, Tag, Lean, and Contact, how do they apply?

For the next hour he continued to research the theories behind the application of these four concepts.

Soon the light became increasingly brighter and more and more farmers headed to their fields. As they passed by, only a few looked to see the fighter standing near the tree. Yangban eventually gathered his belongings and began walking down the dirt path towards Lichuan. For hours he steadily walked and saw no one. Eventually he arrived at the small village and found a small secluded area to sleep.

The following day several hours after his morning practice, Yangban was walking towards Mingshui when two men stepped into the road from a small path leading to a field.

These are not farmers. He thought as his hand instinctively tightened around his spear.

Instantly he began walking directly in the center of the path. If I stay in the middle, I can deal with them easier from here. He quickly moved the pack on his shoulder to the center of his back.

As they drew near, they immediately separated and began walking along the edges of the path; each one held one hand behind their back as they approached Yangban.

"Hey you! We are the twin tigers Lauxi and Weifa and we want everything in your pack and if you give it to us, we'll let you live." The bigger stranger said as he turned and faced his opponent.

"Go back to where you came from and leave me alone!"

"Nobody talks to us like that and lives!" the second shorter bandit yelled.

"I just did, now go home and leave me alone!" he shook his finger at both strangers.

Weifa rushed forward and swung his two hook swords from side to side while sliding his feet in the loose soil. Instantly Yangban stepped back twice and readied his sharp spear by pointing it at the stranger. The moment Weifa was within range he kicked a small amount of dirt up at Yangban's face and reached out to hook the spear with his hooks. Yangban stepped across with his right leg in front of his left while swinging his spear in a large circle; down and over the top, bringing the sharp point down at his opponent's ear. Weifa quickly twisted into a low crouched position while driving his swords up to avoid the razor edge. As he was blocking the spear Yangban jumped forward and kicked him in the face; sending him rolling backwards towards the shallow ditch filled with weeds.

Instantly Yangban turned and quickly stepped forward to engage Louxi; who was still watching his friend fall into the thick weeds.

"Fttt, ftt, ftt," the razor spear tip danced back and forth in the air with the red tassel fluttering behind as the point drew near to its target.

Louxi's eyes grew wide and his jaw dropped as the tip danced and continued to draw nearer. "Ftt, ftt, ftt" and suddenly it was gone as Yangban quickly dropped the point and targeted the stranger's groin.

"Ahh!" Louxi screamed as he frantically raised his leg while twisting to stop the impending injury.

"You…, you'll pay for that!" he yelled while chopping at his attacker's waist with his two-hand broadsword. As the sword spun wildly across in front of Yangban, he leaned back enough to let the blade speed off into thin air. Once it passed, he quickly shuffled in and swept Louxi's supporting leg out from under him.

"Thud." His head hit the ground, sending up a small puff of fine dust.

Yangban turned to confront Weifa, who finally climbed out of the ditch and was walking towards his opponent with the swords spinning circles on each side of his body.

Yangban walked in a semi-circle with his spear drawing large circles in the air in front of his opponent. The moment Weifa stopped his circling Yangban reached forward and stabbed at his leg; forcing him to drop his swords and block the exposed limb. The moment he dropped his swords Yangban withdrew the spear and stabbed at his shoulder.

"Thud.' The sharp tip penetrated the ragged cloth and layers of skin before stopping at the bone below.

"Ai-yaa!" he screamed as the blood began to stain the shirt.

While he was focused on the wound, Yangban again withdrew his spear and attacked the opposite shoulder. "Thud, thud, thud" he stabbed the joint.

Weifa dropped his weapons and tried to address the two wounds as Yangban stepped in and kicked him in the chest.

"Thud!" his feet suddenly left the ground as his body was propelled backwards towards the ditch.

Yangban returned his attention towards the other opponent and yelled, "If you don't want to end up like him, you better drop your weapon and step to the side."

"We're the twin dragons and nobody beats us!"

"Okaaay…" He stood straight up and shook his head.

Louxi raised his sword and began slowly walking forward. Yangban instantly stepped sideways with his spear pointing at his opponent's face, then stopped, shook the tip to make the pellets inside rattle like an agitated snake, and lunged forward while sending the tip at his feet. Louxi quickly pulled his foot up to let the spear shoot underneath and reached out to chop with his sword at his attacker's shoulder. Again, Yangban stepped to the side and avoided the blade while swinging the spear overhead and downward at his ear. This time his opponent was too late to stop the impact. "Thud." The sharp edge hit the top of the ear and sliced down until it hit the shoulder; taking the small flesh appendage along before it fell to the ground.

"Ahhh!" Louxi grabbed the wound with one hand while waving the sword with the other.

"With the next move I'll do the same to your arm."

"Ahh, ahh, ahh!" he screamed as he stepped back.

"Wise decision, now get out of my way!" he shook his spear again to make the pellets rattle.

Cautiously Louxi stepped back and to the side while staring at his opponent. Meanwhile, Weifa stumbled out of the ditch, tripped and fell on his weapons before frantically standing to watch his opponent walk away.

Yangban walked slowly past Louxi with his spear still pointed forward, then turned and continued down the dirt path without looking back.

Hmm, twin tigers, huh, more like sick cats! He looked up at the sun as it began to sink towards the distant horizon.

It was now 1861. It had only been three years since the Middle Kingdom was once again defeated by the foreign devils over the importing of the deadly opium. As Yangban walked northward, he began to see more and more of the white-faced devils living and working in the major cities of Shandong Province.

Hours later he walked through the gates of Zhoucun, looked around at the vendors lined up on each side of the opening before heading further inside.

"Where can I get some tea and a bowl of rice?" he asked the barber sitting on his small bench.

"Go straight and turn right at the first intersection." He gestured while looking down the street.

Later, after finishing his meal, he walked back towards the gate and found a corner to sleep in for the night. Looking around he noticed several of the vendors had already closed their booths and were settled in for another night's quietude, while the remainder searched the area for yet another client.

"What do you mean I will never have any children?" the lady sitting next to Yangban screamed as she stood up and pointed at the old bearded man sitting behind the small table.

"I'm just telling you what I'm finding on your palm."

"But…but we want to have a son and not just a daughter."

"Your future does not contain that, according to your palm."

"Are you sure?"

"Yes."

"Can you read it again?"

"Okay, but it's not going to change." He shook his head while motioning for her to sit back down.

"Hey, could you trim my queue before you close?" Yangban asked the man across the path.

"Sure, sure come over here and sit down."

Twenty minutes later the barber finished trimming and re-braiding the hair. Afterwards, Yangban walked back to his spot, situated his belongings as a small pillow and quickly fell asleep.

In a seemingly short time, he heard a distant rooster crow to signal the upcoming morning. Time to begin another piece of my journey. The walking will help keep me warm after that cold night. He looked around to see everyone else was still asleep.

After walking through the large opening, he noticed the thin layer of white covering everything on the ground. "Crunch, crunch," I guess with all this frost covering everything, it was colder than I thought.

"Chirp, chirp, chirp," a solitary bird sat on a branch nearby looking for his friends to come out and talk.

I should have no problem making it to Cingzhou by tonight and from there it will only be two more days before I get back to Pingdu. He adjusted his backpack, turned towards the east, and headed away from the city. Days later he saw the faint outline of an old familiar friend off in the distance. Ahh, Pingdu at last. Instantly he increased his pace as the excitement of returning home finally settled in to his consciousness.

"Creak!" the old door complained. "Hey, Shoushan, how have you been? I haven't seen you in years!" he said as he stepped into the familiar office.

"Yangban, I don't believe it, you're back." He stood up from his chair and walked over towards his friend before bowing.

"Yes, I retired from the rebel group and plan to live at the Hua Lin Temple."

"That's great. They could use someone of your skills to help improve their fighting."

"Oh, I don't know about that, I hear an old friend of my grandfather's, Zhan Tingfa, is now the abbot and I know how good his Kung Fu is. My father and grandfather told me many stories about him and his exploits as a fighter in his younger days."

For the remainder of the afternoon the two fighters sat and caught up on each other's lives. Soon the shadows began to stretch across the compound and up the walls, while the light slowly yielded to the darkness. Yangban bid his friend farewell and headed towards his family compound before the darkness engulfed him and the entire town.

Two weeks later he headed north towards the secluded temple off in the distant woods. The late October weather had suddenly turned cold overnight, leaving everything with a thin coating of frost that lingered until late in the morning, when the sun had finally warmed its way through the cold air. I'm glad I learned the art of Dian Xue, because those special exercises will definitely keep me warm while I walk, he thought while walking past the barren fields.

Early the next afternoon as he was passing Kuantao village, he watched as a raggedly dressed couple seemed to be lingering along the road near a small grove of trees. Instinctively a sudden chill ran down his back as he observed their actions. They continually looked around as if checking to see who was walking by. As he approached, they quickly turned and only looked down the road in his direction. I wonder what these two, think they are going to attempt to pull off. As Yangban grew closer, he could finally see their weapons hidden behind their backs and now as they moved into the middle of the road, he noticed their movements were definitely not farmer-like.

"Hey could you help us out?" the man with the tattered outfit asked as he stepped forward.

"No, and you need to move out of my way."

"Hey, I think you need to help us," the woman snapped as she walked up and stood next to the man.

"I think you need to find someone else to try and rob."

"No, I think we will have no problem taking everything that you have!" she leaned forward and pointed.

"If you want to see tomorrow so you can rob someone else, you need to step out of my way and let me pass."

"Ha! Who do you think you are?" the man raised his long sword above his head.

"I've killed many men much more experienced than you two losers, so move out of my way!"

"Losers? I'll show you how good we are!" the man rushed forward while circling the sword on each side of his body. Yangban stepped back two steps and exhaled deeply while watching the stranger

swing his sword wildly around his body. The moment he knew the man was within range, he slapped the sword to the side and then instantly pulled the spear tip back towards his opponent and cut a deep groove in his neck before kicking him in the chest. "Thud" echoed through the cold air as the foot drove the man backwards. "Use your sash to stop the bleeding!" the woman yelled as she watched her accomplice frantically try to close the wound.

"Ai-yaa!" she yelled as she turned her attention towards the solitary figure standing in front of her.

As she stepped forward, Yangban noticed the half circle stepping pattern she was using and recognized it from a unique style he had encountered years earlier in Jinan. Dong family style. I recognize that style of movement, he thought while watching her move closer with her twin daggers cutting vertical circles in front of her body. As she neared, she suddenly jumped up and kicked towards her opponent's chest. Yangban quickly stepped to the side and chopped at her elbow with his spear. Instantly she turned to avoid the sharp tip and swung her right dagger at his shoulder, but Yangban's momentum carried him too far away, so the short blade only cut through the air. Instantly Yangban dropped to one leg and swept her feet out from under her, causing her body to suddenly turn in midair until it was almost upside down. "Thud!" her head hit the frozen ground followed by the daggers dropping from her hands.

Yangban turned and pointed his spear at the man tying the cloth around his neck. "Get out of my way or you will die today!" he yelled as he stepped forward. As he took several more steps, the man began to raise his sword, but Yangban quickly jumped forward and kicked the man in the chest again; sending him backwards into the deep ditch.

As he turned, the woman finally stood back up and was rubbing her head as she tried to maintain her balance. "Back up!" he yelled as he paused and pointed the sharp point at her head.

After the woman stepped back several steps Yangban turned and continued on his journey northward without looking back.

"Banfen, Banfen! Are you okay?" he heard her say as he walked away.

Several days later Yangban turned to begin climbing the hill leading up to the solitary dwelling hidden in the dense growth of trees.

Minutes later he could detect the faint smell of burning wood, Ahh, I must be getting close, he thought as he continued his climb. Soon he began to see the outline of an ancient looking structure peeking through the trees ahead.

14. CHANGING SEASONS

1862. The Middle kingdom had just been dealt another blow by the white devils over the influx of opium. The economy was continually weakening while the people endured even more struggles. Vast amounts of materials and equipment along with land were destroyed or stolen due to the war.

"Boom, boom, boom," he dropped the large ring of metal against the wooden gate and heard it echo through the interior compound.

"Screech, boom," minutes later, the gates slowly began to swing back and allow a solitary monk to step through. "May I help you?" the stranger asked.

"Yes, my name is Cheng Yangban and I would like to ask the abbot's permission to live here." Yangban said as he humbly bowed to the monk.

"We don't have much room, but I'll ask anyway." He turned and stepped back through the opening.

After the gate closed, Yangban walked over and stood in the warm sunlight near a large tree, placed his belongings on the ground and glanced forward to see several young cardinals hunting through the weeds for their next meal. As he stood up, he raised his head and watched the small solitary clouds hurriedly dash across the open sky. While they raced forward a tiny shadow sped through the trees, across the ground and back up into the distant trees in a desperate attempt to keep pace.

Down the hillside where the path turned and followed the stream, a fox scurried along the side while sniffing for the scent of small rodents that might have passed by recently. Suddenly, it stopped and sniffed the area more intently before turning and dashing into the underbrush with its nose still barely off the ground.

"Who, who, who," he heard off in the distance from over his left shoulder as he looked around to admire the landscape and vibrant foliage with its lush emerald green leaves, array of bright flowers and thick ferns. "Whoosh" the large owl flew past a few seconds later as and effortlessly dodged every branch and limb like a seasoned fighter before diving towards the ground.

"Screech, boom." the aged gates complained thirty minutes later as they were once again forced to work.

318

Quietly the monk stepped out through the opening and turned towards the visitor, "You can enter now," he said while holding the wooden gate.

Yangban stood up, picked up his belongings, walked over to the gate, and the two turned to walk inside the quiet temple walls. Inside the gates they passed by a large open grass area, then a fishpond with numerous lotus leaves covering the surface and then several small structures connected by a narrow pathway before heading towards a dwelling sitting alone at the end of the path.

"Knock, knock, knock," the monk lightly tapped on the wooden door frame and stepped back.

"Enter," the soft voice said from behind the door after several minutes.

"Creak." The monk cautiously opened the aged wooden frame and gestured for their guest to follow him inside.

"Master, I brought the stranger who was at the front gate." He said as he entered the room and bowed.

"Thank you Finxu. You can leave us now." He placed his calligraphy brush back in its holder and turned to face Yangban.

"Cheng Yangban... is your family originally from Pingdu?"

"Yes."

"Ahh, so your father was Cheng Zhangfu. I knew him many years ago when I worked for the Li family." He looked directly at his visitor.

"Yes, I remember. When I was young, he would tell me about you and your skills as an escort."

"Yes, that was many, many years ago when Old Li's father first began his business." He leaned back in his chair. *"What brings you to our humble little temple?"*

"I have traveled to many provinces as an escort and also while rebelling against the corrupt officials, but now I have had enough of that life and would like to spend my last days in peace and solitude."

"So, you fought against the government?"

"Yes, I didn't like the way they treated the people and how corrupt the officials were while telling everyone how much they were helping the people."

"Are any officials looking for you?"

"Not that I know of. I quit fighting them several years ago so I wouldn't be arrested."

"Ah good, the last thing we need here is a group of angry officials looking for someone." He stroked his beard and looked at the ceiling.

"With so much travelling and working with other rebels, you must have acquired skills in many different styles of Kung Fu." he stood up and walked closer.

"My family style was Long-fist, after that I learned a unique style called Praying Mantis, a little White Crane and then I learned some Hua style from my friend in Jinan."

"Praying Mantis and Hua style, hmm." He walked across the room while stroking his long thin beard, stopped and delicately added a single brush stroke to the scroll. After several minutes of looking at the scroll he turned, placed his hands behind his back and said, "Very well, I'll allow you to stay as long as no one arrives to arrest you over your past. I assume you are willing to teach us your style, and I knew your family and their reputation." He walked over to his guest, and placed his hand on his shoulder.

"Tell Finxu to show you to your room and assign you some chores for the morning cleaning." He walked back to his chair and picked up his brush.

"Thank you, Master, for accepting me." He bowed and turned to leave.

Walking outside he quietly closed the door and turned towards Finxu.

"Well, what did he say?" Finxu stepped closer.

"he said, I can stay as long as no one is looking for me and I'm willing to teach everyone my Kung Fu.

"Great and welcome. So, what styles did you learn?"

"My family style is long-fist and then I learned Shuai Jiao Praying Mantis, White Crane and Hua style."

"Wow I can't wait to learn those. It'll go well with my Cha family style."

"He wants you to show me where I'll be sleeping, and then explain what my duties will be in the morning."

"Okay, let's go over to the other building where everyone sleeps, get you a bed and then go over to the kitchen," Finxu said as he turned and began walking away.

The following morning as the sun announced the beginning of a new day, everyone began their daily routines before gathering in the large open area for training. Soon Abbot Fu arrived and said, "Everyone, this is Ching Yangban from Pingdu, I have granted him permission to live with us. I have known his family for many years and believe he'll be a great addition to our temple.

"I want everyone to welcome him and teach him our Kung Fu."

"He knows a new style called Praying Mantis and over time he will be teaching us this unique type of movement.

"Ready everyone, bow to our newest member." Everyone turned to salute Yangban.

"Finxu, take our newest member over by that tree and begin teaching him your Black Tiger style basics. I want everyone else to practice the weapons we discussed yesterday." He walked over to the tree and sat on a small stool.

"Chuling, what did I tell you about your stances last week? It doesn't appear that you've made any adjustments or improvements. You're still shuffling your feet around like you're sliding on the ice. Your techniques will never have any real power or effectiveness if you don't learn how to root to the ground." He shook his head while pulling his fan from inside his sleeve.

"Yes, Master."

"Watch your brother Dawei, see how he sticks to the ground when he punches and kicks? Then as he moves, he allows his feet to float across the ground like the morning mist."

"Fighting must be a combination of very different concepts, sometimes they even sound like they are completely opposite and could never complement each other, but they do. Just like when I told everyone about the different natures within each weapon, remember?" He casually moved his fan through several techniques.

"Yes, I think so."

"Okay, tell me what I said."

"Ah, you kind of said…"

"Kind of said? Ha! You forgot." He leaned back against the trunk of the aged sentry.

"Here is what I said. I told everyone about how a hard weapon should be able to demonstrate qualities of being soft, while a soft or flexible weapon should be able to perform hard techniques, remember? Within each weapon there should be its opposite. If a

weapon is only hard, it can be broken and if a weapon is only soft, it can be breached. It's the same idea for your body and its movements. Whenever you move you need to incorporate several concepts simultaneously in order to be truly effective. You must glide like the smoke across a still lake and still be rooted to the ground like this old oak." He reached over his head and patted the old friend.

"Your techniques should be as soft as a gentle breeze meandering through the trees and as powerful as the raging waters of the Yellow River in the spring. Softness boiling within the hardness and hardness hidden within the softness. Do you understand?"

"Um, I think so."

"It doesn't sound like you're too sure." He began to smile while closing the fan before tapping his forehead with the metal weapon.

"You're right, Master. I am still trying to figure out how the weapons can be both hard and soft at the same time. Because when I try to make my stick movements soft, then Finxu laughs and says it looks like a bowl of limp noodles. when I try to make it hard so that I can attack and defend myself Dawei says it looks like I'm trying to hit with a 500-pound boulder." He looked at the ground and kicks a rock across the training area.

"Well, that's quite an interesting description of your techniques." Abbot Fu looked at the large white clouds overhead and smiled.

"So, what are you focusing on in your training, in order to change those interesting descriptions?"

"Well, every time I try something that I think might help, it always falls apart and causes more problems. So now I don't know what I should try because I don't need any more problems with this issue." He looked around at everyone training and shrugged his shoulders.

"Hmm, it sounds like you've come to an all-too-familiar crossroad in your training. Just to let you know, everybody goes through the exact same issues during their training career and it's only those who are willing to delve deeper into their situation that will succeed and discover the truth about these ancient concepts. So be careful and don't let your ego continually wear you down and make you feel as though you aren't good enough, talented enough or capable of understanding or comprehending these ideas. Everyone can grasp them, if they persevere and maintain their desire to succeed."

"But… somedays my mind throws these thoughts at me about my life and the training, and it makes me feel…"

"Inadequate?"

"Yes, how did you know that, Master?"

"That's a very simple question to answer, because I've been there also, and had the exact same thoughts go through my mind as the ones you're having right now. My master told me the same things I'm telling you now. But it was only through my own personal dedication and desire to master the art that I succeeded, as it will be yours that either makes you improve or not." Abbot Fu leaned forward and put his elbow on his knee while pointing at his student.

"Yes, Master, I'll keep trying because I believe if you say that that is what you had to do, then that is what I'll do also because I want to be as good as you are." Chuling stood up straight and placed his hand on his hip.

"Good, good you're beginning to learn. Now whenever you begin to hear those whispers in your ears, always remember what I just said and you'll quickly forget the thoughts and move on in your training. Before you know it, you'll be a master.!"

"Baomin! Raise your arm more when you strike with your sword. Otherwise, you'll never be able to scare anyone." He stood up and demonstrated the technique.

"Finxu, how's our newest student coming along?"

"Great, Master, he definitely has many years of experience because I'm learning as much as he is."

"Good, keep at it."

"Zhuping, show me your tiger hook swords form. I've seen you practicing everything else but not those."

Zhuping instantly began jumping forward while twisting and turning to imitate grabbing the ankle with the hooked blade and cutting the tendons. He followed by jumping high in the air while twisting overhead and chopping down on the top of his imaginary opponent, before stepping in and driving the blades into his opponent's throat.

"Yes, that's getting better but don't let your mind wander so much while you attack. I can tell you're not always paying attention by the way you move your swords."

Zhuping turned and bowed as his facial expression gave away his secret.

"They need to be moved as though you are a dragon soaring through the sky in search of an unsuspecting victim, while darting between the clouds in an effort to hide his position." Abbot Fu effortlessly danced through the techniques as though he were tying a delicate bow.

"Wow," Zhuping said as he watched the aged warrior demonstrate the intricate series of attacks and defensive movements.

"Okay, if I can still do it, then you should have no problem."

"Yes, but you're a master." He said while shaking his head.

"Zhuping, see how the swords are sharp on the inside and outside of the hooked end? That's so you can cut while moving the sword forward or backwards. So, don't think they can only attack in one direction. Just like a tiger they will attack as they move forward and also while they are retreating. They will not leave a single opportunity left unchecked, so you shouldn't either." He walked back over to his stool and sat in the shade.

"When you walk in a pattern to imitate a snake moving through the grass, you need to move the hooks as though they are slicing through an illusion in life that you are trying to advance past. Then when you pause in your horse stance, it is to demonstrate that

327

you succeeded and are now in a position beyond the veil. Don't just wiggle the hooks as though you're afraid of them and they're desperately trying to keep up with your steps. No, you're the one trying to keep up with the hooks!" he pointed at his temple and then the sky.

"Huh? An illusion?"

"Yes, an illusion. Life is always trying to cast another illusion over your mind in an attempt to make you feel as though you are less of a person and cannot accomplish what you are visualizing. Fear not, for all your energies and efforts are the very substance that propel you forward and help you to succeed. So, if your body and movements are supposed to imitate Yinglong, the dragon in the sky, then have the courage to try and allow yourself to experience the feeling of being a dragon. Otherwise, how will you ever know what it feels like to be an imperial dragon flying through the sky without any effort or fears from their enemies?" He slowly began to stroke his long thin beard.

"The dragons have always been revered in Chinese culture for their unique and individual characteristics. We have nine different dragons and I hope your parents taught you about all of them. If so then what I'm going to say will be old news. As I said, we have nine dragons, and each one has a very unique characteristic, which is why you will see a different expression and body position on each one. And each one will be strategically positioned throughout the house or family compound." He began to slowly draw a sketch of a compound in the soft dirt.

"Now try again and as you move the hooks, let your spirit soar like Yinglong."

Chuling scratched his head and immediately began the hook swords form.

"Yangban, watch how you position your hand as you strike. The Black Tiger style has a unique theory about striking with the fingertips and palms." He raised the arm and pulled back on the palm to change the angle of attack for the fingertips. "See, the direction of the force is now upward and at an oblique angle to the muscles in the stomach, which means their ability to resist the impact is diminished greatly."

"Ah, so you're not trying to drive them backwards only. You're uprooting them from the ground first and then backwards."

"Yes, yes that's correct and that's why when we strike, we're using the heel of the palm as well as the fingertips. And then as you're hitting, your claws dig into the flesh and rip just like a tiger." Finxu pressed his palm against Yangban's chest and curled his fingertips as if they were claws, causing the shirt on his friend to tighten.

"Now that I've taught you some of the basics, I'll show you the beginning of our first form." He stood next to Yangban and gestured for his friend to follow.

Suddenly an unexpected gust of wind raced across the ground and swirled in the middle of the open area. The dust gathered into a circle and danced wildly as it spiraled upward before rushing off over the distant wall with the wind and disappeared. Only to leave the area calm once again.

The routine began with a series of upward and downward claw movements to gather energy and focus the spirit. Next was the traditional salute, followed by several raking claw techniques diagonally across the body of the imaginary opponent, followed by a series of upward and downward rips with each hand to imitate a raging tiger slicing its opponent from top to bottom.

"I like that series," Yangban said as he walked over to the tree and sat in the shade.

"It's a great opening, isn't it?"

"It really expresses the attitude and spirit of a raging tiger." Yangban sipped some cool water.

"Next I'll teach you the Tiger circling the sun techniques." Finxu said as he walked back out into the open area.

"I'm ready," Yangban said as he jumped up and followed his friend.

"Now as you finish the diagonal ripping techniques, the next series teaches how to move forward and rip up and down the body with each tiger claw. It goes like this, first you step forward and rip down the body, step forward again, turn the hand over and rip back up. Afterwards, repeat the entire sequence on the other side, followed

by a double punch and a raking technique down the face." Finxu stopped and turned to watch Yangban perform the series.

"Watch how you rip with the claws. They need to rip straight up or down the body to maximize the attack on your opponent. And when you step, it must be very strong like a tiger attacking its prey, so use your entire body. This style uses very strong footwork which must be rooted to the earth, just like a tiger." He demonstrated several stepping techniques.

"Visualize a tiger as you move and feel the power radiates when attacking. Your mind must become the tiger and absorb its spirit."

"This series is powerful." He stood up and started again as the sweat continued to pour down his face.

Over the several hours the newest member at the temple focused on learning this unique style of Kung Fu, while the remainder of the class reviewed and researched the theories from the previous day.

"Okay, I think it's time to finish for today and begin our evening chores before we eat," Abbot Fu said as he stood up and began walking towards his private quarters. As he walked past the first building, he stopped by the ancient fishpond and threw several small pieces of food into the still water. Instantly its surface sprang to life as the residents rushed to the surface and consumed the welcomed treat. After several minutes of observing the silent friends, he continued on his journey.

An hour later as the abbot walked into the dining hall he said, "Finxu, I want you to spend the next several months teaching Yangban your entire Tiger style."

"Yes, Master, I'll teach him everything I know."

"Good, and tomorrow you can have him help with the gardening." The abbot said as he walked to his seat, sat down and began eating rice from his small bowl. "Everyone, eat." He said to the students patiently waiting while pointing at the steaming dishes.

Early the next morning as everyone began to prepare for the morning meal, a cool breeze slowly crept through the temple and whispered that the harvest season would be arriving soon. The leaves on the low hanging branches danced excitedly from the breeze in anticipation of the impending cooler weather and the release from the summer's heat, while several fallen leaves jumped and skipped across the bare soil.

Weeks later another cool breeze drifted between the weathered structures and announced its delivery of the autumn season, while the temperature continued to drop throughout the day. Eventually, the afternoon was cooler than the nighttime low and everyone pulled their robes a little tighter as they trained.

"Yangban, I want to show you one of the Black Tiger energy exercises, so that you can use it to help you warm up on the cold mornings," Finxu said as he walked out into the training area the following morning. As he walked, the cold night air caused the ground and grass to crack with each step while his breath became visible with each exhale.

"Good, I know several exercises but I'm always willing to learn more, especially if they are an improvement."

"The first one is called "Tiger pushes the Mountain." It's designed to help stimulate the energies flowing throughout the body, strengthen the back muscles and open the hip joints." He demonstrated the initial movement.

"Now follow me, move your body exactly like I move mine and I'll explain each detail as we practice." Yangban stepped next to his friend and began mirroring every motion he saw Finxu perform.

"As you sink, make sure to keep your back straight and you'll find your hands never reach past your knees. Also, this is the point when you exhale and focus your energies on the tips of your fingers. Now as you rise up to turn towards the other direction, you want to inhale and draw your tiger claws in close to the body before sinking and extending everything outward with another exhale."

"This is great. I can feel the stimulation building in my lower energy gate."

"Now the next section of this exercise is called "Whirling tiger pushes the mountain" and this will help to spiral all the energy and collect it in between your arms before you direct it into your fingertips. So, we'll do the same beginning but now we're going to add the whirling tiger movements which look like this." He demonstrated the added motions.

"As you do this section, you need to maintain your body position so that your hips stay parallel with your knees, to help stimulate the *joints and strengthen the legs. And when you extend your arms beyond your knees the back must lean slightly forward like a tiger pouncing on its prey."*

For the next hour the two fighters continued their practice and decided to focus their attention on the stimulation and projection of their internal energies. Eventually, the abbot slowly walked into the area and said," Everyone come over here I want to explain an important concept to you."

"In our traditional medicine we have a concept about the energy that runs throughout the body. We know that there are two basic types called congenital and acquired qi. Congenital qi is the essence you get from your parents before you are born. Each person has a certain amount at birth which you use and slowly exhaust as you age. The other, acquired qi, is the energy you build up and store from day to day through the food you eat, the exercises you do and the way you develop your mind to think." He sat down on his favorite stool under the tree.

"Congenital qi, or essence, determines your lifespan and overall health during that time frame and it's not something that you can acquire or develop more of. The amount is already predetermined. So, the emphasis should be upon trying to preserve and maintain the amount of qi your parents gave you at birth. How do you do this? Well, it takes years of diligent practice and determination to understand all the intricate and subtle details which make up this process. But you must first be taught the basics about the fact that the process is even part of you." He looked at each student.

"First, as I said earlier, this process is part of everyone, so now we can begin to explore how it works and what we can do to maximize its affect upon our daily lives.

"Your parents acquired their congenital qi from their parents and ancestors, so yours is a mixture of each of your parent's ancestral qi combined together in your body. So, to a certain degree your life is determined by your ancestors and their congenital qi. After that the remainder is up to you and the decisions you make in life."

"Decisions we make?" Chuling asked.

"Yes, each day we all make numerous decisions in our lives that help to shape our lives and assist or deplete our internal qi. How you think and what you think about has a direct affect upon your congenital qi. Thoughts are far more powerful than most people understand and the effect they have on your body is usually overlooked. That is one of the reasons that we focus so much time and effort on development of the mind during our training." He pointed at his temple with one finger.

"Next we have the acquired qi. This is from the things we do in our daily lives. Acquired qi is like a storehouse that continually has its reserves rise and fall depending upon the actions of our daily lives. When we spend the day preparing and eating food with nutritious benefit, the outcome will be an increase to our reserves. Additionally, when we practice various exercises specifically designed to promote healing and energy movement, our reserves will increase. And as we continue to raise the level of our qi reserves, this will directly affect the amount of congenital qi we need to use

during that day. So, your mindset from day to day should be to keep these ideas as an important cornerstone and continually strive towards maintaining a high level of acquired qi through your food, actions, and attitudes. Each day we begin with good food and then when we start our training, we always begin with the energy building exercises to help promote the circulation and quiet the mind. In that way, we develop a daily habit of promoting and prolonging our lives. Hopefully, the routine becomes ingrained to the point where we spend our entire lives cultivating and storing qi while reducing the amount of congenital qi required each day."
The abbot slowly looked up at the clear sky.

"Today I want you to contemplate these ideas and research your daily lives to see if there are areas where you can make small adjustments and improve your congenital and acquired qi. Okay everyone, go out and resume your training." He pointed at the open area.

"Hmm, another indication as to why he's the abbot," Finxu said as he walked aside Yangban back to where they were training, while watching the birds fly from branch to branch during their morning ritual of saying hello to all the neighbors.

"Yes, that's true. All the things he has talked about since I arrived are an enhancement of what I have been told over the years. I've learned many different types of qi development, some good and some just so-so. But his explanations have helped to make the mediocre exercises so much more effective." Yangban shook his head as he walked.

"I think for the rest of the day I'd like to focus on my qi exercises and integrate the ideas I just heard." He said as Finxu placed his water beside the tree.

"Good idea."

Hour after hour the two fighters stood silently focusing on various qi development exercises that each had acquired over their years of training and traveling. After what seemed like mere minutes, it was now time for the noon meal, so they finished their exercises and slowly walked towards the dining area. "That sure didn't seem like we were practicing very long, but here it is already past the noon hour," Yangban said as he stepped inside the room and walked over to his assigned seat.

"Later today we'll have to pick up where we left off." Finxu placed his hand on the shoulder of his friend.

"Finxu, did you finish teaching Yangban all of your Black Tiger style? It's been three years since you started." Abbot Fu asked as he sat down at the end of the large table.

"We should be finished in several months, Master."

"Good, because I want him to begin teaching everyone his praying mantis style."

"Okay, I'll make sure we get finished by the August moon festival."

"Okay everyone, Finxu informed me yesterday that he has finished teaching Yangban, so today Yangban's going to begin your training in praying mantis." Abbot Fu said as he turned the corner and headed towards his favorite tree. Overhead the chorus of birds chirping to announce the new day and remind everyone about the boundaries of their individual territories seemed to excite the squirrels who were hunting for acorns and caused them to dash even faster from tree to tree. The air was exceptionally cool and crisp and as the abbot walked, his breath could be seen with each exhale.

"Make sure everyone warms up their muscles really well today," he said as he walked past several younger students. "It's weather like this that will cause you to get injured if you don't spend extra time warming up the body."

"Yangban, you can stand over here near me while you teach the others." He pointed at the small clearing next to his seat.

Yangban walked over to the area and turned to bow to his teacher. "First, I'd like to explain where I learned this style and a few details about what makes it unique," he said after he turned towards the group, looking up to see a single white flake slowly float towards the ground.

"Years ago, when I was working in Pingdu as an escort for Old Li. His son Li Zhizhan, returned home from his travels, and told me about this unique system of praying mantis kung fu that he learned from Sheng Xiao Dao ren, while near Qingdao." He began as he scratched the ground with his foot as another solitary remnant of

the water from the sky softly touched the soil near his shoe and disappeared.

"Actually, his father told me he had learned the style, so when he arrived, we questioned him about it and he was willing to demonstrate. Needless to say, as soon as he started the first series, I knew I wanted to learn every bit of it. It was that powerful."

"Like so many other styles of kung fu, this one is also based upon the movements and actions of a creature in nature. He said it was invented over 500 years ago by a man named Wang Lang who observed the actions of a praying mantis catching and subduing a cicada." He placed the fingers of each hand in a unique arrangement to imitate the position of a mantis's front arms when attacking.

"After many years of observation and research, Wang Lang then added some theories and applications from other styles together to assist in enhancing the natural motions of the praying mantis."

"So, if everyone is ready, we can begin with some of the fundamental movements and drills." He stepped forward and motioned for everyone to follow behind him.

"The first position is the one I just showed you. It's called "praying mantis catches the cicada", so your hands and fingers should look like this with one hand extended further out than the other. It imitates catching an arm and locking the elbow to control an opponent."

"Make sure as you apply this technique that you turn your shoulders to help maintain the lock on the arm." He said as he twisted his shoulders to demonstrate. "Also, your front foot should be only on the toe so you can attack with the leg." He added.

As each classmate practiced forming their hands and fingers into the correct positions, Yangban continually walked from person to person and adjusted the technique to ensure its proper position.

"Now that everyone understands that movement, we'll move on to the next one. This series is called "jade ring and chop step" and looks like this." He instantly executed the series.

"It's used to lock an opponent's arm while chopping the throat and sweeping the leg. Finxu, step over here so I can demonstrate how it works." He motioned for his friend to step forward.

"Punch at me with your left arm."

As Finxu punched towards his friend's chest, Yangban instantly grabbed the arm, swung his other arm over Finxu's head, chopped the opposite side of his neck while sweeping the front leg out from under his friend. "Thud!" Finxu hit the ground and momentarily laid there from the shock of the impact.

"Wow, that sure was unexpected," Finxu said as he slowly stood up and rubbed the back of his head.

"Now I'll show the series to you slowly so you can see how it applies." He motioned for Finxu to step forward.

Step by step he demonstrated the individual techniques and explained their applications and then had everyone try the series on a partner.

Over the next several hours Yangban continued teaching the basic techniques and their applications to everyone until the abbot said, "I think we'll stop there for now, go inside to eat and continue later." He stood up and pointed at the buildings.

"After I teach everyone some more of the fundamentals, I'll explain a few of the theories specific to praying mantis," Yangban said to Finxu and Zhuping as they walked towards the kitchen to help prepare the noon meal.

"Hey Chef Wei, what would you like us to do to help out?" Finxu asked as they stepped inside the kitchen door.

"Go over there and finish cutting those vegetables for me so I can add them to the water, and then we need the rice cleaned and poured into the that water over there." He pointed at the two large metal containers partially filled with boiling water.

Minutes later the group began carrying the various containers out into the dining room, placed them in the center of the large table and returned to the kitchen. "Okay Chef Wei, we have everything ready. Are you going to join us?" Yangban asked as he headed towards the door.

"I'll be there in a minute," he yelled over his shoulder while stirring another pot.

Eventually, the meal was finished and everyone walked outside to complete their mid-day chores prior to the afternoon training.

"As we begin this afternoon, I want to finish the fundamentals and then explain several of the primary theories unique to praying mantis," Yangban said as he watched the other students arrive and begin loosening their joints.

"The last basic I want to teach you is a special stepping technique. It's used to quickly cover the distance between you and your opponent. It's called "beng bu" or crushing step. As I said, it's used to quickly close the distance without the need to execute a complete stance change. All you need to do is quickly shuffle the back foot in to the other and then slide the front foot out." He walked to the middle of the group and demonstrated the technique.

"Wow!" Dawei said as he watched.

"This step is essential in praying mantis for covering the distance and not losing your attacking ability, so make sure you connect the footwork with the timing of your hands." He executed the series again to reiterate the previous statement.

Later, as everyone stopped and drank some water, Yangban said, "Now one of the fundamental theories in praying mantis is as your opponent is attacking, you need to attack in response to their intent. You will be reacting to their movement, yet you need to get there first with your attack." He looked around to see if anyone had a question.

"Chuling, do you understand the concept?"

"Yes, what it means is that our opponent will be moving first to try and attack, but with our praying mantis fighting strategy we need to arrive first with our attack."

"Yes, very good. Now let's research the theory with a partner," he said.

Initially, everyone seemed to struggle with the concept, so Yangban walked from group to group and explained subtle details to help clarify their confusion.

Eventually the sun slipped below the distant treetops and signaled the end of another day's training. Slowly everyone turned and walked back to their rooms before beginning the evening chores. The sun quietly disappeared below the horizon, the birds finished their last conversation with their neighbors and the forest was quiet. The only sounds lingering through the temple were the echoes from the chef in the kitchen hurriedly trying to finish the meal preparations.

Day after day the routine continued until Yangban completed the task of passing on to all his classmates the praying mantis style.

"Master, I've finished teaching my entire praying mantis style to my classmates," he said as he walked over to the tree where the abbot was seated.

"Good, cough, cough. I'm confident that it'll be a valuable asset to each of them for the rest of their lives, cough."

"Are you not feeling well today, Master?" he knelt down to look straight at his teacher's face.

"Oh, it's something that's been coming on for some time, but I think my herbs will help." he patted his student's shoulder as he stood up. "I think I'll go back to my room and rest." He slowly walked away.

"Finxu, is the abbot feeling any better? He doesn't look very well." Yangban sat down near his friend.

"I'm not sure. He tells me he is but I'm not seeing any improvement yet and at 95, I don't know if his body can take much more." He looked at the ground and shook his head.

For several weeks the students diligently maintained a constant vigil over their master and watched as his health slowly rose up and then abruptly dropped slightly lower, with each drop in health taking another piece of his spirit. Their continual efforts to help boost his strength with herbs, acupuncture and energy techniques were having little effect, while his body was showing signs of decline.

Soon, his body was no longer able to recover from the loss of spirit and he quietly slipped into a deep coma. For several days they continued their efforts and daily vigil until the saddening moment *when Abbot Fu drew his last breath and drifted off into forever. Solemnly the residents quietly began the task of preparing his body for its final home and finished the monument honoring his life's journey.*

Over the next several weeks everyone mourned the loss. All training was ceased and replaced with solitary time for reflection upon the moments spent learning from their teacher and his words of wisdom. Each student was required to dedicate his meditations to the enhancement of Abbot Fu's journey and the committing of his teachings to their memories for future generations.

Eventually the focus of the monks slowly changed from mourning their abbot's loss to determining who would be qualified and willing to accept the position as the abbot. Each day time was set aside for the members to gather for a meeting and discuss the position.

"Finxu, I think you would be the best choice for the title," Dawei said when he was given permission to speak.

"I'm too old and would prefer not to be the abbot," he said as he placed his hand on the back of his neck.

"Yangban, I believe you're a better choice for the position than I am, and if nobody is against his accepting the role, I think we should pass the position to him." Finxu said.

"Agreed." Everyone in the room said in unison.

15. WINDOWS AND MIRRORS

Quietude, tranquility, peacefulness, and balance of life drifted slowly from moment to moment and day to day in this accumulation of simple structures. Each day was organized and structured around a simple series of events. Upon waking everyone gathered to enjoy the simple meal of vegetables and rice. Afterwards, the morning training was commenced in the large open area, warm-ups to invigorate the muscles and internal energy, followed by stretching and practicing of individual forms. Then researching each movement in the form through applications with a partner, and finally a discussion about the movement's theories for fighting.

Throughout his time in the temple, Cheng Yangban learned a variety of Kung Fu systems from the other members, as well as teaching his family style along with the praying mantis style to them. Over the years he gradually became a senior student and finally when the presiding abbot died, he was asked to take the position.

It was now 1886 and the tensions between China and the remainder of the world continued to grow as each country invaded the Middle Kingdom and forced another series of cessions. Yet few knew of this solitary compound deep in the woods and away from the remainder of civilization where life was still lived – simply.

"Changde, I want you to take your younger brother Xiawu and manicure the inside walls near the front entrance after your training this morning." Abbot Cheng said as he walked towards his house.

"Yes Master, I'll make sure and have it done before our afternoon training." He bowed.

"I'll be in my house if you need to ask any questions."

"Xiawu, the abbot wants us to go out and trim all the growth on the wall by the front gates." He pointed at the area.

"Okay, I'll get a couple of tools we can use to help cut everything back to where it looks good and isn't crawling up the walls."

Originally the Chinese evergreen shrubs and cedar trees had been planted to allow for pruning from the back side, but over the years they had begun to grow taller and wider. So now it was time to remove all the excess growth and return them to their original size and shape. This required cutting numerous large branches from the trees which were reaching out over the slower growing shrubs and stealing their precious sunlight. The high reaching tree tops struggled to gain an opening between the even larger trees on the opposite side of the wall and needed to return to a more manageable height.

"Let's start with trying to bring those tree tops back down and then we can work on the wide branches," Changde pointed up at the newest growth at the very top.

"I'll put the ladder up over there and climb up to cut the trunk so it's even with the top of the roof."

"Be careful so it doesn't fall."

Several hours later as the sun reached its peak in the sky before beginning its downward slide towards the trees, they finally finished cutting the tops lower and cleaned up all the debris. "Now let's start cutting back all the lower branches away from the wall." Changde walked around to the back side with a small saw.

"I'll cut the branches loose and throw them to you so you can carry them out to the debris pile."

"Okay." Xiawu prepared the small flat cart and as the branches were thrown out, he arranged them on the cart and secured them

349

with a small woven bamboo strand rope. Load after load, he removed the unwanted growth and soon the pile outside the wall was almost as tall as the temple walls.

"Changde, Xiawu, it's almost time for our afternoon training." Junior monk Feixing said as he walked up and observed the progress of the fresh new look.

"We'll cleanup and head over to the training area," Xiawu said as he began arranging the tools on the cart.

The following morning the two monks returned to their project, focused on finishing the shrubs on one side of the front gate before the noon meal and then began on the opposite side. After their small meal they returned and Changde started cutting the branches and throwing them out. As Xiawu pulled the loaded cart out to the pile he noticed a stranger off in the distance climbing the small dirt path towards the temple. "Changde, I see someone coming up the path," he said when he returned, as he released the handles on the cart.

"Okay let's go out and meet him." He set the saw on the cart.

"Hey, where do you think you're going?" Changde asked as the stranger began walking towards the opening between him and Xiawu.

"What?" the stranger said as he stopped.

"Hey, I said where do you think you're going?"

"I'm here to see Abbot Cheng Yangban."

"*What is your name?*"

"*I'm Li Yutang from Pingdu.*" *He began to walk inside but Xiawu stepped in his path. After the long climb in the hot sun Yutang was completely drenched in sweat and as Xiawu stepped in front of him Yutang's facial expression instantly changed to an intense glare at the stranger in his way.*

"*I have been sent here by my father who is a good friend of the abbot's. He wants me to ask permission to live here. So, could you tell the abbot that I have journeyed far and would like to begin my training?*"

"*You stay right here and I'll inform him of your arrival.*" *Changde turned and headed inside the large opening.*

"*Omm, omm, omm,*" *Xiawu quietly began chanting to alleviate his fear from the stranger's intense glare and calm his shaking legs.*

Eventually, Changde returned and saw the young stranger appearing to ready himself for fighting.

"*Wait, wait, I just talked to the abbot and he said you can come in.*" *Changde raised his hand as if telling Yutang to stop.*

"*Good.*"

"*Xiawu, please go get some tea and pastries and take them to the abbot's quarters,*" *Changde pointed at the kitchen area.*

"*Follow me and I'll take you to see the abbot.*" *He turned and began walking into the temple and as they walked neither said a word.*

"Knock, knock," Changde lightly tapped on the weather worn door. "Come in." He slowly pulled back on the old handle and allowed the stranger to enter the humble quarters first.

Abbot Cheng sat writing at his small table. As the door slowly opened the flame from his single candle wildly danced from the incoming rush of air. After he finished his letter and gently placed the delicate brush back in its holder, he turned towards his guest.

"So… you're the son of my good friend in Pingdu city? So how is my old friend?" he stroked his long white beard.

"He's doing well."

"My student tells me you want to live here with us."

"Yes, Master, that is correct." Yutang nervously shifted as he replied while handing the scroll to his host.

Abbot Cheng carefully untied the delicate red ribbon and then opened the scroll. "Hmm…hmm" he said while reading the carefully written characters. "I see your father wants you to learn my Kung Fu style. I know of your family Tan Tui style and its effectiveness, so why does he want you to learn my Praying Mantis?" he leaned back.

"I guess he thinks it will be a great addition to what I already know."

"Interesting." He stood up and walked towards his guest, who was still nervously shifting. "Relax, I'm not going to hurt you." He stopped only a few feet from his guest and looked at the open scroll.

After several minutes he slowly rolled the delicate scroll back up and said, "Well... if your father is so confident in my abilities, I guess I shouldn't let him down." He tapped the scroll in his palm.

"Changde, take our newest member and show him where he will be sleeping."

"Yes, master." Changde bowed and turned to leave.

Hmm, we'll have to see if he's as good as his father says, Abbot Cheng thought as the wooden door finally closed.

I think I'll write a letter to his father and tell him his son arrived. He turned and walked back to his small chair sat down and picked up his brush.

"My good friend Li" he began on the fragile fabric. Several minutes later he finished the letter, placed his brush back in its holder, rolled up the small scroll and tied it shut with a short piece of ribbon.

The next morning as Abbot Cheng walked outside, he noticed a new songbird sitting by the fishpond excitedly singing to the other birds in the trees. Hmm that's interesting. I've never seen one of those in this area before, but now that I accepted a new student, it arrives. He thought as he walked towards the training area.

"Everyone, come over here, I want to introduce our newest member to you" he said as he pointed to the center of the training area. This is Li Yutang. He's from Pingdu City and I've accepted him as a

student, so I want everyone to welcome him and teach him our *Praying Mantis Kung Fu.*" He placed his hand on Yutang's shoulder. "*Xiawu, I want you to take our newest student over on the side and teach him the basics of the Shui Shou (wrestling hands) Praying Mantis system.*

"*But…*"

"*Is there a problem with my request, Xiawu?*"

"*No, master, no problem at all.*" He lowered his head as he bowed to his teacher.

"*Everyone else, today I want you to focus your attention on the various elbow techniques. That means keep track of how many different strikes you know and where are they attacking. How are you and your opponent situated when you attack and what would their defensive movement will be for your attack?*"

"*Xiawu, teach him all the basic stances, punches, kicks, praying mantis hand techniques and briefly explain the praying mantis fighting application techniques,*" he said as his students walked off to the side of the training area.

"*Changde, I want you to research how each of the eighteen elbows are being used in the newest form I taught you. Where are you when you initially attack, how are you positioned when you attack, what part of his body are you focusing upon?*" Abbot Cheng walked over to where his student was practicing.

"*Master, is this elbow technique used against a single or double fist attack?*" Changde asked as he demonstrated the movement.

"It depends. Sometimes you will encounter an opponent using a double punch technique, and other times they may only use one fist. If you only need one elbow, then the other can be used as a lever to strengthen the first elbow."

"Oh, I see what you mean, the second elbow helps to make the single elbow stronger by giving it an opposite direction leverage."

"Yes, exactly." He raised his thumb in approval of the insight.

"Master, I have a question about this circling movement in the small wheel form." Feixing walked up as the Abbot turned back towards the group.

"Show me the movement."

"It's this one," Feixing demonstrated.

"What is your question?"

"How do these two hand circles apply?"

"Well, as you circle the arms, you are executing a movement that can be used in numerous applications. You could be trapping a single arm at the wrist and elbow, or you might be blocking the arm while you deflect the incoming kick, or you could be throwing your opponent. It will all depend upon what your opponent is doing to make you use that specific movement."

"You must be very careful when you are researching the applications of a technique, because your mind will try to find only one solution for the move and with each technique there are hundreds of applications."

Three hours later Abbot Cheng stood up from his chair in the shade of the large tree and said, "Okay we have trained long enough for today, but I want everyone to reflect upon the concepts of praying mantis fighting. Next week we will discuss them again, but for now we need to finish our daily duties before we eat." He slowly began walking towards his private quarters.

In a couple of days, I'll explain to everyone about the fundamental theories of the White Crane style, he thought as he passed by the fishpond and observed the same bird still singing.

After allowing the students several days to focus on their individual assignments, Abbot Cheng walked out one morning and said, "Today I want to talk to you about the White Crane Style of Kung Fu." He opened his arms to demonstrate one of the systems typical movements.

"In the White Crane System, one of the fundamental principles is patience. A crane will always demonstrate immense patience. That doesn't mean he won't strike first because he will, but his primary objective is to wait. A crane will wait until the absolute last second before striking because he wants to make sure his opponent has completely committed to attacking before he reacts.

"What does that mean? It means a White Crane practitioner will wait until his opponent is committed to attacking to the point that he cannot retract or change the direction of his movement. Then the crane can avoid the momentum by slipping to the side and striking from an oblique angle. White Cranes have learned how to develop immense amounts of light qi or energy, they can make their

bodies very light on the ground and when they jump, it is almost effortless.

As the crane avoids an incoming attack it will immediately turn and strike with their beak or use its large wings to slap and shield its body. Turning is a crane's natural tendency for avoiding an opponent.

As the abbot continued to explain the characteristics, a gentle breeze drifted across the open training area. First the leaves on the far side began to gently flutter and twist, then the few tall weeds in the field slowly leaned and bowed towards the abbot, next the soft air reached the students and surrounded their bodies while gently caressing the sweat from their clothes. As the breeze finally touched the abbot he paused, tilted his head towards the sky and allowed the experience to absorb into his being.

"That is how a crane experiences life, by allowing it to absorb completely into its core. When it fights, it will be totally consumed in the situation but not by the situation," he said while pointing at the sky. "Several years ago, when I stopped in Weixian, I witnessed a fight between Master Zhou, a White Crane specialist and Master Tang Fendu, an Eagle Claw specialist. It was very impressive to watch the skill level of Master Zhou in relation to his ability to act and move like a crane. Each of his techniques was truly white crane at its core and as he moved, I only saw a crane.

"I want everyone to practice their latest series of movements and reflect on what I just said as you execute each movement."

For several hours Abbot Cheng sat under the large tree and observed his students as they practiced. "Hey, that's not correct!" he occasionally would tell a student he observed incorrectly executing a technique. "Now try it again, but this time use your waist and not your shoulders."

"Immerse yourself in the techniques but don't be controlled by them. Understanding and insight comes from being one with the technique. If you analyze too much, you won't feel the inner essence and will miss its true core.

"Yutang, not like that! You're young and full of energy, but you're wasting it all by trying too hard and not feeling or listening to what the movements are saying. Each movement is an entity in its own space and time and has much knowledge to convey, but you need to be present and decipher the language of your body. Your body speaks to you through your feelings, and that is its unique language, so you need to develop an understanding through your practice of what each sensation means. Execute each movement but connect to it and become one with it." He demonstrated several movements.

"Like this, Master?"

"No! You're still trying to show everyone how good you think you are and that is going to be your downfall unless you correct the attitude. There have been many people over the centuries who learned the art of kung fu, but not all of them ever became high level practitioners. Why? Because too many of them were consumed by their ego and never returned to normalcy. Consequently, they only achieved a small amount of proficiency available through

their training. Some of them died because their ego convinced them their techniques were better than they actually were, and when they fought a true master, their delusion broke apart. "He hit his palm with the other fist.

"Changde, please show Yutang how it should be done so he can see the difference."

Changde bowed and instantly began the form which his younger brother was struggling to understand. Each movement was clear, precise and showed a complete immersion of the mind. As he moved his body seemed to effortlessly drift from one technique into another while radiating the true inner power developed from years of practice.

"See, see how he moves and how his body and mind are one. He's not trying to show off to anyone or achieve any type of status. He's simply becoming the techniques and consequently they are a perfect execution of movement and power. I know your father taught you better than that, so now you try and before you start, clear your mind of your ego because it's holding you back." He pointed at his temple.

The abbot watched as the young recruit struggled with the concept of oneness and repeatedly performed the routine. "It looks like you're starting to understand what I was referring to about connecting to the movements." Abbot Cheng raised his thumb in approval when he was satisfied Yutang was beginning to acquire the proper mindset.

"After we eat, I want you to spend the afternoon developing this concept and don't start thinking you've mastered it in one day. It'll take years of focus and diligent practice to acquire the level of ability that your older brothers have attained." He stood up and began walking back towards the small dwelling while placing his hand on Yutang's shoulder.

An hour after the sun began slipping towards the tops of the distant trees, the students and their teacher walked back to the open training area. "So, Yutang, did you come to any conclusions about your training while you were eating?" Abbot Cheng asked as his student walked past.

"Yes master, I thought about what you told me earlier and I'm beginning to realize that I have a long way to go before I'm as proficient as my older brothers." He slowed down his pace and walked with his teacher.

"Why?"

"I was talking with several of the older students and they told me that they were my age, they too had trouble with their mind convincing them about the greatness of their techniques."

"Yes, that's true of everybody. Even I had to deal with my mind trying to make me better than my abilities at the time. Eventually, I became aware of the tricks the mind continually whispered in my ears and realized if I wanted to become like the fighters in the Water Margin (Outlaws of the Marsh), I needed to overcome all the distractions I was hearing and realize that I was making them all up myself. So, if I changed how I thought, I could make the

majority of the delusions disappear." He slowly headed towards the large shade tree.

"Changde, I want you to show me the "Crushing Step" routine. I need to see if you've corrected the mistakes." He sat down and leaned back against the bark of the aged sentry.

"Xiawu, have you finished learning the double broadswords?"

"Yes, Master, my older brother Xingwei showed me the ending this morning." He pointed at his classmate who was stretching in the shade.

"Good, I want you to practice only that routine this afternoon and focus on where the blade is cutting." Abbot Cheng circled his arms around his body as if guarding himself with the swords.

"Lingshen, remember that routine from your family style you showed me last week. I want you to teach it to Xiawu.

"Okay, Yutang, you need to return to the routine you were working on this morning."

Hours later as the shadows crept across the open field and began climbing up the bark of aged sentries, Abbot Cheng slowly stood up and motioned for everyone to finish their practice and begin walking back to the buildings. Within minutes the sun had fallen behind the horizon and turned the clear sky bright orange, signaling that the dark would soon surround them.

Later as everyone finished their evening duties, the sliver of moon slowly climbed over the horizon while everyone returned to their practice in the small space next to the old fishpond. Slowly the air began to cool and release the thick humidity. Gradually several small animals returned to their task of searching for sustenance. Everyone continued their personal research and eventually the moon was high overhead, marking the end of another day for the solitary practitioners far below.

Slowly one by one the students finished training and headed back to their rooms for another night of sleep and reflection. Xiawu and Changde remained behind deep in conversation about the subtle details of an advanced form. Suddenly, as the abbot stepped out the doorway to his small dwelling, a lone owl called out from off in the distance searching for a friend. "Tell everyone tomorrow we will focus our attention on their short weapons," he said while looking off in the direction of the small winged friend before turning and walking back inside.

The following morning as everyone finished their warm-ups and stretching, Abbot Cheng said, "Today I want to discuss the principle of using the short weapons." He sat down on the stool, waved his hand for everyone to join him and waited for everyone to step in closer.

"First, we will start with the flute. This weapon is primarily used to attack the soft areas of the body since it isn't strong enough to break any bones. An old saying about the flute goes, "If the flute comes out someone is going to die." Anytime it's used to block, the block is primarily a deflective movement instead of an attempt to stop the incoming force with a direct hard-barring technique." He held up one arm and rested the other on top in a cross pattern.

"Your accuracy must be very precise in order to hit a soft vulnerable spot such as the throat, solar plexus or groin while your opponent is moving. Also, you will need to be willing to move in very close to your opponent in order to execute these attacks, since it is a short weapon. Wrap the arm to defend and then flick the end into the eyes, deflect a strike and drive the end into the throat or chest, circle around an attack and hit the temple, or drop below an attack and hit the groin." He touched Lingshen lightly to show the location of the strikes.

"When defending against another weapon the concept I mentioned earlier about deflection is even more important. A flute is very adept at slightly changing the direction of an opponent's strike without trying to stop his momentum. Afterwards, you can effectively attack exposed body parts because you will be positioned on the inside of his defenses.

"From now until we stop for our noon meal, I want everyone to find a partner and practice attacking and defending against the flute's techniques." Abbot Cheng turned and walked towards his small bench under the tree.

Later as everyone returned to their training, Abbot Cheng walked out into the open area and said, *"Everyone, come over here. I want to explain about another short weapon, the Double Daggers."* He carefully pulled the two knives out of his sleeve.

"These knives carry the spirit of a serpent. When striking they move with the speed of a snake biting its prey, explosive and exact. When defending they will coil like a snake wrapping its victim, tight,

controlling and deadly with the edge cutting deeply while moving inward. Also, they can spin to attack like a furious dragon whipping its tail to defend its eggs in the lair.

"As you defend, make your body as fluid as a young willow branch, supple and capable of moving in any direction without hindrance. Then your energy can freely flow and allow you to strike every target from any direction. Additionally, when you jump to avoid your opponent, you should become light like a floating leaf dancing on the summer breeze, then land and become solid like the base of Mt. Tai so you can strike and drive your power from the center of the earth.

"Coordinate the movements of the two thieves' in the night so that as one is defending and misdirecting, the other is stealing the exposed fruit from the exposed areas of the body." Abbot Cheng walked over and sat down before continuing. "The daggers must act in total unison while guarding your body, yet maintain their deceptive nature to lure your opponent into their trap."

"I've seen many fighters who are truly masters of deception with their daggers and others who should give them up and use a feather. The choice is all yours. If you pick them up and decide to carry them, make sure you control and wield the serpents correctly or else the dragon's tail will strike you down.

"Now, I want everyone focus on becoming the serpent, and learn to tame the dragon so its spirit will be your ally."

As everyone practiced integrating the essence and spirit of the serpent, the abbot watched to see who was correctly grasping the concept. This was a concept and nature that would demand many hours of diligent practice to effectively absorb into the core of the practitioner. Abbot Cheng knew from personal experience that the mannerisms he observed from his younger students as they tried to imitate the theory were just that, vague imitations. Years from now they would finally merge with the concept and wield the twin dragons effectively.

"No, Yutang, you're not moving the daggers as though you're in control. It looks like you're trying to keep them from biting you!" Abbot Cheng imitated the scared looking movements. "Who's in charge while you're executing those techniques, because it looks like they're leading you around by the tail? Move with more command of your weapon. Otherwise, your opponent will never take you seriously or fear their power."

"Stronger, stronger, more relaxed and shoot the power from the blade out into its target without any hesitation, now spin quickly, like a millstone turning. Yes, that's better." He leaned back against the bark of his old friend, watched the routines of his students and remembered when he first arrived. It's been so many years since I first arrived and began teaching these forms in this same open area. Now I've become their window into the past so they can see how the past generations trained and what they might have achieved. I hope they will mirror my teachings well in the future. He stroked his white beard.

The sun still had several hours before disappearing behind the horizon, but suddenly a cold breeze rushed across the ground and violently shook the leaves above the abbot. I guess the cold winter is going to arrive early this year, he thought while looking up at the delicate leaves struggling to hold on.

"Changde, have we gathered enough wood to burn for the winter?"

"Yes, Master, Lingshen helped me find extra last week when we went out into the woods."

"It appears the cold will be arriving early this year, so we might want to find more."

"Okay we'll go out tomorrow and take Yutang along to help."

"Xiawu, I want you and Xingwei to find something to cover the extra wood your brothers are going to bring back."

"Let's go in and start making preparations in the rooms for the coming winter. I don't want to wait until it's snowing before we start." He stood up and slowly began walking back to his house.

Three months later the Chinese New Year of 1887 arrived as the winter maintained a strong grip on the land. The snow that blanketed the landscape and wrapped tightly around the trunk of each tree in the woods shielded the roots from the frost and was transformed into a crusted layer of white. Now the few remaining animals out searching for the last remnants of food cautiously scurried across the hardened surface from one dead bush to another.

Inside the temple the residents began making simple preparations for their celebration. A small ancient red scroll proclaiming a prosperous new year was hung outside and the small mirror chasing away bad energy above each doorway was meticulously cleaned, while several good luck scrolls were strategically placed inside to enhance the feng shui (geomancy) of the dwelling. Everywhere inside the dwelling was cleaned to sweep away the previous year's bad energy to make room for the upcoming celebration the following day and a simple meal prepared to welcome the new year.

"Pop, pop, pop!" echoed through the temple, out across the frozen ground and through the barren trees surrounding the temple the following morning as each student was allowed to light a strip of fireworks outside their home in order to scare away any bad spirits on the first day of this new year. "Xing nian kuai le!! (Happy new year)" everyone yelled as they greeted each other in the courtyard and exchanged red envelopes filled with coins.

Soon Abbot Cheng stepped outside wearing a bright red silk jacket with large gold "Longevity" symbols embroidered everywhere. "Xing nian kuai le!" he yelled while walking into each dwelling to greet his students.

"Dress warm for today's training, I sense this is the high temperature for today," he said as he turned to exit the room.

"Today we will focus on rooting to the ground when it's slippery." Abbot Cheng said as walked up to the tree and placed his blanket on the small stool.

"As everyone can tell, now that the ground is frozen, it's harder to stay rooted and not slip. Your awareness, sensitivity and belief must be even more rooted to the ground and it's these three that will keep you anchored. When you move you must become light and stay relaxed and when you stop you must root deeply into the ground to

hold your position." He suddenly rushed across the ground and stopped without slipping or falling.

"Find a partner and I want you to push against each other and practice holding your position, no matter how hard your partner pushes, and then try pulling him towards you." One by one Abbot Cheng walked from group to group and showed them how to achieve the technique. "Now that you are understanding the concept, try jumping and kicking to see if you can land solidly," he said as he walked over to sit down. "This concept is very important because you will not always fight someone in perfect weather conditions."

"Next, I want everyone to stand completely still and focus your energy on the bottom of your feet. If you focus correctly the ground will not feel cold and your energy will not melt the snow, because your energy will create a shield between your feet and the ground. Relax your body and focus on the bottom of your feet, but stay perfectly still." Abbot Cheng stood up and stood in between all his students while directing the exercise.

"Now that I think you are ready, take off your shoes and stay standing." He removed his shoes and stood motionless while talking.

"Focus on the soles of your feet and send your thoughts, intentions and energy to that location. Stay relaxed and breathe deeply." For the next hour no one moved while the abbot continued explaining the intricate details about the exercise in order to help increase their belief and abilities. "Okay, everyone slowly move away from your spot and you'll notice the snow is still intact. Now put your shoes

back on and walk inside for a warm meal." He said while watching everyone begin to move as he remained still. Eventually, the moment his students began walking inside, he returned to his shoes by the tree, put them on and followed everyone inside.

As everyone began eating the hot vegetables and rice, Abbot Cheng sat at the end of the table and continued explaining about the exercise. "Your mind is capable of abilities far beyond your comprehension, but in order to achieve them your belief in the abilities must be just as strong. If your belief was strong enough you could perform the techniques instantly. Unfortunately, the mind has many doubts and even more fears which stand in the way of your success. So today we started slowly by trying to connect to the ground through pushing and pulling and finally by removing your shoes. These were only the beginning steps in this technique and eventually as you progress, I'll show you the more advanced levels." He saluted all his students and began eating.

For months the daily practice included training in the art of directing the energy and controlling its usage in specific locations. Soon the thick layer of snow on the rooftops began sliding towards the edge before falling to the ground, signaling the arrival of the spring season. Small buds began appearing on the branches of the trees and whispers of green started to peek through the ground where the sun had melted the snow. The unique sounds of the first migrating birds echoed in the trees as a lone fox shuffled across the open ground in search of a rodent. Suddenly, the gray canvas that had painted the sky for many months began to retreat and allow the sun to announce its return.

"Changde, I want some of the junior students to go out and begin tilling the soil for our garden," the abbot said as he walked towards the fishpond with a handful of rice.

"Yes, Master, I'll send three of them out to start digging before we start training."

"Good, because tomorrow I want to begin planting." He threw the rice into the swarm of hungry koi anxiously waiting at the edge of the water.

"Also, tell everyone to bring their spear out to the training area this morning."

"I want to explain to everyone today the ways of the spear." Abbot Cheng held out his spear and shook it until the small pellets inside the tip began to rattle.

"As you know, this is called the king of all the weapons, and when you wield it, you must make its nature shine through, if you want to be successful. It must dance in the heavens like the mischievous monkey king jumping from cloud to cloud to avoid the gods. Its direction is unknown and its intent shrouded in confusion. The red tassel flutters in the air like a butterfly dancing on the wind. As you plant the handle on the ground to block, it should be as solid as Mt. Song at the Shaolin Temple. As the tip is thrust forward to strike, make its speed like a meteor dashing across the night sky.

When you wield the spear, it should feel as light as a feather, but when you strike down it should fall as heavy as a pillar in heaven. It should create confusion with its movements and illusion through its deception. Never swing the spear in desperation, patience should always be your ally." He demonstrated a properly executed thrust and block.

"The spear has a long reach and if you wield it correctly, you can deceive your opponent into thinking it has no use when they step in close. Ah-ha! This is when you have successfully confused them, for it is just as effective in close as it is far away." He raised his finger and pointed at the clear sky.

"Your sensitivity should extend to the end of the sharp tip so you can feel your opponent's weapon and know his intention without looking. Then as you wrap your spear around his weapon it will become a useless piece of metal or wood. Make your spear an extension of your body yet as flexible as a strand of delicate silk, so that when you strike it becomes as hard as steel, but when it dances it's relaxed and its depth becomes peerless.

"Centuries ago, during the Tang Dynasty (618 – 907 AD) lived a woman by the name of Fan Lihua who was an exceptional spear practitioner. Many fighters believed her spear held magical powers because she was unbeatable with her techniques because of her size and flexibility. So many of the techniques required agility along with superb range of motion and consequently, numerous Kung Fu styles have all incorporated a form into their system that is named after her.

"Your footwork must be fast, precise and stable in regard to placement during each stance, the speed of each movement and coordination between the feet." He quickly executed several intricate stance changes from the spear form.

As the tassel dances like a young dragonfly on the water, you must use its movements to confuse and distract your opponent. Then you can easily neutralize their desperate attempts to penetrate your defenses. But, as you dance effortlessly on the summer breeze with your spear, you must always be aware of their techniques and watch out that they are not drawing you in to their lair." He pointed at the sky with one finger.

"The tip on your spear should be useful in both directions as you make it shine in the bright sun. Driving it forward you make the point strike like a snake while cutting the exposed flesh, and as it returns you twist the tip and slice a vital vein in the arm or leg and release the body's life force." Abbot Cheng slid his fingertip across his elbow joint and then the knee joint to show the target area.

"Be aware of some masters wielding a spear that has turned completely dark, because they have soaked their spear in a special herbal mixture which makes the wood shaft extremely flexible. This allows them to utilize the spear as a whip when it's blocked, wrap around the opposing weapon and continue striking in addition to being a long hard stick. But to perfect this ability will require the practitioner to spend many years of practice to perfect, consequently they will be hard to defeat." He manipulated his spear into a large semi-circle to show its flexibility.

For hours, the students practiced trying to attack and defend with their weapons in relation to what their teacher had just emphasized. Soon, the warmth from the sun reminded everyone that the hour was at the mid-day point, so they slowly retreated to the shelter of the aged buildings and enjoyed their simple meal.

Minutes later they heard, "Rumble, rumble, crack!" as everyone sat enjoying the vegetables and steamed rice.

"It seems the heavens would rather we stayed inside and practiced for the afternoon." Abbot Cheng said as he stepped inside the doorway of the small room. "Once you are finished eating, please move the tables over to the side." He turned and stepped out into the dark noon-day light.

Minutes later Abbot Cheng stepped back in through the opening and looked around the room and said, "Good, you moved all the tables to give us sufficient room for practicing." He placed his large bamboo hat on a chair.

"Let's review what I explained to you this morning and practice the concepts on a more in-depth level." He said while walking to the center of the room.

"Yutang, show me what you learned from the class earlier."

The newest student stepped forward and said, "Well, when you said the spear tassel should dance on the clouds like the mischievous monkey king, I finally grasped what you meant. My father told me something similar but I never quite knew what it meant because I was always confused about how the tassel could act that way while moving through the air. This morning as you explained some of the principles about how the spear should act as we use it to attack and defend, I remember how my father demonstrated the techniques and the words he kept repeating to me as he moved from technique to technique and his words finally made sense.

"Good, so all those years of training and listening to him explain the principles were not wasted. Oftentimes we need to hear the principles explained by someone else before we can truly understand their meaning. That doesn't mean whoever we heard the words from first is wrong. It just demonstrates how the mind will hear the exact same phrases differently depending upon who is speaking," the aged warrior said as he slowly sat on the chair near the door.

"Oftentimes, as children we hear our parents tell us things on a daily basis, but because they are our parents we block out or ignore many of the things they are trying to teach us for our own improvement. Later, someone else will step into the role of teaching us and end up telling us the exact same theories, philosophies and strategies as our parents, but then we will be at a point to be willing to listen. It's partly because we are older but also because it's someone other than our parents who is talking. Learning is the underlying principle. Don't be concerned with who is in the position of teacher, just allow yourself to be open and receptive to whatever they have to offer at the moment," he continued as everyone sat on the floor in a semi-circle.

"This afternoon I want everyone to find a partner and spend your time training with the spear and as someone explains a theory to

you about how they feel the technique can be applied, don't block out their thoughts just because you think your idea is better. Always remember, ALL ideas have value, your responsibility is to research the movement and find out how each of them can be utilized." The abbot began to slowly clean the aged brush before preparing his small scroll.

For several hours the students diligently trained on the concepts their wise and experienced teacher imparted to them. Soon as the clouds began to finally break apart and allow the final rays of the sun's warmth to penetrate the thick dark wall, Abbot Cheng stood up and headed towards the open doorway. "Okay everyone, it's time to finish the training and prepare for our evening chores before we eat."

The following day as the sun gently threw its rays of light through the trees and everyone was preparing for their morning training, Abbot Cheng walked up to Xiawu and Yutang and said, "I need you two to go into town and gather some supplies."

"What would you like us to pick up?" Xiawu asked as he turned to face his teacher.

"Here is the list and I don't want you spending hours looking at all the non-essential trinkets in the store windows." He said while shaking his finger.

"Yes, Master." Yutang said as he bowed.

Quickly the two gathered their weapons and headed back to their simple quarters before walking to the main gates and beginning the journey down the hill towards town. Several hours later the two fighters walked into the small village and searched out their usual clients. Suddenly, Xiawu stepped closer to the first store entrance and stopped in front of a large notice pinned to the wall.

"Hey Yutang, look at this!" Xiawu said as he pointed at the large paper.

"Wow, does he really think he's that good?" Yutang asked as he stopped to read the notice.

"I guess so, but I don't think he knows much about our Praying Mantis style."

"So, what do you think?" Yutang asked.

"I think he needs to be educated about our style and about being such a braggard."

"I don't know. Master said not to waste any time."

"Yes, you're right, let's split up to buy the items and meet at the large tree."

"Okay, I'll go down there while you go inside this store."

Slowly the two fighters turned and headed in different directions to buy the items on their list. Once they finished it was time to go out to the edge of town and sit under the large shade tree and relax before heading back to the temple.

"I signed my name at the bottom of that challenge," Xiawu said as he sat down and leaned against the trunk of the old tree.

"What... are you serious?"

"I think I'm ready to test my skills."

"Are you going to bring anyone with you?"

"No, I want to do this on my own, so don't tell our Master." Xiawu said as he turned and looked at his friend.

"O...kay." Yutang looked at the ground and shook his head.

"I'll be fine, I can handle just one braggard."

"O...kay."

Eventually the two fighters gathered their supplies and began the long walk back home. Throughout the entire trip neither fighter said a word about the challenge match and soon they arrived back at the front gates.

"Remember, don't tell Master," Xiawu whispered as they walked through the gates and headed towards the kitchen.

Yutang didn't say a word as he sighed and continued walking.

The following morning as everyone was busy preparing for the simple meal, Yutang observed Xiawu quietly heading towards the main gate before turning and heading down the hill. Quickly he turned and focused his attention on arranging the vegetables on the large wooden plates and then carrying them to the tables.

The sun had just begun to climb over the horizon and minutes later the first rays reflected off the moisture on the plate of food as Abbot Cheng stepped through the doorway and headed towards the opposite end of the table. Suddenly, he stopped and quizzically glanced around the room as if looking for something. "Where's Xiawu?" he asked while sitting on the simple wooden stool, but no one answered.

"Changde, have you seen your younger brother?"

"No, Master."

"Hmm." He said while picking up his chopsticks and eating the steaming mix.

Later, after Abbot Cheng left the dining hall and retreated to his personal dwelling, Xiawu limped through the main gates and headed towards his sleeping quarters.

"Xiawu, what happened?" Yutang asked the moment he stepped inside and saw his friend lying on his bed.

"I guess that stranger was better than I thought."

"Are you okay?"

"Yes, but I have several injuries that will require some healing before I go back."

"Go back?"

"Yes, I don't plan on letting him win on just that one challenge match." Xiawu adjusted his position on the bed.

"When will you go back?"

"Probably several months from now after I heal and can train more on the areas where I was weak."

"Next time I'll go with you."

"No!" he sat up on the bed and grabbed his side as his face winced from the pain.

"Are you sure?" Yutang helped him slowly lie back down.

"Yeess!" he said while exhaling deeply.

For the next eight months Xiawu focused on healing from the injuries and improving the techniques that caused him the defeat. Eventually after another four months, he informed his friend that he thought he was ready. "Yutang, I think I'm ready to go back to town and even the score with that guy."

"Are you sure?"

"Yes, so I'm going into town tomorrow, but please don't tell Master."

"Okaaay, but if he asks us where you went, I hope he doesn't ask me personally." Yutang scratched his head.

"I'll see you when I get back later today." Xiawu patted his friend on the shoulder as he walked towards the large wooden gates.

Yutang stood and watched his friend disappear around the corner and then turned and headed to the training area. Throughout the morning Yutang maintained a low profile whenever the abbot was in the vicinity and successfully avoided answering questions about the location of his friend. Eventually, as the sun began to fall towards the hills and the dark sky to fill the trees, Xiawu finally stumbled into the temple and limped across the grounds towards his bed. The moment he opened the door Yutang walked up and said, "Xiawu, where have you been?"

"I just got back from the fight."

"You look worse now than the first time you fought him. What happened?"

"He beat me really bad and said that since I came back to fight again, he wasn't going to show me any mercy."

"He said that?" Yutang prepared an herbal medicine patch.

"Yes."

"Here, put this on your larger wounds, I'll be back later to check on you!" he hurried towards the door.

"Where are you going so fast?"

"I'll tell you when I return."

Yutang closed the door and rushed towards the front gates, turned the corner and headed down the hill.

I don't believe it. How could he be so dis-respectful to a Kung Fu brother? As his thoughts raced, he began picking up speed and soon he was running towards the village. Upon reaching the outskirts of the small settlement, Yutang stopped and scanned the area in search of his opponent.

Ah-ha, there he is! He walked towards the man sitting under a large tree.

"Hey, are you the guy that beat up my friend this morning?" he yelled while pointing at the man.

"Why, are you a friend of that young punk who thought he was so tough that he could challenge me?' the man replied while leaning back against the trunk of the large tree.

"Yes, and I'm here to teach you a lesson about respecting your Kung Fu brothers!" Yutang stepped closer and stared at the man.

"Ha, go home or I'll teach you the same lesson."

"Get up and we'll see who gets taught a lesson!"

Suddenly the man jumped up, rushed towards Yutang and instantly they were furiously launching attacks and counters. Over the next thirty minutes the battle raged back and forth from one side to another. As it continued, a crowd quickly gathered to watch the two seasoned fighters apply their techniques. Eventually, the fate of each fighter was sealed in the memories of time and their lives would forever be altered. The stranger immediately succumbed to the stopping of his heart and Yutang was now destined to a life with the memory of a life extinguished.

Minutes later, Yutang finally turned to begin the long walk back to the temple and inform the abbot of the events, as he walked, the scenario continually replayed in his mind.

Hours later as he was lying in his bed reliving the experience, a dark cloud of sadness continually engulfed his spirit and emotions. The night seemed to stretch further and further into eternity as the emotions welled up inside, then softly subsided before building like a wave and crashing into his brain once again.

Finally, the sun began to lighten the dark as it edged closer and closer to the horizon and signaled the moment when he must inform his teacher of the event and its outcome.

"Knock, knock." He lightly tapped on the fragile wood door of Abbot Cheng's quarters.

"Enter Yutang." a seasoned voice from inside replied.

"So, what brings you here at this time of day?" Abbot Cheng asked as his student slowly entered the room.

"Master, I need to talk to you about something that happened yesterday." He looked at the floor.

"Oh, you mean about your trip into town?"

"Yes."

"I already know about it. So how did the fight conclude?" he sat next to his writing brush and ink well.

"I killed him." He turned and looked at the ceiling as his shoulders sank further.

"Did you intend to kill him when you left the temple?"

"No, Master, I only wanted to teach him a lesson about respecting his Kung Fu brothers."

"You realize the authorities will come here and investigate and then take you in for more questioning?" he leaned forward and placed his elbows on the table.

"Yes."

"I suggest you finish your morning chores and then gather your belongings before leaving the temple. When they arrive, I will tell them you left and I don't know in which direction you headed." He turned and looked at his student.

"Yes Master."

As everyone was training in the open grass area, Yutang eventually walked up with his faded backpack hanging from his shoulder. Slowly he bowed to his teacher, stood up and watched Abbot Cheng return the courtesy. "Everybody, feet together and bow to your fellow classmate and lifelong friend." Immediately, everyone stopped their training and bowed to Yutang for the last time. "Good-bye, Yutang, we will all remember you and your spirit," Abbot Cheng said as he placed his hands on his student's shoulders.

"Good-bye, Master." Yutang turned and headed towards the wooden gates for the last time, stopped in the opening and turned around to look at the humble series of dwellings he had called home for so many years, lowered his head and turned to begin his journey into the world.

Acknowledgments

At this time, I would like to thank the following individuals for their assistance and continued support throughout the development of this book.

Cynthia Swann-Haase: my wife, and dedicated companion.

Elizabeth Swann: tirelessly willing to assist and edit the evolving stories.

Jeff & Ellen Schmidt: inciteful suggestions throughout the development.

Randall & Roseann Rossing: continued support and excited anticipation for the release of the sequel.

Sally Olson: meticulous editing and patience.

About the Author

Thomas J. Haase is a Master of the Chinese martial arts and recently published the first book in the series, "Pugilist from Shandong"

While living and teaching in Tampa, Thomas has travelled throughout the Orient, acquiring extensive knowledge and understanding about their culture, which he has woven throughout each book.

www.ingramcontent.com/pod-product-compliance
Lightning Source LLC
Chambersburg PA
CBHW071149020726
47502CB00002B/344